RED DUST ON THE GREEN LEAVES

A Kpelle Twins' Childhood

Go up-country, so they said,
To see the real Africa.
For whomsoever you may be,
That is where you come from.
Go for bush, inside the bush,
You will find your hidden heart.
Your mute ancestral spirit.
And so I went, dancing on my way.
. . . .

An overladen lorry speeds madly towards me
Full of produce, passengers, with driver leaning
Out into the swirling dust to pilot his
Swinging obsessed vehicle along.
Beside him on the raised seat his first-class
Passenger, clutching and timid; but he drives on
At so, so many miles per hour, peering out with
Bloodshot eyes, unshaved face and dedicated look;
His motto painted on each side: *Sunshine Transport,*
We get you there quick, quick. The Lord is my Shepherd.

The red dust settles down on the green leaves.

I know you will not make me want, Lord,
Though I have reddened your green pastures
It is only because I have wanted so much
That I have always been found wanting. . . .

From *The Meaning of Africa* by Davidson Nicol.

Red Dust on
the Green Leaves

A Kpelle Twins' Childhood

BY JOHN GAY

With the editorial advice of
John Kellemu
Introduction by Jerome Bruner

Photographs by
Harrison Owen

Published by InterCulture Associates

The title is adapted, with the author's permission, from
"The Meaning of Africa," a poem by Davidson Nicol,
a portion of which is quoted on page i.

Sketch of Balama Town on pages vii-ix by Elizabeth Stull

Copyright © InterCulture Associates, Inc., 1973

Published by InterCulture Associates, Inc.
Box 277, Thompson, Connecticut 06277, U. S. A.

Library of Congress Catalog Card Number 73-77698
ISBN 0-88253-219-7 (cloth), 0-88253-220-0 (paper)

Printed in the United States of America by the Vail-Ballou Press

FOREWORD

This book is about two boys. These boys do not actually live, except in my mind, in the life of the Kpelle people as a whole, and hopefully in the minds and hearts of the readers of the book. Yet the book is not a novel, not a work of the imagination. Rather it is a careful reconstruction of Kpelle life in the 1930's and 1940's, based on extensive research. No person and no institution appears as an exact replica of any model past or present, and any resemblance is due rather to an attempt to represent Kpelle life in a single narrative.

I wish to thank John Kellemu, a graduate of Cuttington College and my research associate for many years, for helping make this book an accurate reflection of Kpelle life and culture. Mr. Kellemu read the book critically at two stages in its development, eliminating what was not true to the life of his people and adding many details I would otherwise never have known. I must take full responsibility for all errors, of course, but Mr. Kellemu must receive major credit for much that is true in the book.

This book is based on a multitude of sources, and could not have been written without extensive research by others. I cannot possibly single out the contributions of each individual, but I wish to thank by name persons who have contributed in many and varied ways. If I have omitted any, which is very likely, then to those persons, I say only—I am sorry.

My hearty and sincere thanks, for the work they have done on and for the Kpelle of Liberia, go to Christian Baker, Beryl Bellman, Jean Bissell, James Bomberger, Moses Bono, Isaac Browne, Joseph Campbell, Robert Christiansen, Thomas Ciborowski, Gregory Cleveland, Michael Cole, Jane Collier, David Crabb, Warren D'Azevedo, Yakpalo Dong, Christopher Dorweh, Philip Dorweh, Francis Dunbar, Franklin Dunbar, Richard Fulton, Judith Gay, Sulongteh Gbemeneh, James Gibbs, Joseph Glick, Harry Greaves, Daniel Gweh, Svend Holsoe, Festus Hooke, Joseph Kamara, Musa Kamara, Joseph Keller, Helen Kohler, Kiemue Kollie, John Korkoya, William Kromah, Akki Kulah, Arthur Kulah, Ronald Kurtz, Morris Kutukpu, Johnny Kwiipor, David Lancy, Charles Lave, Jean Lave, Theodore Leidenfrost, Chapman Logan, David Lukens, Eleanor Lukens, Robert McAndrews, Richard McFarland, John McKay, Kylkon Makwi, Melvin Mason, Barbara Meeker, Margaret Miller, Leonard Moody, James Mueller, Benjamin Mulbah, Paul Mulbah, John Norris, Harry Ododa, John O'Grady, Vincent Okafor, Corahann Okorodudu, Kenneth Orr, Melissa Pfeiffer, Paul Ricks, Rose Sambolah, Wilton Sankawulo, Willi Schulze, Augusta Scribner, David Scribner, Sylvia Scribner, Thomas Seavers, Dieter Seibel, George Seymour, Donald Sharp, James Sibley, Henrique Smith, Samuel Smith, Otto Spehr, William Stewart, Ruth Stone, Betty Stull, James Stull, Paul Sulongteh, Saki Suah, Albert Swingle, Gabriel Swope, John Tamba, Sylvester Tamba, Henrique Tokpa, Koli Tokpa, Zephaniah Ukatu, Jeremiah Walker, Fletcher Watson, John Wealar, Karin Weisswange, Charles Wellington, William Welmers, Dietrich Westermann, Albert Wolokolie, and Albert Wungko.

Finally I must acknowledge my immense debt to the Kpelle people who have been gracious hosts during my 14 years in Kpelle-land. It is to the Kpelle people, and particularly to the children among them, that I dedicate this book.

John Gay

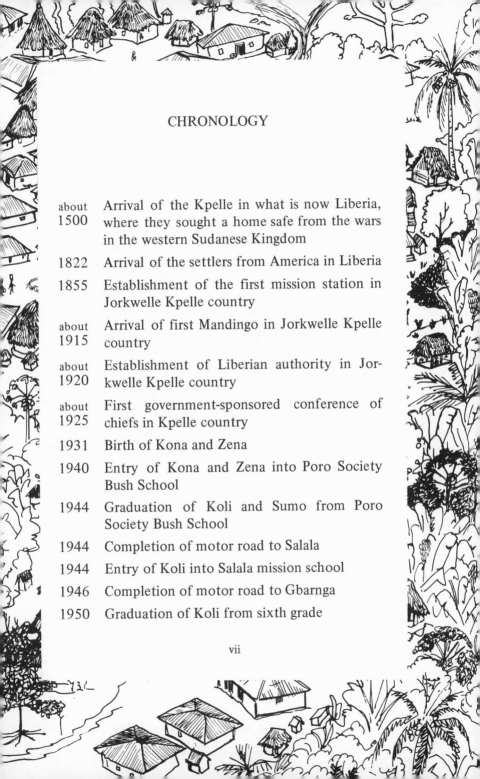

CHRONOLOGY

about 1500	Arrival of the Kpelle in what is now Liberia, where they sought a home safe from the wars in the western Sudanese Kingdom
1822	Arrival of the settlers from America in Liberia
1855	Establishment of the first mission station in Jorkwelle Kpelle country
about 1915	Arrival of first Mandingo in Jorkwelle Kpelle country
about 1920	Establishment of Liberian authority in Jorkwelle Kpelle country
about 1925	First government-sponsored conference of chiefs in Kpelle country
1931	Birth of Kona and Zena
1940	Entry of Kona and Zena into Poro Society Bush School
1944	Graduation of Koli and Sumo from Poro Society Bush School
1944	Completion of motor road to Salala
1944	Entry of Koli into Salala mission school
1946	Completion of motor road to Gbarnga
1950	Graduation of Koli from sixth grade

CONTENTS

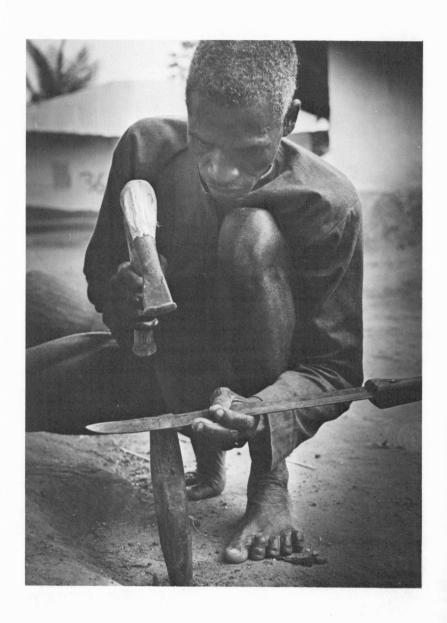

RED DUST ON THE GREEN LEAVES

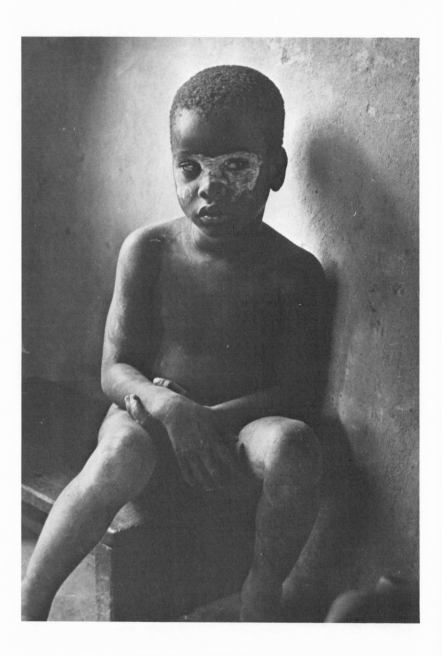

INTRODUCTION

BY

JEROME BRUNER

This is a book about a culture, about the Kpelle people and their way of life and thought. It is told through the medium of two brothers, Sumo and Koli, growing up as Kpelle in the heart of Liberia. It follows them from birth into adulthood, through crises of great and often heart-rending intimacy. One sees them becoming not only members of their own society, but strikingly different human beings, almost opposite sides of the same coin. The one becomes a cosmopolitan, interested in the new and the foreign, the other a traditionalist, steeped in the ways of his culture. By their different directions, they come to stand for the deep split that develops within Kpelle culture, looking as must all tribal societies in Africa, to the new for opportunity and excitement, and to the old for reassurance and ballast.

Yet it is more than a documentary, the recounting of the "lives of two brothers." These pages depict the "real," to be sure, but they evoke a sense of the human side of being a Kpelle to a degree that is extraordinary. Mr. Gay writes with a distinction and a compassion that surely reflects his fourteen years of deep involvement with the people he is describing, or evoking. For there runs through the book not only the structure of daily life as lived, with its cadence and intricacy, but also the emotional subtleties and the ambivalences that surround the day-to-day actualities. There is hunger for power in these accounts, the shame and the compromises of adultery, the humiliations of being put down — the universals of the human plight that can be recognized in any culture so long as one looks with care and with humanity. The author helps us to do that.

But there is one thing beyond all others that I treasure in this book. I have never visited the Kpelle, but I have always heard from friends and students who worked with them, either as teachers or as anthropologists, of the extraordinary use of proverbs and of formulaic ways of dealing with human difficulties. These were their means of putting things into the perspective of the traditional. Here one finds it in the concrete: the poetic and linguistic subtlety of the well-chosen proverb, the consensus that exists about what needs saying and what should be unsaid. These are a delight.

I have commented on the separate ways of Koli and Sumo, one toward the white man's world, the other toward the traditional way of ritual, secret society, village life. John Gay happens to be one of a small band of world-recognized experts on the subject of the Westernization of traditional societies, particularly the impact of this Western-ization on the thought processes. It is not surprising then that his account of the two different ways rings so true. But his expertise never intrudes, one does not feel him to be lecturing. Rather, one feels that it is Sumo and then Koli who are telling their story and making it possible for us all to understand better — without losing sympathy for either.

In the past, anthropologists like Radin and LaFarge have used the device of the well-told life history to describe the subjective side of a culture. *Crashing Thunder* and *Laughing Boy* have been in my imagination ever since I read those finely-wrought biographies. Sumo and Koli join them there now, and I am in John Gay's debt. I think the reader will share this pleasure with me, whether he is expert in exotic cultures or making his first venture. John Gay teaches as he delights.

Oxford
May, 1973

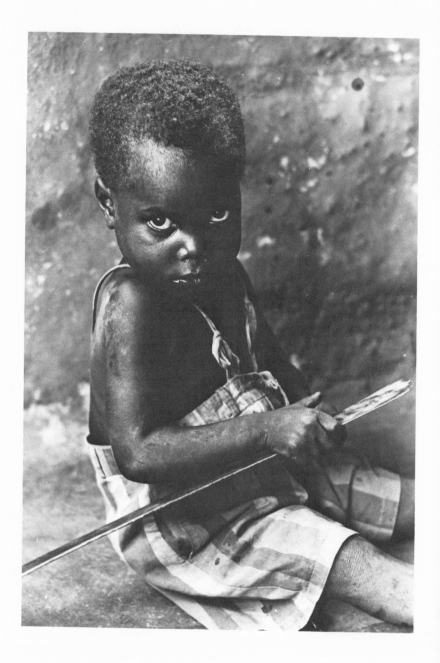

CHAPTER I

The Wind Blows Twice

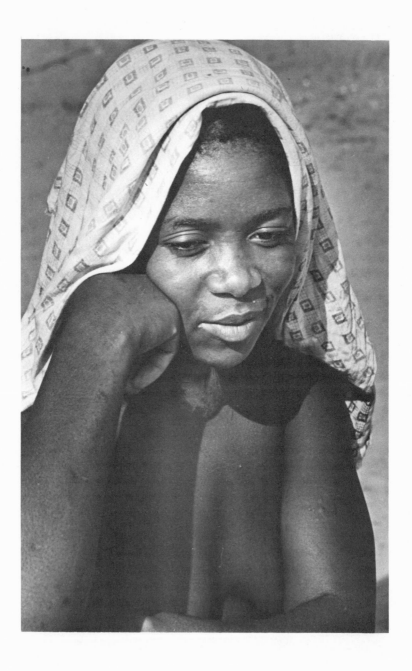

I: THE WIND BLOWS TWICE

Yanga had increasing difficulty bending to cut the heavy red-ripe stalks of rice. Pains had come irregularly at first, but later, after each handful of rice she cut, she had had to rest. It had not been so bad in the cool of the morning, as she and the other women had cut their slow way across the farm, leaving only the stubble for the forest to reclaim. But after the sun had moved halfway up the sky, Yanga felt she could no longer continue.

Yanga and the rest of the women in her group were responsible that day to work for her neighbor. Next week the women would come to Yanga's own farm, to cut and stack her family's rice.

Yanga was fairly sure her time had come, but had not yet told her friends. She knew she was large, unusually large, but she was not sure how many times the moon had gone behind the hill since she had last slept with Flumo, her husband. She had taken care to eat only the right meats, so that the child would not resemble a bush pig or an anteater. She had not dared eat an egg, since that would surely cause the child to be stillborn. She had not eaten bush cow, even though her husband had killed one during that very month, since if she had the delivery would be difficult. She wanted to be sure nothing would go wrong this time.

Even so, as the sun reached the top of the sky and stood over the women's heads, Yanga became nervous and very tired. The pains increased. This was not her first child. Three others had been born. One had died only a few days after birth and a second had died even before it had walked. The third, a little girl, was big enough now to tie a stick on her back and call it her own baby. If Yanga's time had come, and if this baby decided to stay, the older sister, Toang, would now have a real baby to carry, instead of that stick.

It had taken a long time, and many requests to the spirit in the huge cotton tree, the one which had been planted when the *town* was built, before Yanga was pregnant. She must not lose this child. Only if it were a witch would she wish it dead. But her dreams had been good, and she was sure that this child would come to stay. She had even dreamed that she would bear a girl, and thus felt in her heart she would have a son, which her husband Flumo so much desired. The spirits always speak indirectly.

Yanga finally told her friends she could work no more. She and her sister Noo, wife of Yakpalo, their town's weaver, stopped cutting rice to return to town, a long walk over three hills and through two swamps in the heat of the day. Her husband's head wife, Toang, stayed on the farm to complete Yanga's share of the work, to cut the rice and give it to the farm's owner for him to tie and stack in the loft of the thatch shed on the farm. Yanga and Noo were tired, and the pains, even though reassuring, tired Yanga even more.

When they reached town, she went to find her husband so that he would call the old midwife. The midwife worked well, but even so Yanga feared a long labor. She might well be forced to confess the names of all her lovers, or even be severely beaten, if the baby did not come promptly.

Yanga's husband, Flumo, was in town that day. He was working, as he usually did at this time of year, in the blacksmith's shop at the edge of town, an open-sided, thatch-roofed, round shed. When his wife returned from the farm he was sitting on the low wall of the shed, waiting for the knife blade in the coals to become hot enough for him to work. A young apprentice worked the animal skin bellows, so that the air rushed through the flaming charcoal and heated the blade which he was about to shape into a rice-cutting knife. Many

women in town had asked him for knives, now that they
were cutting the new rice.

Flumo saw Yanga return early from the farm, and, before learning her reason for leaving the farm so early, asked
why she was always so lazy. He knew her time was near, but
it was not his business, nor the business of any man, to bring
a baby into the world.

He hoped very much he would have a son, but did not
express this hope to Yanga. She was his second, younger, and
more beautiful wife, and to show too much interest would
make his head wife, Toang, jealous. Moreover, if she did not
bear him a son, he might suggest to Toang that she look for
another young girl for him to marry.

He had often seen a beautiful girl in the next town,
Yanga's home, and half hoped he might take her as his third
wife. It would bring him higher status, and perhaps also the
son he wanted. Moreover, Yakpalo, Noo's husband and
Flumo's main rival in town, now had five wives and four
sons.

Flumo realized that Yakpalo had inherited three of
these wives as the eldest son when his father died. But even
so they were Yakpalo's property, though one was beyond the
years of child-bearing. Yakpalo had given one to a younger
brother and another to a poor stranger who had come to
town, keeping the one who was too old to bear more children. All this made Yakpalo seem so much more important
than Flumo. Flumo realized he must have a son this time, if
he was to maintain any standing in the town.

Very soon Flumo would know what the ancestors had
given him, and there was nothing he could do now to change
things. Yet, when Yanga told him she needed the midwife, he
was afraid suddenly, but said nothing. He called for the midwife, but found she was on her farm. He sent her grand-
daughter there to bring her back to town, urging the little girl
to hurry because Yanga's time had come.

Flumo stayed in the blacksmith shop to complete the

knife and then begin working on the axe blade his nephew wanted. The hot, tiring sun which preceded the cold winds of dry season was going behind heavy clouds which could now be seen above the trees. The rainy season went out this way every year — heavy, hard days, and threatening, black clouds. He wondered whether today's clouds brought rain with them, or whether, as in the past several evenings, they would drift away and leave the hardening ground unsatisfied. But as the wind began to pick up, he decided the rain would come. Leaves were brushed up from the ground and tossed in the sky — perhaps by some ancestral spirit that wanted to announce itself when Flumo's son (would it be a son?) was born.

The rain in the sky brought early night with it. Flumo finished the axe, and told the boy who was working with him to stop the bellows and scatter the coals. Flumo thought of his own father and grandfather, neither of them long dead. He thought also of those many other ancestors, whom he could not name but whom he knew were helping him, and were perhaps present in the gusts and swirls of wind that kept the coals alive even after they had been scattered. He knew his family had buried them in the right way, and so their visit could mean no harm. He had made sure to give them new rice on green leaves at the crossroads each year after harvest, and he had promised them a sacrifice if he had a son.

Flumo and the boy left the shed to reach home before the rain fell. On his way, he met the midwife hurrying into town. Flumo greeted her, but said nothing about the business at hand. It would not be right to show too much concern or weakness now — what was going to happen would happen. If the midwife needed anything, she would let him know.

He went to his house, a small round, thatched hut near the edge of town. His head wife Toang had by this time also returned from the farm, the rice cut and stacked. She was preparing Flumo's supper, even though it was not her night to do so. He commented to her only, "When black deer is in the forest, spider sleeps in his bed."

Toang understood the proverb immediately, with a mixture of anger and satisfaction. She had cut rice and cooked food for Yanga that day. She also knew that her husband preferred Yanga to her. Moreover, Toang could bear no more children and here was Yanga perhaps about to give Flumo the son he wanted.

And yet Flumo's proverb had granted Toang's cleverness at getting what she wanted. She had cooked palm butter, crushing the fleshy exterior of the palm nuts in the mortar, and adding to the rich thick oil dried fish which she had caught and dried on the rack which was suspended over the fire in her house. The palm butter smelled good, and Toang knew it would please Flumo. Let Yanga have a male child. Toang would take Yanga's place in other ways. Only as a last resort might Toang use witchcraft to get rid of the new child, or cause Flumo's love for Yanga to grow cold.

No further word passed between Toang and Flumo. None was necessary. Both knew where Yanga was, and nothing either said could change what would happen. The midwife had not sent for help, and so Flumo offered none. Flumo ate his palm butter in satisfied silence.

His two daughters came to the house while he ate, fresh from dancing with their friends. Flumo was always pleased to see how cleverly they were able to match the intricate steps of their friends in the dancing game. One girl would challenge another to dance in the center of the ring, and that other would have to match the steps of the first. If she failed to follow the steps she would be out of the game.

Flumo's daughters danced well, particularly the older one, Lorpu, Toang's fourth child and the only one to live. Flumo had often praised her as she danced down the other girls. He would take her by the shoulder, pull her to himself, wipe her brow, and dance a few steps with her, as the onlookers laughed with approval.

Small Toang still had much to learn. Her mother helped

her when she fell, and encouraged her to try again. Yanga was a good mother, Flumo felt. She had already given small Toang her first fishing net; she had shown her how to beat the rice in the mortar to loosen the kernel from the husk; how to winnow the beaten rice by tossing it into the air from a large flat basket and catch the grains while the chaff floated away in the air; how to bring water from the stream near the town; and how to keep the living area around their houses clean from grass, goat dung, leaves and sticks. Soon Flumo knew Yanga would be teaching small Toang how to care for her baby brother.

The older daughter, Lorpu, was to enter the forest next year to learn the history and the secrets of the *Kpelle* people in the *Sande Society Bush School,* and to learn as well the skills which would allow her to come out as a woman three years later. He would miss her, he thought, as she and small Toang came running to him.

Small Toang and Lorpu waited for their father to finish his palm butter. They felt he was in a good mood that night, and so they knew they would eat well. Their meal was to be the rice crust from the pot, covered with what was left of the palm butter. But they hoped for more, and they were not disappointed. Flumo left them two pieces of dried fish in the pot, even though he could have eaten all himself.

When the palm butter was finished, Flumo asked Toang and the girls about their farm, how soon the work group would reach there, and inquired whether Lorpu and small Toang had done their work well in driving away the hungry rice birds, which had last year eaten so much rice on the farm of Flumo's brother, Saki, who had been away working at *Firestone* at the time. Flumo told his daughters a story of the girl who had slept instead of driving away the rice birds, and was carried away while she slept to be married to an evil mountain spirit. Toang and Lorpu joined in the song after each part of the story. They knew the story well, but small

Toang could not help being afraid and promised herself never to sleep when she was expected to work. She had heard too many stories of the terrible spirits and ghosts which can harm the lazy or stupid child not to know well the danger she faced.

Dark had come now, proper dark, not the dark of the rain which had remained in the sky instead of falling to settle the dust. The clouds were there still, but Flumo now believed it would not rain that night. The wind had stopped — surely proof that the ancestors had been present in the wind, and not merely the threatened rain.

Flumo left his house to walk to the town chief's court, a round open-sided shed like his blacksmith's shop. He and the other elders had been called to hear a case. On his way there, he found that he had walked away from his usual path, and was not far from the midwife's house. Then out of the dark he heard a cry, Yanga's cry, and mixed with it were the calming words of the old women who were helping her. He walked faster, because he was not supposed to be nearby when his child was born. Would it be a son this time, and would he live beyond those few days or months of the others?

Despite his fear, Flumo felt somehow satisfied. Yanga's cries sounded healthy and good. Moreover, the wind began to blow again, raising the dust and leaves around his feet, and blowing them beyond him toward the midwife's house. This was another good sign. He was sure his grandfathers would not leave themselves without a boy to carry on the family. Without a son, Flumo's ancestors, indeed Flumo himself, would be nameless and faceless, would die the second death.

This time the wind brought the rain from the sky, another good sign. Flumo reached the chief's *palaver* house, and ducked under the eaves in time to avoid a good soaking. The rain brought with it thunder and lightning, the shot-gun of the sky, which came still closer until the whole town was lit by the flashes. Flumo could see first the outline of the chief's house, and then its every detail as the lightning struck on all sides of the town.

Flumo found it hard to pay attention, what with the rain and the lightning, and with his wife in labor. But he listened dutifully. He had to, as chief of his quarter of town and as blacksmith. As quarter chief he tried to settle quarrels within his quarter so they would not have to reach the chief's court. And as blacksmith he was important in the men's secret society, the *Poro Society,* in which every man in town defended and passed on what their ancestors had taught them.

The case was brought by a man who accused his wife of not working on his farm, and then remaining away from home for a year and a half. The wife wanted a divorce be-cause her husband slept with other women when she was pregnant, had taken a second wife without her advice, re-fused to cut the bush for her rice farm, and would not visit her family. She said she had left home for her grandfather's funeral, and he would not come to bring her back again.

The woman would not give up trying, and the men were almost as restless as Flumo. The chief and his elders had done many of these things themselves, and had received no com-plaints from their wives. What right had this woman to leave her husband, and get damages from him? The case had been taken earlier to Yakpalo, the chief of their quarter, to help settle the matter. He had tried to hear their complaints, and get them to apologize to each other. He had told them "the truth about the world is apology," but they had not listened. He had brought Flumo into the matter, since as blacksmith he had helped arrange the marriage. Flumo could not help, and even the chief was unable to force them to stay together. Thus the case was now near its end, and the men were im-patient to finish it.

The rain lulled and then stopped, and the lightning,

thunder and rain were carried toward the next town. So must the case end, Flumo thought. The woman will go with the rain to the next town, her town, and carry her troubles with her.

Flumo was relieved when the chief began to question the woman. He picked at the weakest point in her case, and questioned her hard. His comment was, "A palaver is just its head." He found that she had stayed at her father's home for a year and a half. Her excuse, that her husband had not come for her, was poor. She should have sent for him instead of sitting down and doing nothing. She says her grandfather died? That is no excuse for disobedience.

The elders were of one mind when the chief called them aside. The woman's guilt was obvious from the moment she had folded her mat and left home. The case was finished. The divorce was granted, and the woman's father agreed to return the bridewealth her husband had paid: two white chickens, a goat, seven bunches of iron money, two containers of salt, and five bolts of white cloth.

The woman was not surprised. Only she knew that she was now pregnant, and that her new man very much wanted a son. He would pay the bridewealth to cover her father's loss. The new marriage would take place quickly and quietly by giving a white *kola* to her father, and then she would enter her new life. She reminded herself that "sitting quietly reveals crocodile's tricks." These men had been so busy and noisy in their own self-importance that they did not see her game.

The chief was settling the matter of the bridewealth when the silence left by the passing of the rain was interrupted by a baby's cry. The fear which Flumo had kept hidden in his heart was relieved. He was sure that all was well now. He knew the cry had to be his new child, because he knew all forty houses in town, and there was no other new baby. He was preparing to leave the chief's palaver house and make a sacrifice to the ancestors, when he stopped. It was not one cry. He could hear two voices. The other men also heard the voices, but said nothing.

Then the midwife came dancing up to him, leaves, fresh green leaves in her hands, and a satisfied smile on her face. She brought the leaves to Flumo, and with them the words that he had a son. He reached into the pocket of his robe, the robe he wore when listening to a court case, and gave her a white kola nut. She then asked for another, telling him in the same quiet way that he had two sons, not one only, and so he must give her a second white kola. When he did so, she told him that his wife's labor had been easy, and the boys looked fine.

She danced quickly away, so Flumo could go to prepare the sacrifice. Flumo now knew why the wind had blown twice. It was not for nothing that this had happened. The ancestors had come to his house two times, once for each of the boys, and then they had brought rain to water these new plants and soften the ground for them to grow well. The boys would grow in his house, and both of them *zoes*, gifted with special knowledge of and power over medicine and spirits. Twins were always zoes, a blessing to their house.

Flumo left the chief's palaver house satisfied with himself. The case he had come to hear was closed, and the men were still in control of the world. The woman had been put in her place, his head wife had given him a good meal, and he had two sons.

His wives' houses sang with activity. Toang supervised matters at Yanga's house, busy and satisfied. If she could not bear sons herself, at least she could show herself a good household manager. Though jealous in her heart, she did not let it show. The midwife and her helpers continued to dance, as they always did for twins.

Flumo could hear Yanga inside singing quietly to herself. He thought of her nursing the babies, even though no milk had yet come. "Will she have enough milk for two?" he thought. It had been a hungry year when Yanga's first son was born, the rains had come late, and then not often enough, and Yanga had found it hard to feed the boy.

Flumo had always believed that Toang had bewitched the child, sending him back to the ancestors. He had thus been pleased when Yanga gave the name Toang to the next-born, the very girl who was now bringing a bucket of water from the river to wash the new babies. This had seemed to satisfy Toang, and the jealousy in his house quieted down. Even black deer sometimes has the wisdom of spider.

Death comes from many causes. There is no one thing which kills a person. Perhaps Toang had eaten the baby boy in her dreams. She admitted later, when pressed hard, that she had dreamed of flying through the air, and eating the flesh of a bush pig. Only witches have such dreams, and she and Flumo knew it. Yet that had been a hard year, nor could a scanty milk supply, frequent force-feeding of rice-water, or the special leaves which old Noai prepared, help the boy.

Before he even took his first steps, he died. One day he refused the breast, as if he knew there was little nourishment there. He grew hot and dry, and before night he was gone.

Flumo thought to himself as he heard Yanga singing with the twins that he must suggest to Noo, Yanga's sister, that one of the new-born boys should be named "Good-for-nothing" and the other "Dirt," so that the ancestors would not try to take either back again. When they were initiated into the Poro Society, then they could be given new names, proper Kpelle names.

The healthy cries of the boys drove these thoughts from his mind. There had been good signs at their birth. The spirits had come twice, and they had watered the ground. The boys would surely live. He went to Yanga's house, and thanked her for the boys. He picked each up and silently blessed them. They had to live. Yanga knew all the precautions, he was sure. But just to be safe, he warned her not to eat crabs, crawfish or catfish, lest the boys get sick, and he warned her not to bathe in still water, where these animals live.

He left Yanga and went to his own house to sacrifice the chicken. In due course, the town would see his boys. The women would bring them out to show the world on the fourth day. He would then hold the feast for the midwife and all other women in town who had themselves borne children. In the meantime he would do his part. He and his nephew went to the grave of their grandfather near the edge of town. They cut the throat of a white rooster, let the blood fall on the grave, and silently gave thanks.

From there Flumo went back to his house and slept. There was nothing to do but be patient. He would spend his time at the blacksmith shop for the next three days. Women could not trouble him there, and he could wait until the boys entered the world.

CHAPTER II

First, Taste the Palm Wine

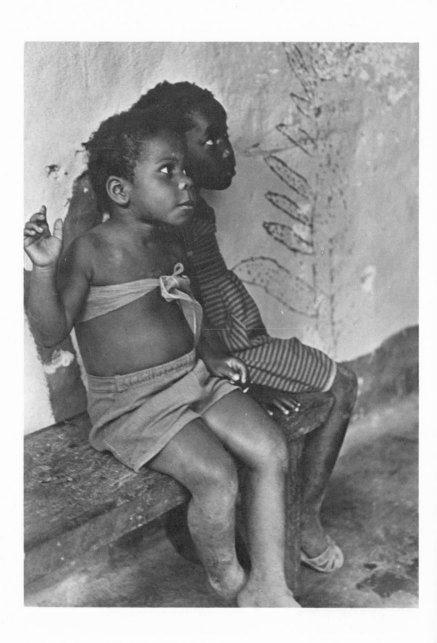

II: FIRST, TASTE THE PALM WINE

Yanga returned to the farm after five days. Though weary and not yet as strong as the other women, she did her work. She laid the babies on a cloth and joined the others cutting rice. After two weeks she would tie one of the new babies to her back, while the other would take the place of the stick doll small Toang had so delighted to carry on her own back.

The other women rejoiced with Yanga, and gave her the easiest place in the line, where she could keep her own pace and stop when she needed to feed the boys. It tired her to produce milk for two, and she like Flumo feared that she would not have enough. The women knew this, and let her stop frequently to rest. They knew that if the boys died, Flumo would marry again to keep his name alive, probably that young girl from Yanga's town. And if Flumo married again it would surely hurt Yanga, caught in the middle between that clever spider, Toang, and the new young wife.

The rice had grown well. Flumo quickly filled the loft of the shed on his farm with the red-ripe bunches of new rice he tied on the day the women cut his farm. The fence that Flumo and his nephew had built against hungry animals had not broken, and Lorpu and small Toang had done well in driving away the rice birds. The rains had been full and steady when needed, and the late showers had been few and gentle as the rice ripened. Only on the night when the boys were born had heavy rain fallen, sent by the ancestors. And even that heavy rain had not broken the full grains of rice from the bending stalks as happened some years when furious rainstorms, mixed with hail, had beaten down the fields.

Yanga felt sure in her heart that the twins would stay with her. On the fourth day, she had shown the boys to the world, and all had rejoiced at the feast for the midwife and the other mothers of the town. Flumo had brought palm wine, four chickens and a goat for the women, as well as a special present of a new knife for the midwife herself. At the feast Yanga's sister, Noo, repeated Flumo's own suggestion that the boys be called, for the time being at least, "Good-for-nothing" and "Dirt." Noo had herself lost three of the children she had borne to Yakpalo, and her fourth, a young boy, was always sick. She knew better than to let her sister take unnecessary risks. Any man, Yakpalo and Flumo included, would show more love to a woman who bore him healthy children.

Flumo was silently pleased when Noo proposed the names he suggested to her. He could not name them himself, but now the names were given, as well as the traditional names always given to twins, Kona and Zena. He nodded his assent, and even gave Yanga's shoulder a strong grip as he looked at the boys. He said nothing more than, "Feed them well," and "You haven't cooked for me for four nights," but she knew he was pleased.

And so Yanga sang as she rested against a tree in the heat of the day. The memory of that feast the day before caused her even to take a few shuffling steps, trying to dance as the women had danced for her boys. The few dance steps hurt, and so she stopped. But in her heart she danced.

She danced, even though she remembered that Toang had borne no sons and would be jealous. Toang would try to steal the boys' love, or else might bewitch them and eat their spirits, as she had done the other boy. She caught herself before she spoke the dead boy's name to herself, because she did not want the spirits to notice these new sons. She had to be careful if her sons were to survive. Black deer must learn from spider if she was not to be hurt by spider.

Every day when the rice was cut and stored, Yanga and small Toang brought the boys back to town. After two weeks, the harvest was done. Now was the time for the women to prepare to open the Sande Society Bush School next year. They had to plan the time, choose the principal zoes to teach the children, and put medicines on the bush to set aside parts of the forest where men and non-initiates were not allowed.

Yanga was given only light work in these preparations because of the new babies. The dry season was fully here, the dust-laden winds from the north were blowing, and the nights were cold. Yanga bundled the twins up carefully. But fortunately, they seemed to thrive, and did not suffer from the cold that had taken that other boy.

Little Toang was a big help also. She had been in the world for four full dry seasons now, and this was her fifth. Yanga had nursed her three years. Some had said it was too long, but Yanga wanted to make sure that the girl lived. Yanga knew that she could not sleep with Flumo until she had stopped nursing the baby, but there was no rush since Flumo had big Toang to enjoy.

Moreover, during the last year of nursing small Toang, Yanga had been enjoying the secret visits of her lover, Togba, Yakpalo's nephew. She thus had felt no real desire to go back to Flumo at that time. Flumo was so much older than Yanga, and Togba was so young and handsome. Noo, Yanga's sister, had arranged the meetings when Yanga knew that Flumo was occupied with Toang.

Yanga had taken medicine from old Noai, the town's medicine lady, to prevent her affair with Togba from spoiling the milk. Otherwise she might have had problems. But, with Noai's help, she had felt secure.

But then Yanga had realized she must come back to her

husband. Her affair had to end before the new rice was planted, lest the crop fail. Thus the year before the twins were born, Yanga had confessed that she and Togba had been seeing each other. A chicken had been sacrificed on the sharpening stone, Yanga admitted her guilt. Flumo had been angry, had threatened to send Yanga home, but his anger had yielded to a new bolt of white cloth that Togba brought as a peace offering.

Flumo had known it would help him if he forgave Yanga. He could always re-open the matter if Yanga failed to do her work. Also, Yanga had been quiet about her affair, just as quiet as Flumo in his own affairs. He had to smile within himself that his wife had played his own game and played it well.

It had been a long time after that before Yanga conceived. Some said that Toang in her jealousy had bought medicine to keep Yanga childless. Flumo suggested Yanga had gone back to Togba. Yanga had denied it and offered to submit to an *ordeal* by poison to prove her innocence. Just to be safe, however, she asked old Noai for medicine, in case the ordeal were administered, because it was true that she had once, but only once, gone back to Togba, even within the year that the twins were born. She had very much wanted a child for Flumo again even if Togba might be the father.

When the twins were born, little Toang was big enough to do part of a woman's work herself. She carried the babies, sometimes even both of them for short periods. She washed them, she brought them clean clothes, she slept with them in her mother's round thatch house on the smooth mud ledge which surrounded the inside wall, she kept them out of harm's way, and she showed them leaves, sticks and insects.

It was not easy, caring for two babies. Little Toang gave what help she could. Flumo did his best to make fine tools so that men even came from neighboring towns to exchange meat for his products, meat which he gave mostly to his younger wife, even though he knew well of big Toang's jealousy. The fine, dry weather allowed them to live outdoors after the worst of the cold had gone. As a result, the babies flourished. They turned their heads, they looked at the world, they laughed, and they filled their stomachs. They liked it especially when their father would pick up one and then the other and toss him in the air. The boys were fondled and praised by all their family, and all their family's family.

When the cold nights were over, the new year came and with it preparations for the new farming season. Next month they would enter the forest. Now was the time for the town. They drummed, they danced and they sang. They mended or rebuilt their houses, kitchens, fences, benches and looms. They repaired chicken coops, and repaired also the town fence that kept cattle, goats and sheep from wandering into the forest. And, as always at this time, they placed newly beaten rice on green leaves where the paths parted at the edge of town to ensure the good will of the ancestors for the coming year.

Flumo and his wives, just as every other family, put their houses in shape. Flumo and his nephews cut new thatch in the swamps and tied it to weak places in the roofs of his wives' houses to keep out the early rains. They provided new straw for beds. They made new mats for sleeping and to curtain off their beds. The twins slept with Yanga, and Flumo made her roof especially strong.

Yanga and big Toang made salt and soap from forest plants. They combed the seeds from cotton and spun and dyed the thread for Yakpalo to weave into the narrow strips of cloth from which Flumo would sew their clothes. They wove mats and tied nets and traps for catching the fish and game they needed to put on their rice.

Noai, the herbalist, collected her leaves and made charms against the difficulties of the coming year. Old Noai also helped Yanga make pots and other containers for cooking and storage. These had to be made in private, using the special techniques and medicines Noai had taught Yanga during her stay in the Sande Society Bush School.

Flumo worked hard to make the tools his townspeople needed to do their work. Cutlass, axe, hoe, knife — all essential for survival. Flumo as the blacksmith helped maintain life in more than material ways. His hands held the tools of the secret society. His heart realized the needs and fears of each of his fellow townsmen. And his mind kept the unspoken words and rituals which ensured the safety and unity of his people.

When all was ready the townspeople would turn to the forest. There they found the food to maintain life, harvested from roots, vines, trees and shrubs. There lived animals of all kinds, animals which ran on hoofs and claws, those which crawled or slithered or burrowed through the dense undergrowth, those which leapt or flew through the tangle of trees, and those which swam in the swamps, creeks and rivers.

The forest made life possible, but in it also were the spirits which sought to trap men, the dwarfs, genii, evil ancestors who had not received proper burial, witches, and even the mysterious *Forest Thing* known only to members of the Poro and Sande Societies, but feared by all.

Just last year, Flumo's brother, Saki, had seen an evil spirit, tall and threatening and white, on the trail as he was returning late at night from six months working at Firestone. He had arrived in town, breathless, ashen gray, and unable to speak until the next morning. Mulbah, the head zoe of the town, had washed Saki with special medicines to free him from the spirit's power. The elders had often warned townspeople not to walk in that area of the forest alone at night, but Saki was always taking risks, and this time he had been caught. No one could make his farm in that area, lest the spirits bring harm to the town. Yanga never walked there with the twins, even in full daylight.

It was time for Flumo to choose where to make his

farm. He wanted a good rice crop to feed the boys, no danger from spirits, a short walk from town, and friendly relations with the other townspeople. Once he had tried to make his farm just beyond the land his grandfather had left to the family. He had known it was not his land, but the place looked good. But no sooner had he marked the spot by clearing a small patch near the main trail than Yakpalo, his rival, chief of the other quarter in town, and husband of Yanga's sister, Noo, said he would make his own farm there, since the place was his by long tradition. Flumo had found another farmsite, to preserve harmony in the community, but he had had to hide his anger against Yakpalo.

This year Flumo first thought of the place he had made his farm when Lorpu was only a baby. The trees had grown again and refreshed the soil with their dead leaves, and rice would once more grow there. Cutting the young trees and clearing the undergrowth here would be easy. A simple blow of the cutlass would remove a tree. The same oil palm trees and the one great cotton tree he remembered from that earlier farming season were still there, nor would they be cut down. They would only have to clear away the new growth, and the farm site would be ready to burn.

But he decided against that location. He needed plenty of rice to satisfy Yanga and the twins, and he knew rice would grow better deep in the high forest. He selected a piece of forest where Flumo had hunted only last month. It was there that Flumo had killed the bush cow that Yanga had feared to eat, lest it harm her unborn child. Moreover, others had brought him black deer, monkeys and civet cat killed in that area, with which to buy their tools. These animals Yanga could eat, although the twins could never eat black deer or cassava snake.

Yanga had thus already eaten well from this part of the forest, and she and the boys would eat well again when they harvested the good crop of rice Flumo knew would grow here. He would have to work hard to cut the big trees, but the harvest would be good. Flumo planned to cut the forest himself, with the help of men who work for the tools Flumo made them. Flumo did not join a work group this year, since he had to spend most of his time in the blacksmith shop. But a work group would help him clear the forest and make his farm in return for tools.

But to make the tools, Flumo had to have more iron. He had heard that some blacksmiths were now using iron brought by the *kwii,* those strange people, some black and some white, who had come from the coast to his own *Jorkwelle* Kpelle country during the year when his daughter Lorpu was born. And now Lorpu was big enough to enter the Sande Bush School.

Flumo did not want to yield to the kwii people by using their iron. Before the kwii had come to his people, his town had been free, free to fight its own wars, free to take slaves from the *Mano* people who were always troubling them, free to live their own lives, even free to be hurt by the very wars they fought. Flumo wanted to remain free, and smelting his own iron was important to him.

Flumo thought back to the year that Lorpu was born. Strangers had come, strangers with rifles, saying they came to protect the people. Their chief — they called him the *D. C.* — lived at the new town of Gbarnga, and sent his soldiers to Flumo's town two or three times a year. They demanded money, something Flumo and his people had before only known in the form of iron rods which came down from the *Loma* people to the north. Kwii money consisted of small round white things, worth nothing to Flumo, but worth food and hard work to the kwii. The soldiers also collected rice and palm oil for the D. C., and took men from the town to plant rubber trees at Firestone.

The kwii did not let the people settle serious disputes in their own way, in the Poro and Sande societies, as they always had. No, they had to take the matters to Gbarnga and let the D. C. decide what should be done. That was not all they had to take to Gbarnga. The kwii came with rifles to force the people to bring their rice, oil, cassava and kola nuts to Gbarnga to a market held by the *Mandingo* people. In return, the Kpelle got money, cloth, tobacco, salt — and also iron, iron which some blacksmiths now used to make their knives and cutlasses.

But that iron meant a kind of slavery to Flumo. Ever since he was initiated into the highest grades of the Poro Society, he had made the long walk into the deep forest every two or three years to get his iron. It was a secret the Kpelle knew, a secret which made the Mano and the Loma jealous and which forced them to come to Kpelle country to buy their iron. And now even this secret was being taken away from him. No, Flumo would go to the forest for his iron this year, even if he never did so again. He wanted to do it for his boys and for the ancestors, who watched over his boys. Other blacksmiths might use kwii iron, but he at least was still a true Kpelle man.

Flumo had to prepare himself for the work ahead. He kept himself clean, avoided his wives, and purified himself to make sure the iron would be strong and workable. Toang knew enough to leave him alone. Yanga would not, of course, come to his house while the twins were so young. He was sure, moreover, that both would remain faithful to him during his absence to make sure the iron was not spoiled.

The night before he and the boy who helped him left to join two other blacksmiths from farther in the forest, they sacrificed a white chicken at the grave of his grandfather. They asked the ancestors to be with them, and to help Flumo keep the tradition he had been taught. Flumo had heard that once a young girl had been sacrificed in his town to make the iron good. But that was not necessary now.

The men walked into the high forest, not far from the great river, to a hill they knew had good rocks from which to make iron. Still there from the last time was the furnace they built by packing termite clay around a banana stalk and then burning out the stalk, leaving a strong, smooth column. Flumo and the other men packed the hard dry charcoal, the dark rich ore, and the wood of the corkwood tree in layers in the furnace. They made another sacrifice at the foot of the cotton tree which had been planted there when the place was first used. They rebuilt the hut near the furnace to house the bellows, and then began the hot, tiring but serious business of smelting iron.

For three days they heated the furnace, until finally the rocks melted and the liquid began to flow and stiffen at the base of the furnace below the hole which they had cut into the side. They reheated and mixed the liquid iron until the blend was right for tools, working until they had enough iron for the next three years.

Flumo returned home, laden with new bars of iron. He washed himself with medicines and then sacrificed two white chickens and new rice to the ancestors, before taking the iron to the shop to test it. It was strong and clean, fit for the finest cutlass and axe he could make. He was sure it was better than the kwii iron from Gbarnga, even though his brother Saki laughed at him for all his hard work. But Saki had lived with the kwii at Firestone, and no longer understood.

Flumo set to work at once to make a cutlass and axe for himself. They were two days in the making, the best wood for their handles, the edges sharp and sure. He did not work so well for others. He knew that, and so did his friends. But they did not have twin boys at home, twin boys who, God willing, would stay this time, and not return to the ancestors.

Flumo knew well the men who would cut his farm. Most were from his own quarter, and before he had become blacksmith for the town, he had often cut in the bush with them, shoulder to shoulder, striking blow after blow at the tangle of vines, at the young trees, even at the forest giants. Flumo knew how to work, his body next to his neighbor's, how to move in rhythm against the green wall, how to follow

the beat of the drummer who sang with love and admiration
for their strength and skill, how to accept the admiration of
Yanga and big Toang when they wiped the sweat from his
brow.

The sound of the red deer horn called the men early in
the morning. The men were ready, warned by the town crier
the night before that the work group would go to Flumo's
farm. Only Togba was absent, a fact which worried Flumo.
Togba would have to pay his fine of a freshly killed deer to
the group. Had it something to do with Yanga? He wished he
knew if that affair was really over. Perhaps the twins. . . .
But he stopped himself before he completed the thought.

The men made sacrifices to the ancestors for a fruitful
farm, and before the sun had broken through the morning
mist they were deep into the forest. Dark was on the earth,
and remained unbroken where they were to cut the farm.
Even at mid-day, when the full strength of the sun would
burn last year's rice farm, dry and brown with the broken
stalks that had once fed the swelling rice, the forest remained
cool. A spot of sunlight here, an elusive shadow there, were
all the men saw of the sun.

A small troop of white-faced monkeys jeered at them
from a safe distance. Flumo noticed that the monkeys were
more afraid now that the kwii people had brought rifles to
the forest. He was glad the twins could still see the monkeys.
Frustrated birds cried out at not being able to seek grubs in
the earth that the men disturbed. And butterflies danced
along with the dry, dead leaves that fell from the trees at this
season. It was a good day, and Flumo felt the strength of his
loins as he prepared to lay low the forest for his sons.

Before the work began, the leader of the group offered a
sacrifice for the farm. He poured out some palm wine, while
another man roared and pawed the earth like the wild buffalo
which he had known was his animal double ever since eating
buffalo meat had made him sick, and his grandfather had
warned him in a dream to be more careful in the forest.

All the men had ties with the forest. In order to be a good worker, one must have an animal behind him. It was even said by some in the town that Flumo's brother, Saki, must have no animal, since he did not like farming, and spent so much of his time at Firestone. Flumo's own double was the bush hog, and he must not kill it and most certainly not eat it, lest he sicken and die. The twins would not know their doubles until the ancestors showed them. Flumo hoped neither would be like Saki.

For Flumo and his friends the town and the forest were things apart, both necessary to life. Their job now was the dangerous and serious business of bringing the town and the forest together, so that men might eat and live. And so the sacrifices they performed were important. Without them, the harvest might not be good, and the forest might even strike back. One of the giant trees which dominated the land and protected it from the sun might fall and kill a worker. A leopard might attack their party on the way home. Surely it is better to do what is required than to risk trouble.

Another risk would be to cut down the great cotton tree which spread its branches at the edge of the farm. It is foolish to disturb the spirits of a cotton tree. These spirits had often befriended Flumo, and he respected them. Once, when passing under a cotton tree, he felt suddenly he had to stop and look ahead of him, and there was a large cobra prepared to strike. He had thanked the spirit of the cotton tree, and later made a sacrifice in town.

The earth was thick with fallen leaves and branches. There was a steady rustling as the termites tried their best to clear the earth of these fallen trees and limbs. Termites helped make the soil rich for the rice that would later be planted. Flumo thought to himself that the ground here would be good, after the fallen trees had been burned and the ash mixed with the soil.

Before the men started working, the leader cut a vine and set it aside. If Flumo and his wives entertained them well that day, the vine would be given to Flumo. If not, the members of the work group would use it to make medicine to spoil the farm. Flumo knew what they were doing, and so couldn't help take a quick look where the women were getting ready to cook the food.

The women and children had come to the farm not long after the men. Yanga had small Toang to help with the twins while she and big Toang supervised the cooking. They had palm wine to refresh the men and speed their work. And they brought rice, oil, greens, dried fish, dried red deer, salt and the small, hot red peppers the men loved, with which to cook the day's food. The women who were not cooking watched while the men stripped to the waist, put on animal skin gloves and cut into the first trees. The women clapped in rhythm while the men aimed blows in unison at the trees.

Flumo himself set out to cut the biggest of the trees. He hoped the twins might see as he built a platform from small saplings so that he could strike his axe blows above where the buttress roots spread out to support the vast bulk of the tree. He cut deeply into one side with careful strokes, then moved to the other side and made a deep matching cut, somewhat below the first. When the tree was ready to fall, he called a warning to the others, and with a few last blows, toppled the giant. The tree carried with it smaller neighbors and opened the area to a long-absent sun.

When Flumo's tree fell, the drummer sang Flumo's praises as he increased his beat. The audience and the work excited him. He danced as he made his instrument resound, and he sang of the excellence of the workers, the greatness of the forest and the rich harvest of rice which was sure to grow in that place.

Shortly before the sun reached the top of the sky, the leader of the work group sounded his red deer horn. The meal of rice, richly laden with palm oil, fish and meat, was ready. The men left their work and went to join the women who had food waiting for them in large pans and *calabashes.*

Flumo asked the ancestors' blessing on the food and called on God, the head of all the ancestors, to guard them. Then all ate, and ate heavily.

The men rested until the sun reached the top of the sky, and then returned to work. There were more and more patches of light on the forest floor, where the protective umbrella of trees had been cut away, and they shifted position as the sun began to turn downward. The afternoon lengthened into evening, and soon it was time for a second break. The men ate the rest of the rice and soup, and then finished cutting the areas assigned to them. They would return the next day to finish the job. As Flumo took off his gloves and shouldered his axe to start home, Yanga swelled with pride. He turned to her and looked affectionately at the boy on her back and at his brother on small Toang's back. No words passed. None were needed.

Flumo had hired the work group for two days, since he had to make a farm big enough for his two wives and his children. When the second day was completed, he was grateful that the work was done well. Only one man had cut himself with his cutlass. The women had found the right leaves in the forest to stop the bleeding and had tied it with vines and strips torn from an old shirt. The man had gone back to work, but knew that he would need old Noai's help that night to keep the sore from growing worse.

The work group planned to work the next day on the farm of one of its members. Flumo gave them all axes or cutlasses, and even added a whole red deer which he had killed after the first day's work on the farm. The deer, when smoked and dried, would give food for all the farms still to be cut. There was no need to hold back the vine from Flumo's farm. The men gave him the vine with pleasure, and went on with their work. But before they had completed the last of the farms, the air was beginning to grow heavy, as if the rains might come early.

The other work group in town, the one organized mostly within Yakpalo's quarter, was late cutting the forest. As the air grew heavier, they had only begun to cut their farms. Flumo asked himself if the man from Yakpalo's quarter who had asked for Lorpu to marry his son when she finished the Sande Bush School would be a good husband when his people could not cut their farms on time. Not only did Yakpalo's people try to steal his wife, but they were lazy.

The twins were moving about on their mother's and small Toang's backs. They smiled at their father, they made noise, they even tried to sit up on the ground. The first night of rain was the first time they sat up without falling — another good sign. The air had been heavy all day, and, as night came on, the clouds that had built up refused to go away. The town slept, but in the night dogs wakened and roosters began to crow. As the wind blew, the thunder rumbled in the distance, and the horizon was lighted in brief, intense flashes, showing the huge clouds that built up rapidly around the town. The rain fell, and fell heavily, wildly.

Small Toang was excited. She knew that the termites would fly, liberated by the rain that had finally come. She had seen them waiting in the earth when she dug in the forest for yams. They would wait there, perfectly formed, until the first heavy rain released them to fly. The next night, just before dawn, they would fly by the thousands.

That next night small Toang took a clay bowl and joined the other children and even those adults who were not too old to enjoy the hunt. Torches were set on poles around town to draw the mating insects to them. Great numbers of the insects clustered around the torches, as well as on fences, house tops, tree trunks, and kitchens, only to fall back exhausted from their marriage flight. Small Toang scooped them up by handfuls and filled her bowl, polished smooth inside so the termites could not crawl out.

When her bowl was full, she ran back to the house to drop the termites into a hot, dry pot to parch them. She added salt, made sure they were properly dry, and winnowed the wings in a flat woven basket. The feast was ready, and she ate hungrily and noisily, burning her fingers and her mouth. She didn't care. The termites were too good. She even tried to give some to her little brothers, but her mother slapped her hand before she could put the termites in the boys' mouths. They were still too young for most of the joys of life.

Before Flumo's farm could be burned, the trees, limbs and leaves must dry. If it rained too much and too early, the farm would not burn well. There was nothing to do but to wait and hope for a break in the rains.

During that first heavy rain, water had wakened Flumo from his sleep. The night the twins were born, his house had stayed dry, but during the dry-season months insects had eaten even more deeply into the thatch cover. Flumo realized that he had not put new thatch on his roof for five dry seasons, even though he had thatched his wives' houses two years ago. Therefore he and his nephews went into the swamp to cut thatch for the roof. He wished it were his sons, but he knew he would have to wait many years before they could help him. There was little water in the swamp as yet, and so it was not difficult to cut the large piassava palm fronds he needed for his roof.

Flumo had been told that just last year at Gbarnga the D. C. had put kwii iron on the roof of his house. He had not been to Gbarnga to see it, but his brother Saki had seen the house as he passed through Gbarnga coming back from Firestone. No water passed through the roof. Insects and snakes could not live in it. Saki wanted such a roof himself, if only he could save the money the next time he went to Firestone. Flumo hesitated to try something so new, although he also didn't like having to replace his roof every five or six years.

He and his nephews stripped the old thatch from the high round roof that topped the circular, windowless house, after moving his medicines from the eaves. These medicines protected him, helped him be a good blacksmith, and gave him power when he went into the forest on Poro society matters. He checked the poles that underlay the roof, and found them all solid. However, he had to replace many of the vines with which the roof poles were tied.

The men then tied the thatch to the vines, starting with the lowest level, overlapping the thatch so that rain water would run off the steep roof. The layers were thick and the thatch was carefully placed to please the eye. Flumo thought with pleasure of the day when Yanga would once again sleep with him there, proud in the possession of a good house and two fine boys.

While they waited for the rains to stop, a dispute reached Flumo's family. Last year, his brother, Saki, had quarreled with Togba, Yakpalo's nephew, the same Togba, that had slept with Yanga. Before Saki went last to Firestone, the two men had gone in the forest hunting and had killed a black deer. Togba had wounded it with an arrow, while Saki had tracked it down in the forest and killed it with a knife. Togba claimed it was rightfully his, but Saki insisted that the animal would have easily recovered if he had not killed it, and that therefore the animal was his. The quarrel was quickly settled, because the elders agreed that any animal belongs to the first man to wound it, in this case Togba. But Saki felt wronged, and told his friends his heart was not satisfied.

The quarrel had grown a few days later when Saki had offered Togba some palm wine. Togba had been sick later that night and accused Saki of trying to poison him. They had taken the quarrel to Flumo as chief of Saki's quarter as well as Saki's brother. Saki had had a witness who had drunk the same palm wine with no ill effects. However, Flumo had warned Saki always to taste palm wine before offering it to anyone, even his best friend. Flumo had asked each to say all that was on his mind and then apologize to the other. Saki had told how Togba had been mean to him, and had given him none of the black deer, not even when Saki admitted the deer was rightfully Togba's. Togba in turn had described how

Saki had almost thrown the palm wine gourd to him, without taking a polite and friendly taste himself before passing it.

Flumo had let them say what they wished, and then had asked Togba's grandfather, the oldest man present, to say a blessing. The old man, half-blind but greatly respected, had recalled the old days to the people gathered on Flumo's porch, and had asked the great ones who had been alive in those days to bless these young people as they came back together. Both had been wrong and both must bring a token. He had waved his fly whisk at each in turn, and in response each had brought a gift for the other. Saki had brought a head-tie from Firestone, to give to Togba's sister. And Togba had sent to his house for a dried front leg of the black deer he had won from Saki. And both had agreed to forget what the other had done and said.

After a year at Firestone, Saki had returned and heard how Flumo was still angry with Togba. Thus no one was surprised to hear that Togba and Saki had fought in the forest. They had met at a narrow point on the trail that leads to Flumo's farm. Each had tried to force the other off the road so that he could pass, and then Saki threatened Togba with the proverb, "If owl goes up in the sky it must come down and drink water."

Togba knew what Saki meant and asked Saki what kind of water he must now drink. Saki invited him to come taste it, just as he had tasted the palm wine that other time. Togba agreed, and the two began to fight. When they came back to town, Saki's head was bruised where Togba had thrown him against a tree root, and Togba had trouble walking because he had caught his foot on a rock.

They were brought to the town chief, and Flumo and Yakpalo were called to see about their young relatives. The town chief reminded all present that fighting in town is bad, but fighting in the forest is worse. If no one is present to witness the fighting, then anything might happen. He said sadly, "Animals know each other, but human beings do not."

Saki wanted to sue Togba in the chief's court, but the town chief, seeing Flumo did not like that idea, suggested instead that they sit there on the chief's porch and discuss the matter as friends. He pointed out that no blood had been shed, and thus there was no need to perform a sacrifice. If blood had flowed, then more serious measures would have been necessary, but this affair could be settled easily to bring the town together again.

Once again Togba's grandfather was called on to give the blessing. He had grown older and could walk to the chief's house only with Togba's help. In a shaky voice, he asked that his own grandfather, who had known the town when the cotton tree was only a small sapling, be present to keep his town in order. He then sat down to listen. The chief called on Togba and Saki to question each other. Each claimed the other had started the fight. Saki almost wanted to wrestle Togba to the ground again, but Flumo stopped him. Togba re-opened the old matter of the palm wine, claiming Saki threatened in the forest to poison him. Saki in turn accused Togba of trying to destroy Flumo's family, but again Flumo quieted him.

The outcome was clear, but each had to speak his mind fully. Togba said that Saki had been on Yakpalo's grandfather's land, and warned him, "Rooster should not crow in his friend's town." There were general murmurs of approval at this, since everyone knew Saki crowed far too much. On the other hand, Saki's reply, "A rascal is like a bowl because he has a deep inside," was well received, since everyone knew Togba had slept with Yanga.

Flumo and Yakpalo could not show favorites, even though Flumo tried to put in a few good words for his brother. The decision was unanimous, and the chief voiced it by asking, "Does leopard call bush cow a dangerous animal?"

First Togba and Saki must apologize to each other again. They did so, although reluctantly. Flumo gave Saki a white chicken for Togba, and Yakpalo gave Togba a bolt of white cloth for Saki. Both accepted their gifts, although Flumo realized he had been outdone by the generosity of Yakpalo's gift of cloth.

Second, both had to pay a fine, but not a fine in money or goods. The trail was too narrow at that point. Saki and Togba must go together and widen the path, so that two men could pass easily. And if they fought again, both would be driven from the town. The worst thing to happen, the chief stated, would be for the town to lose its unity. There were always quarrels but rarely open fighting. Such brawling could kill the town. Flumo knew he had to agree to the verdict — but nevertheless he made his brother a fine cutlass with which to do his part of the work.

CHAPTER III

Thorns and Rice

III: THORNS AND RICE

As the rainy season drew near, Flumo and his whole family went to the farm to burn the now-dried trees and limbs. Flumo knew he must be careful. The fire must be started down-wind on a calm day, so that it could be easily controlled. Flumo remembered when Yakpalo's younger brother, then a boy just the same age as Flumo, had been trapped on a farm. He had been in the line of men lighting the dry brush with long piassava palm torches, when the wind had shifted and had caught him between two lines of fire. There had been no way to escape, no way to rescue him. They found his body as soon as the ashes were cool enough to let them pass.

Flumo would never let that happen to him or his family. Small Toang was to keep the twins safely out of trouble. They started the burning at a corner of the farm at the top of a slight hill. There was little wind, but what little there was blew beyond them into the surrounding forest. Yanga had brought a live coal in a green stick. She gave the boys to small Toang and set the coal in a handful of palm nut husks, well soaked in the palm oil itself. She blew hard on the coal, and soon had fresh flames. She dropped the burning husks in a pile of grass, leaves and sticks, and the flame sprang up.

The men then took their torches, taller than a man, and lit them from the flames. They carried their torches to other points to spread the fire. Soon the billowing smoke cut the men off from one another, and sound replaced sight. They called to find where each man was in the line, lest any be trapped. The fire moved irregularly, leaping from one pile of brush to the next. The smoke rose high from the ground, column joining column to form miniature thunder clouds. Flumo could see similar columns of smoke from other farms, and so knew he had chosen the right day to burn his farm.

However, there was rain in the air. Even as the farm burned, a few drops fell on the men, and Flumo looked up, concerned that it might rain heavily, spoiling the day's efforts, and requiring him to come back again to re-burn the farm. It was always harder the second time, when there was too little unburned brush for a good fire. Flumo could hear thunder and thought it came from where the columns of smoke joined above him.

Yakpalo too heard the thunder while he worked at his loom in town, and was concerned. His work group had cut its farms late, Yakpalo realized. A relative had died in another town. He had wanted to finish weaving cloth he had promised as bridewealth for his nephew, the son of his older sister. Other men in the group had likewise put off cutting their farms, one until his brother returned from Firestone, another because he had been sick with fever.

The very night that Flumo finished burning his farm it rained heavily. Yakpalo was resentful and suspicious. Perhaps it was caused by the smoke from all the farms burned by the men in Flumo's work group. Perhaps Flumo had medicine to make the rain hold off until his own work was done. Whatever the cause, Yakpalo would not be able to burn his farm until the rain stopped.

It rained heavily for a week, for two weeks. Yakpalo's head wife was restless, and when, after two weeks of rain, she cooked his evening meal it was small and tasteless. She never told him directly when she was angry. But Yakpalo knew something was wrong.

She answered, when he asked her about the food, "Did you put a rock in a clump of mud in order to hit me with it?" Yakpalo did not press the point. He knew it would hurt his family, if they were forced to plant late. The crop might fail if the rains came too soon and stopped equally early.

In the meantime, Flumo and his family were busy cleaning and piling the burned sticks around the larger stumps. When the rains stopped, they would have a final burning of the charred sticks, and then the farm would be ready for planting. He protected himself by getting Mulbah to place unburned pieces of the torches used to set the fire at the entrance to the farm to keep off witches and others who would harm the crop.

But before the rain stopped, one of the twins, the one they called "Good-for-nothing," refused to eat. The untimely rains were falling. Yakpalo was visibly unfriendly to Flumo. And the boy was restless and hot, crying almost steadily. Yanga hoped that the ancestors were not seeking him. After all, was he not "Nothing" to them? She was concerned more that someone was making medicine against the boy. It could be Toang, but she had been more friendly recently. It could be Yakpalo. Could it even be Togba?

It was said in town that Togba had joined a medicine society to make him a better fisherman. He often went to the big river, and lately he had come back with heavy loads of big river fish. Some said that he was in alliance with water spirits, that in his dreams at night he went under the water, broke down the fence that kept the fish safe from attack, and found those he wanted to catch. Then the next day he would go to the river and catch those very fish. But he would have to pay the spirits of the water, pay with a member of his own family. What would be better than his own son, a son he had not acknowledged? Perhaps the twins . . . . No, that was a thought better not brought into mind.

Yanga took the boy, Kona, to old Noai, the medicine lady. She had to use his twin name, Kona, with a zoe woman, even though she had to call him "Good-for-nothing" before the ancestors. Noai was Flumo's father's sister, a woman who had known the whole history of the town. She was old, even older than Togba's grandfather, but still strong.

Noai had lived in the town since it was founded, remembering the very day when she, as a young girl, had been brought to live in the first houses built here. Her family had moved from the old town, which had become so big that it had been attacked by the Mano people from across the river. The Mano had come late one night in the dry season, stolen the rice from the storage sheds, burned five houses, taken off three young girls, and all the while shouted to one another in their harsh, ugly way.

The Kpelle all knew the Mano were lazy and had to steal their rice from others instead of growing it themselves. That time the Mano must have heard of the fine rice harvest and come to take it for themselves.

Noai remembered that she had barely escaped being taken prisoner herself. She had hidden between the buttress roots of the town's cotton tree, where she had been safe. She too might have been taken over the river, perhaps forced to marry a Mano man, perhaps even eaten. She thanked God they had not taken her with the other five girls.

They had left the town the next day to find a new town site. The diviner had thrown his kola nuts on the ground to consult the ancestors. The halves of the nuts had all fallen face up on the third throw, which he had said meant they should tie a stick to a hunting dog's neck, and let him run loose in the forest. Where the stick was caught, they should build the new town. The dog had run into the forest, stopped at a stream to drink and then climbed a hill. Near the top the stick caught in a thicket of vines, and there the new town had been built. It was a fine town site, high on a hill, near a good supply of water, surrounded by high forest, and easy to protect.

Her father, Flumo's grandfather, and the other men had cleared the hilltop, and built the first houses. They had then performed the necessary sacrifices. They had surrounded the town with a vine to mark it off from the forest. In the center of town they had set up the town guardian, a small carved head, put three clean, white stones around it, and built a tiny thatch house over it, scarcely big enough for the smallest child to stand inside. Around the house, they had put more-rocks and a fence. This would guard the town, and be the visible home of the ancestors. When the town elder, grand-father to the present town chief, died, they buried him be-fore the small thatch house, within the fence. Every year, after the harvest was complete, they brought him new rice in green leaves.

The day the town was founded, the elder had been the one to give the blessing. His nephew had sacrificed a sheep, and fortunately it had not cried out. The old man's nephews and all the children of his younger wives confirmed the bless-ing. Some persons had decided to remain behind in what was left of Noai's birthplace, which thus remained the uncle town to the new town. The old man's head wife had remained behind with her children, and he had moved with his younger wives to the new town, and so he continued as elder of both towns.

Even today the relation lived on. Flumo had married Yanga from that town, even though now it seemed small and unimportant. Moreover, he still thought of marrying that pretty young girl, herself a relative of Flumo's mother's sister. Yanga would have to accept the girl if he brought her, because it would help keep all the old ties.

Old Noai knew all these matters, knew all there was to be known about the relations between the people in the two towns. Even more important to Yanga was that Noai knew the relations among all the people who now lived in the new town. If Toang or Yakpalo or even Togba were responsible for Kona's illness, old Noai could help find it out.

Before that, however, Noai would use the leaves she had learned as a girl whom all knew to be a natural zoe. She had played all the games in town with her friends. She had run from house to house with the other girls, begging gifts. She had joined the girls to tease and entice the boys. She had done her best to avoid laughing when other girls told funny stories, and when to laugh would have meant punishment. She had swum with the other girls in the river where they also washed clothes and got water, hoping the boys were watching, diving to the bottom to bring up sand to keep from being caught. But best of all she had enjoyed the games that showed her the ways of the forest.

In one game that small Toang also knew, the children taught each other the ways of animals. The leader would sing, "Put goat's horn on the plate" and the group would respond, "Plate" if goats really had horns. But the leader might trick the group by saying, "Put dog's horn on the plate," and anyone who responded "Plate" would be required to tell the name of her boyfriend. Noai had rarely been caught, and soon had learned all about the animals of the forest and the town.

In another game she had enjoyed the children had to name only plants of one type, such as plants with edible roots or trees with thorns. Noai had rarely been whipped by the other girls for naming the wrong plant. She had been even better at the game they all called "sensible person," in which a string of leaves would be shown to the children to name in order. The leaves, even as many as 25 different kinds, would be tied to a vine, and the child had to call the names rapidly and without mistake. The other children tried to bring the hardest leaves possible, but Noai had known them all. Everyone had said this was proof she was born a zoe.

But even the born zoe must be taught. Noai had learned medicine from her grandmother, learned which leaves, which roots, which bark, which fruits could heal the many diseases which caught the people in town. She had learned how the world of forest things is divided. She had learned the types of root crops, the trees of the bush and the low and high forest, the different types of vines both useful and useless. Without being told she had found the vine which has in it cool, fresh water for the thirsty traveler. Even the small shrubs have names, and she had learned them. Grass is of little use, but soon she had learned which to avoid because it could cut the unwary passer-by, and which could be ignored.

She and her grandmother often had gone into the forest to collect leaves, and she had been forced to repeat over and over again the names and qualities of every leaf that man can use. And on these trips, when the leaf collecting was over, they would stop and collect mushrooms. Noai knew the small delicious kind, which make the soup so tasty, and knew also the red, dangerous mushroom, from which deadly poisons could be derived. She knew also, although she was told never to reveal the secrets, which leaves and barks could be mixed to kill quickly, to kill slowly, or merely to weaken an enemy.

She had learned the water foods, oil, honey, palm wine and the sweet juice of the right forest fruits. She knew which kind of bee gave the sweetest honey, and which to avoid. She knew the very earth itself, the types of rock and sand and clay that could be used. Some clay was for pots, pots made only within the Sande society. Another type of clay could make a girl beautiful to a man, and still another should be rubbed on the face and chest of a sick child. She knew them all. And finally she had learned all those evil things in the forest which must not be angered.

Thus when Yanga brought to Noai her child, Kona, whom she desperately hoped was "Good-for-nothing" to the ancestors, she was sure the old lady could heal him. And even if healing were not possible, she could show Yanga the next step. Noai could stop a running stomach, could cure a fever, could staunch the flow of blood, could heal most common ailments, provided it was not a matter of witchcraft. But if witchcraft were involved, Noai would know who might be involved and what to do next.

Noai asked what was wrong, and said they should wait

until she made the medicine. She went into the bush behind her house and brought leaves Yanga did not know. She mixed them with bark from a pot in the corner of her house, pounded them in a mortar, added palm oil and poured the liquid down the boy's throat. But she warned if there was any evil matter involved the medicine would not help.

And indeed it did not help. For a second day the boy refused to nurse, and his fever did not leave him. He cried less and looked dry and old. His mother forced rice water down his throat, and some of it he spat up again. By this time, she was thoroughly frightened and went back to Noai. Noai's advice, however, was to go to the head zoe, Mulbah, the town's chief medicine man and curer of witchcraft. Mulbah knew as many plants and leaves as Noai, but also understood the deeper forces that cause serious sickness. Noai was sure there was some matter within Yanga's family which caused this problem.

As soon as Yanga showed Kona to Mulbah, he recognized that this was no ordinary sickness. No leaf could cure it, but only finding the witch who had caused the trouble. If the witch were not found, and did not confess, then the boy would surely die.

Yanga gave Mulbah a white kola nut and a white chicken before he could start. He had to heal the boy and reconcile the family. He sacrificed the chicken, ate the kola nut, and then called on his ancestors, his animal double and Flumo's ancestors. He drew in the sand before him, and the spirits guided his finger.

From these markings he saw that the witch was in Yanga's own household. He told Yanga he would come to her house to find who had bewitched the little boy and was now eating him. If none confessed, he would have to use sassa wood, to find the witch by ordeal. Yanga was surprised, because she had feared Yakpalo's household, had feared even Togba. She was also relieved, since now the problem was made more simple. They knew where to look for the witch.

Yanga knew of sassa wood. She had been present many years ago when Mulbah had found a witch that way. Lightning had struck a house in town, and the spirits had shown Mulbah that someone in town had sent it. No one had confessed, even though the chief and elders had begged the people to avoid the ordeal and tell what they knew. Therefore, Mulbah had made medicine for every adult in town to drink. If a person were able to vomit it, he was innocent. If, however, it remained in the person's stomach, he was guilty and would surely die.

He had brought together all the town adults, male and female, and showed them the medicine, reminding them of what would happen to the guilty party. Still none confessed. He then gave it to three persons, all of whom vomited immediately. They were innocent. The fourth in line refused to take it, confessed his guilt, and rushed off into the forest. Hunters ran after him, and soon brought him back, tied with vines. He admitted that he had bought medicine to destroy that house because he hated the man who lived there. His own children had all been sickly and his farms poor, while his neighbor never suffered. He had been determined to bring the man down to his own level.

This had been a serious case, since the man had waited until three people had taken the dangerous medicine before confessing, and since by his own admission he had destroyed a house. He and his family begged the medicine man and the town elders not to kill him.

Since the matter was so serious, the final decision could not be reached in the chief's palaver house. It could only be made at a secret meeting of the officials of the Poro society deep in the forest, with no woman present. A man who had committed so serious a crime should bring a cow or a sheep before the elders heard the case. However, because he was so poor, the elders let him bring what he could. No one in town would help him, so he sent to his brother for a red chicken and five red kola nuts.

The men then retired to the forest. The head of the Poro society in all Jorkwelle country came from a distant town to help settle the case. The guilty man knew that at the least he faced exile, and that at the worst he could be killed. Everyone had heard the story of the great chief on the other side of Gbarnga who had buried a man alive in the center of the town for no worse a crime.

The man was put in stocks while the case was discussed in his presence. He heard alternatives, and trembled for himself and his family. But his brother argued his case well. The man had suffered too much from bad fortune, and he himself would help his brother work for the injured man to make up the loss. The final decision was to sell the man into slavery to the Mano people, and give his wife and children to the man whose house had been destroyed. The brother also must work one year for the injured man.

Thus, Yanga did not want sassa wood to be used in her family. The results could only bring disaster to all of them. Moreover, the baby was still alive, and perhaps the whole trouble could be avoided and the baby get well if the guilty person confessed.

So Mulbah went with Yanga to her house to test for the guilty person. Flumo's face darkened, and big Toang ran without a word into her own house. Mulbah said he had come to do his duty to the village. If Toang was a witch, she must say so. Toang emerged from her house, her face hiding her feelings, and confessed to Mulbah that she had hated the boys from the very day of their birth. Moreover, the night before last she had dreamed of going deep into the forest to a wild witches' dance with the boy, "Good-for-nothing." There she had given the boy to her fellow witches. When the boy had fallen ill, she knew she was the cause. She begged Mulbah to forgive her, and to heal the boy.

Mulbah then told her she must go through the town, and tell everyone loudly of her dream. She must say to all the spirits who had taken her on that night ride, "I am leaving you; don't bother me any more." After she did so, the boy would recover. Toang hastily left Mulbah and her family, and ran through the town shouting to all the people and particularly to the witches who had secretly invaded the town to dwell in the air, the trees and the dark places. She told them to leave, and she begged the ancestors for help.

Yanga felt an immense sense of relief. She had thought, as Toang talked, of using witchcraft herself, but now there was no need. Her son would recover. She took him in her arms, forced some more of Noai's medicine down his throat, and in the quiet of that moment, he began to nurse again. Toang came to her, touched her shoulder, and said only, "Thorns try to grow when the rice dies."

The rain that had kept Yakpalo and the others in his work group from burning their farms began to lessen, and within a few days the ground began to get dry. But the delay had hurt him, and his farm, unlike Flumo's, was not ready for planting.

The women in Flumo's family were already preparing to plant their rice. They had gathered their seed rice, selecting that type that grew best in the high forest, and were arranging for the women's work group to come to their farm. Old Noai warned that it was still early, that not enough time had passed since harvest, but the others said that the rains were here and that they must plant their rice. It was true that Yakpalo's work group had not burned their farms, but even they knew they were behind schedule.

Yanga, big Toang and the other women in their work group went on the day chosen into the forest. Yanga and small Toang each had a small baby on her back, as did some of the other women. Saki went along to provide music for them. He was the best drummer in town, and it would make the day go faster and be more enjoyable, if he were to play for them.

Flumo had made the short-handled hoes with which to scratch the soil, after the older women had broadcast the

seed rice, saved from the last time they made farm in the high
forest. The old women, including Yanga's mother who had
come to see the twins, scattered the rice from calabashes
while the other women scratched the soil over the seeds.

The ground was soft and firm, just right for working in
the rice. The women sang as they worked, their babies content on their backs. Even Lorpu and small Toang and the
other young girls did their part. They marked off an area for
themselves, and competed to see who could hoe the ground
more rapidly. Everyone except Noai was sure it would be an
early rainy season, and the women were happy with their
world.

However, the dry weather held and no more rain fell,
and within a week Yakpalo's farm was ready to be burned.
His family went to the farm, lighted it and burned it. They
thought to themselves that not much time had been lost after
all, and some even began to think that the farms in Flumo's
group had been planted too early. It had not rained since the
rice was planted, and the ground was hard again.

Toang figured back and agreed with Noai that only five
months had passed since the previous harvest had been completed. Yanga disputed it, saying that the moon had gone behind the hill six times. None could be sure, but it did appear
that the rice had been planted early. No rain in a week, no
rain in two weeks, was bad, and the young shoots which
should have appeared by this time were not yet above the
ground. Yakpalo's wives had of course not yet planted their
rice, and their former anger was turning to quiet satisfaction.
Only Noo, Yanga's sister, was concerned about Flumo's problem.

A gentle rain came just when Yanga was about to give
up in despair, the food for her hungry boys threatened by
the lack of water. The rain was enough to dampen the earth,
and cause the young green rice shoots to show above the
ground. Now the ground hogs and the rice birds would attack
the young plants. Flumo had men build a fence around the

farm to keep out the ground hogs, while Yanga, Toang, Lorpu and small Toang drove away the rice birds with slings. A flock would hover just out of range and then swoop down to steal food where they could get it. A well-placed stone would drive them away again for a few moments. Two weeks of driving away the birds would be enough, after which time the shoots would have taken firm hold. Only at the end of the growing season, when the new rice had begun to swell on the stalks, would they once again have to chase away the birds.

Yakpalo's wives planned to plant their crop after a few more rains. But the rains did not come for five days, a week, ten days. The new shoots of rice on Flumo's farm bent over, turned yellow and began to die. Yanga, Toang and all those who had planted rice early were desperate. There had to be rain. Even if it did come now, the harvest would be poor. They would depend on those who planted late, and they would have to make new farms in the swamps.

Flumo realized that a swamp rice farm was a last resort for women without husbands, or for those whose upland rice farms did badly. A different type of seed — one among the more than thirty varieties that Toang and Yanga knew well — was needed. The bush did not have to be cleared, but only the grass and reeds had to be leveled. Thus the long wait, which Flumo and his wives could no longer afford, between clearing, burning and planting was not necessary.

Flumo looked down on making a swamp rice farm. One had to wade, again and yet again, in the mucky, unhealthy swamp water. He could not join his work group in the joy of hard, satisfying, cooperative work. He could not show his strength in the fight against vigorous forest trees. The family could not join in the pleasure of life together in the forest. Moreover, swamp rice did not taste right, and harvesting the crop was therefore a thankless as well as a dirty task.

Yet Yanga and Toang now had to plant in the swamp. They were sure that the big new farm in the forest would fail.

All that effort would be in vain. Indeed, when the rains finally started in earnest that year, only a small part of the young rice plants on Flumo's farm actually lifted their heads.

Yanga and Toang had to care for this forest farm, but they also had to work in the swamp. Together they still would not produce enough for next year. When they were waiting for next year's harvest to come in, what they had harvested this year would run short — and they would have to turn to Yakpalo for help. Yanga's boys would be in their second year at that time, lusty and hungry, and feeding them would be harder than ever.

The year's work was thus hard and unrewarding. Yanga and Toang kept the weeds from choking the rice on the forest farm. And they broadcast seed in the swamp, after they had cleared it and burned the dry grass and reeds that covered the mucky earth that was more water than soil.

Every day they took the two boys on the round of the farms — small Toang carried one and Yanga carried the other. Yanga could hardly feed both of them and also work the farms. The other women were no help now. They had their own problems with the bad weather and their farm work. Yanga could only trust the good omens that had come the night the boys were born, and work hard for them to live. Big Toang was there on the farms, and so were Lorpu and small Toang. But there was more than enough work for all of them to keep the two farms going.

Finally the rains began to fall steadily. Even the small rice that had survived on the forest farm grew well, and the swamp would yield as much as could be expected. It might not be the best year, but it would give enough to last part of next year. What would happen then was in God's hands.

Everyone was hungry, Yanga thought to herself, as ground hogs and rice birds threatened the farm. Even a pygmy hippopotamus broke through the fence one night and began to eat the rice shoots. Fortunately, Flumo had slept on the farm that night in the thatch shed he had built for his wives and children. He had come to fix the fence, and the rain had kept him on the farm. He didn't mind. It was a pleasure to get away from town, from Yakpalo looking so rich. He was wakened by the noise, and fought hard to drive the animal away. He had only a cutlass, but with it he cut the beast's tail. The next morning he repaired the fence.

There was trouble again when the rice began to swell and ripen, and the rains lessened. There seemed to be many more rice birds than usual that year. They came in flocks especially to the swamp farm, and it was all that Yanga, Toang and the girls could do to keep them from eating the maturing rice.

When harvest time came, the women and the men alike went out to the farm. There was new rice, even though not enough for the coming year. The boys were growing well. Small Toang was a big girl now, and could carry one boy and work at the same time. The women cut the forest farm first, while the children drove birds at the swamp. After putting aside the seed rice, they stored the remainder in the eaves of the thatch shed that had sheltered them on the farm during the rains.

Yakpalo's farm was just beginning to ripen when Flumo's forest farm was cut. Flumo began to wonder if the rice that Yakpalo's wives had planted would have enough rain to ripen properly. But the late rains were generous that year, and Yakpalo's farm produced a rich harvest. Flumo felt hatred growing in him, but said nothing.

Toang's jealousy of the previous dry season was giving way to shared concern for the lean year both she and Yanga faced. She did not like Yanga any better, but she had begun secretly to take pleasure in Yanga's sons. She did not want the boys to die for lack of rice. Perhaps she might be able to ask her mother, two towns away, to help when the hungry season came next year.

She and Yanga could see that the swamp farm would produce little. The swamp had been too sour, and much of the rice seed had simply been eaten by the water. Some had grown, but hardly enough to justify the cutting. It was a group of desperate women who, a month after the forest farm was harvested, picked their way through the swamp, a baby on Yanga's back and another crying on small Toang's back, to collect the few grains of rice it had to offer. Yet they had to cut and store whatever rice they could. The boys were getting big, and Yanga needed enough to keep her family alive. Moreover, Toang realized that she too needed rice, since her daughter Lorpu would enter the Sande Bush School next month.

The rains now stopped, and the dry season brought welcome relief. Just a year before, Yanga had been unable to complete her work because of the birth of the boys. Now they were walking, poking into every corner of their mother's house, and crying for more and still more food. They had moved from sitting to crawling to walking. Yanga began to look forward to weaning them, but it was still too early. It was tearing her down physically to have to give so much milk. She herself was always hungry, perhaps even more than the boys. But she could not stop yet, if they were to grow well.

CHAPTER IV

People Are Like Corn

IV: PEOPLE ARE LIKE CORN

After the harvest was in, Flumo and Toang got Lorpu ready to enter the Sande Bush School. The fence had been built at the edge of town, and the tall Sande drum, taller than the tallest man in town, had been set up near the fence. Lorpu saw women coming and going through the fence, but she herself was not allowed near it, until one morning when the drum boomed out its invitation. Lorpu would spend three years behind the fence, three years learning the arts of womanhood. Flumo was still not sure whether he would accept the offer to marry her into Yakpalo's quarter. Another man, from Yanga's town, had also approached him, and he would have to think the matter over.

The excitement of the Bush School entrance was quickly over, for the time was at hand to make rice farms again. Flumo was preparing new axes and cutlasses for the men, when two kwii men dressed in brown shirts, brown trousers and red caps came to town.

The men carried guns, and acted important. They asked for a house, for food, for bath water, and for girls for the night. The townspeople had no choice, because now they were part of Liberia, now no longer their own people. The Jorkwelle Kpelle had fought hard in the year that Lorpu was born, but they had not been able to resist the guns and the power that the soldiers brought with them.

The townspeople were not happy to see the soldiers come. They knew they wanted something. It was not hard to put up strangers in the town guest house. Often visiting elders or chiefs would pass through, on their way to cross the great river. Sometimes they brought cattle which they would trade to the chief for cloth or rice. The town chief, Flumo and Yakpalo had themselves often enjoyed such hospitality when they had been traveling. Flumo's taboos were red deer and python, animals which he must never eat, and when he found others with the same taboos, he could be guaranteed a warm greeting.

But these soldiers were not even Kpelle men. They were Lomas from the north, and could barely speak the Kpelle language. They had come for taxes, Flumo was sure of that. What else they wanted he did not know. The people were familiar with taxes. They had always paid taxes to the town chief and the Poro and Sande elders. This very year, Flumo was responsible for bringing a bag of rice, two bunches of bananas and a large pile of yams for the Sande Bush School. But the kwii taxes were something else. Last year the town had provided five bags of rice and ten large gourds of palm oil, and in addition each house had paid 84 British pence. The rice and palm oil were no problem, but to get the money they had to sell goods at the Gbarnga market.

Flumo thought back to the year after Lorpu had been born. Soldiers had taken three men with them to the coast, and then over the water to *Fernando Po* to work. Only one had come back, two years later, and nothing was ever heard of the other two. The one who returned spoke of the fear they felt on the big ship, of hard work on a big farm and of not understanding the ways of the people.

The soldiers had come again every year to get taxes and men to work at Firestone. Flumo still was not sure what Firestone was, even though he knew that the men who went there had to clear the ground and plant rubber trees. He also knew that when Saki went to Firestone, he did not make farm but would come back after six months or a year with little other than new clothes and gifts from the coast.

The chief called the people together to find what the soldiers wanted from them this time. He knew they wanted

more workers for Firestone. They had to send three men, or
else the paramount chief and the D. C. would bring trouble
to the town. But, even worse, five men had to help the D. C.
make his own farm. The townspeople knew that when they
went to Firestone, at least they would come back with something. But working for the D. C. was another matter. They
would eat little, work hard, and be beaten if they asked for
pay. They did not know what to do. The men were needed
in town to make their own farms. But if they delayed, the
soldiers would continue to eat the people's small supply of
food, demand hospitality from their wives, and soon begin to
use the whips they brought with them.

There was no choice but to send the men. The soldiers
promised they could come back in two months. They said
that the new law passed by the D. C. said every Liberian must
do two months of work for the government. Flumo's wife's
town had tried to resist last year, but for their efforts they
had only been beaten and the town chief taken to Gbarnga
and put in jail. The government still feared the Jorkwelle
Kpelle, because they had fought so hard the year Lorpu was
born, and so treated any resistance harshly.

The worst thing was when the soldiers forced the men
to carry them in a hammock to the next town. It was one
thing to work for the government, but it was quite another
to carry these Loma men as if they were important chiefs.
The men they chose at first refused, but the soldiers brought
out their whips and beat the youngest one. They had to
obey. But when they reached the stream at the edge of town,
the men looked at one another and realized what they had to
do. They were crossing the log bridge, when suddenly one of
the men slipped. The others slipped too and jumped out of
the way. The head soldier, the one who had insisted on being
carried in the hammock, was dropped and fell headlong into
the muddy waters. The men had managed to drop him just
where the mud was deepest, and he emerged black and soaking wet. They begged his pardon, they apologized deeply, for

being so stupid. But they said they were not used to carrying such loads over rivers and through forests. There was nothing the soldiers could do. The soldiers walked with the men the rest of the way to the next town.

Saki was more fortunate. He was going back to Firestone, where he knew people and where at least he could earn something. But the problem was now what to do with the girl he had married last year. He had gone to Yanga's town and found a girl but had been unable to pay the full bridewealth, giving only a white kola nut and a soft mat to the girl's father. She was now pregnant, and so she could not go with him to Firestone. She at first thought of going home to her mother, but Saki did not like the idea. Since he had not paid the full bridewealth yet, the girl might never return. So he begged Flumo to take her into his house.

Flumo was glad to see Saki go to Firestone. Saki was always in trouble, even now that he was married. It would not be too hard to take care of his brother's wife and his new child when it was born, and would even bring him higher status in town. Moreover, Saki promised that he would bring back cloth and even some money for the family.

However, Flumo was still worried about Toang and Yanga. Toang was quiet and waiting for the family to run short of rice. They all knew that the family's rice supply was not enough for the whole year. Toang's mother had a surplus of rice, but Yanga's family had also had a hard year. Flumo thought to himself, "When black deer is hungry, can he give his horns to spider for rice?" He would have to help Yanga pay Toang for her mother's rice. Flumo could settle that dispute when it arose, but in so doing he must not suggest that Yanga was his favorite. He would have to borrow rice also from Yakpalo, although he hated to do it.

The boys were growing strong and well. One had burnt himself in the fire, but not badly. Both had had fever, and both had passed worms — but Noai had given them leaves to chew to break the fever and get rid of the worms. They ran freely in town, and small Toang was kept busy trying to keep track of them. Other girls had such an easy job, with only one baby brother to mind. She had two, and though she was proud of them, she was often angered and tired by them.

The boys spent time on the large farm that his fellow townsmen were preparing for Flumo. He was busy in the blacksmith shop most of the time, and had little time for farm work, even though there were hardly enough men in town to cut every family's farm.

Flumo's farm itself was hardly big enough for the three families. He would have to collect palm nuts, kola nuts, and coffee berries to sell at the big market in the Liberian town of White Plains. Flumo had walked to White Plains, a one-week walk, two years before the twins had been born. He had more often been to Salala, which was only a three-day walk. But the kwii people had more things to sell and gave better prices in White Plains, because Liberians lived there, whereas Salala was a purely Kpelle town. However, now that the Liberians had put a D. C. at Salala, Flumo hoped he could sell his goods there.

Flumo planted his own coffee trees near town, so that he would not have to collect wild berries in the forest. He knew that the blacksmith in the next town on the road to Gbarnga had planted coffee trees, and was now trading the produce for cloth and even iron. Thus after his rice farm was ready, Flumo went to visit that blacksmith and bought from him enough small, rooted coffee trees to make his own coffee farm.

The rain held up, and the rice grew well. But, as they all knew would happen, last year's rice was finished at least a month before the first of the new rice could be harvested. And now Toang brought her surprise. She announced to the family that her mother had invited her home for a visit, and that she would stay there at least a month. Her uncle had died and she was needed. Toang's home was two towns away, toward the coast, and it took a full day to reach there. Flumo and Yanga tried in every way possible to persuade Toang to come back soon with rice from her mother, but she would not agree. She had her reasons, and could not be talked out of them.

Yanga had counted on borrowing rice from Toang's mother to feed her growing boys. They were strong and hungry, and she needed good food for them. And now Toang was going home, and could eat rice at her mother's house until the harvest. Only when Flumo agreed to go with Toang and to take her mother a present of a fine bracelet, two new cloths, and a goat, would Toang agree to let him borrow some rice to bring home to Yanga. Flumo said to himself, *"Pangolin* showed leopard the way to eat him, and spider was there for the feast." Was not Toang a clever spider, and had not the leopard of bad fortune eaten Yanga? But there was nothing Flumo could do. Bridewealth, he thought, is never completely paid. For the gifts he was taking to Toang's mother he could marry that girl from Yanga's town.

The boys had enough to eat that hungry season, but at the expense of Yanga's status in the family. Toang, the head wife, always distributed rice in the family. But now she was also the provider.

But even this was not enough rice to feed his own family, as well as Saki's wife and child. Flumo hated to do it, but he would also have to borrow two hampers of rice from someone else in town. And that someone had to be Yakpalo, who had plenty of rice remaining in his storage shed.

Flumo did not go directly to Yakpalo, but rather he went to the town chief's brother, Sibie. Flumo and Sibie were distantly related, and had often helped each other. Flumo explained his problem to Sibie, bringing him a white chicken as a way of reminding him of their long friendship.

Sibie in turn approached Yakpalo in a quiet way. Yakpalo was working at the loom, and Sibie came to talk about the weather. He commented on how good the weather had been this year, how it had helped the rice grow well. And then he remembered last year, when Yakpalo had been particularly lucky, even though some other people who deserved as much had been unfortunate.

Yakpalo listened closely to the last remark, sure something was coming. He agreed that it had been a hard year for some people, but gave his opinion that they had not been wise. Sibie countered that Yakpalo shouldn't forget that for a time he had been worried lest he burned his farm too late. Perhaps Yakpalo should help out those less fortunate, lest his own ancestors be angered with him for meanness. The net was closing, and Yakpalo realized it. Who is Sibie talking about, Yakpalo thought?

Then Sibie began to talk about the twins and how they were hungry, about Toang and how she had gone to her mother to stay. There was Yanga, hungry, and there were the boys who would be future zoes in the town. One could never refuse to help a zoe, lest he one day cause trouble. After all, "One tree cannot make a forest," Sibie reminded Yakpalo, and he told him the story of the man who had gone to build his own village in the high bush, so as not to have to share his wealth. But he had become sick, and none had come to help him. He also told of the rich man who did not receive friends in his house, and so when he became poor he was welcome at no house in town.

Yakpalo was reluctant. Did not Flumo bear a grudge against him? Had not people falsely accused Togba, Yakpalo's nephew, of sleeping with Yanga? Was not Flumo caring for the wife and son of that lazy Saki, who went to Firestone to avoid his town work? But Sibie responded, "Antelope's child showed the trap to his mother." One should always listen to the advice of one's friends. Moreover, Sibie said of Flumo, "There are people like corn; if you don't clean the leaves, you can't see the seeds." Yakpalo was allowing the leaves to keep him from seeing the real Flumo, town blacksmith, leading elder in the Poro society, and great-grandson of the town's founder.

Yakpalo agreed. He had to. Sibie had woven a net too strong to escape, a net of words and proverbs. Sibie went and brought Flumo. They talked about weaving, about the tools Flumo was making, about the soldiers who too often came to town, about Flumo's decision not to go again into the forest to smelt his own iron, until finally they came to the matter at hand. Yakpalo agreed to loan Flumo the two hampers of rice, and gave them to Sibie, who in turn passed them to Flumo. Flumo promised in turn that he would give Yakpalo a strong new axe and cutlass in return for the rice when the dry season came. He offered to add a knife, but Yakpalo refused. Had not he and Flumo lived together all their lives? Besides, Yakpalo gained by being generous. The debt should never be paid entirely. Flumo gave his word, and Sibie ended by saying, "A man's word is worth more than money."

Yakpalo and Toang could have their status, thought Flumo as he brought Yanga the borrowed rice. He had two boys, and these two boys were his wealth. Rice too was wealth, but rice was only for eating. The boys would grow and be strong. Toang had no sons, and Yakpalo did not have twin boys. They were welcome to their pride.

The dry season came, and with it a good harvest. Flumo completed the axe and cutlass he had promised Yakpalo, and took them to Sibie. He and Sibie met Yakpalo at the loom. Yakpalo accepted the axe, but said he did not need the cutlass just now. Let it stay until later. Flumo could trade the cutlass to someone else. Flumo did not like it that way, but could do nothing to shake Yakpalo.

The matter was finished. Flumo thanked Sibie — and then realized what he should do with the cutlass. He gave it to Sibie to cement their friendship. Sibie had taken a risk by being the intermediary. They both knew what might have happened if Flumo had not repaid the debt. Yakpalo might have sued him, might have brought Sibie with Flumo into the chief's court. But it was not necessary, and so now Flumo and Sibie were closer friends. Flumo realized it is not good to have too many friends — they are always asking for things. But a few are necessary.

Kona and Zena had been with them now two years. There was hardly need to call them "Good-for-nothing" and "Dirt" any more. Yanga was ready to wean them. She was tired, tired to the bone from feeding the two of them. She was sure she could not make it another season. Moreover, the boys now ate the same food as everyone else — rice, greens, fish, palm oil, and even an occasional piece of well-chewed meat.

So Yanga went one day to old Noai for help. Noai would know the right leaves to rub on her breasts, so the boys would stop troubling her for milk. Noai found the leaves, beat them in a mortar, and helped Yanga rub her breasts thoroughly. The next time the boys came to nurse, they drew away sharply and in tears. They learned the lesson quickly, and weaning was easy. Now they were on their own.

The next two years were filled with watching, waiting, listening and learning. No longer were the boys fondled and carressed by all the women in town. No longer could they run to their mother or small Toang for comfort and love. In fact, for the first few months after weaning, the boys were sent to Yanga's town to live with Yanga's older sister. There they would be strangers, and would learn to make it on their own.

There was so much to learn, whether in Yanga's town, at home, on the farm, or in the forest. Their mother and small Toang took them everywhere, and expected them to learn what they saw. They had to keep their eyes and ears open to what was said. They were praised if they could remember and do what they had been told.

No one told them how to do the easy tasks. Yanga was ashamed of the way that Saki's wife would tell her little boy how to carry wood or how to clean grass or dirt from before the house. Kona and Zena learned simply by being told what to do.

More difficult was learning how to behave toward others. One day when old Noai had come to Yanga's house, Kona, the taller of the two boys, the one they had called "Good-for-nothing," had not bent low to pass the old lady as he left the house. His mother had punished him severely, by putting hot pepper in his mouth. He cried until he thought he could never stop crying, but he never forgot to bend low before his elders.

Kona always seemed to receive more beatings than Zena. He ran where he should not go, took food he had not been given, and tried to be one step ahead of Zena. Flumo was particularly unhappy when Kona acted like this. He did not want his boys to compete with each other. Kona tried too hard. Flumo preferred Zena, who was content to act like the other children. Flumo warned Kona, "Friskiness can bring fish on shore." He was afraid that Kona would someday be caught by his own disobedience, his own curiosity.

Perhaps, Flumo thought, the name he had suggested for his son, "Good-for-nothing" had been a bad choice. It might be the reason why Kona behaved this way. He worried about his son — what would he be as a man? The only answer Flumo had was to warn his son and then to beat him when he ignored the warning. Flumo could not just ignore his sons the way Saki did. Saki left it to his wife to tell the boy what to do. But that was Saki's business, Flumo thought. Let him ruin his son.

The boys also had to learn to speak proper Kpelle. There was so much to learn and Flumo and Yanga wanted them to learn it well. As twins, the boys had talked mostly to each other. Now they had to talk more to others, and it was often hard. Yanga was not surprised that they had their own language. Twins are born to be zoes, and zoes operate in strange ways. But zoes must also talk to others, and talk well. Sounds, names, sentences were all hard to get right.

As the boys listened to their elders, they saw that language is power. Their father was often asked by townspeople for his advice, which he rarely gave directly, in clear, outspoken language. He spoke in proverbs to those who came to him for help. To the person who was reaching beyond his capacity, he said, "A short man does not measure himself in deep water." To the woman who was vexed with her husband for not making a bigger farm, he said, "Can rabbit do the work of elephant?"

One day the boys took a trip with Flumo to Yanga's town for the election of a new town chief. The old chief had died, and his son and nephew both were talked of as successors. The two men tried to see who could entertain Flumo and the boys better.

The old chief's nephew, Flumo knew, was the cleverer of the two, was sure to be elected the new chief. For one thing, he assured everyone that he did not want the job, and thus the town elder asked him to conduct the election. He had delayed holding the election for almost six months, while the assistant town chief had acted in the place of the dead chief. He had used the time to entertain townsmen, make loans, and cement relations. The son of the former chief, on the other hand, said openly he wanted the job, a clear mistake.

At election time, the old chief's nephew greeted the soldiers the D. C. had sent to supervise. He invited them and all the townspeople to a feast welcoming them to the town. But Flumo knew the game. He was using his wealth, even a cow he killed for the feast, to show what sort of man he was. And yet he said he did not want the office. He wanted only an honest election under Liberian law.

After the feast, the soldiers called the nephew to hold the election, and asked for the candidates. The old chief's son stepped forward — and no one else. As a result, the town elders gathered to discuss the problem, and then called the old chief's son to talk with them. Clearly disappointed, he left the discussion and then proposed that he would prefer to see the old chief's nephew have the post. Thus there was only one line for the people to join in voting for the chief.

Flumo's only comment to those near him — and the twins overheard it — was, "The axe that cut the tree, the tree has fallen on it." It was not for nothing, he said, that the nephew won the job. The twins did not understand. There was so much they did not understand. Flumo tried to explain to them that what is unspoken is stronger than what is spoken, but Kona wanted everything explained to him in detail. The new chief held a second feast, and invited everyone to join him. He was generous, perhaps too generous, and remarked to Flumo, "To hold office is better than to hold money." Flumo answered him, "The way the owl sits down determines his share of the feast."

All these sayings sounded strange to the boys, nor did they understand the explanations. They had to figure them out for themselves. The boys did not see rabbit or elephant, owl or axe, but they soon realized that words meant more than they seemed to mean. Zena appeared to understand more than Kona, because he was more willing to sit quietly and listen. Kona asked too many questions, his father felt. A boy who is always asking, always asking, has no time to listen and learn and become wise.

Not that the boys could spend much of their time listening to the elders. Only at special times were they allowed to sit and listen. More often they were with their mothers. They went to the waterside where the women washed clothes, beating them against the flat rock, and washing them beautiful and clean with the soap they made from palm oil and wood ash. At other times, they were at the house or on the farm. They remained close to their mothers, Toang and Yanga, unless their father called for them. Flumo was very proud of them, although he did not often show it.

The boys tried to be helpful when they could, and their mothers praised them for it. They would take branches with leaves and sweep the ground in front of the house. They would put mud in a pot and say they were cooking supper. They would scatter pebbles on the ground and say they were planting rice.

That season, Yanga let them scatter a few grains of rice in one corner of the farm to be their own farm. However, Kona did not want to share the plot with Zena, and so they began to fight. Yanga separated them, and spanked them, particularly Kona, for being so mean. She then settled the matter by giving Zena another corner of the farm, better than the first, so that each had his own spot. She warned them to be careful, not to let birds or ground-hogs eat the rice, nor to allow any weeds to grow there.

Every time they went to the farm, the boys looked hard for weeds. One day, while Yanga was not looking, they found what they thought were weeds, and started to pull them up. Yanga saw what the boys were doing, and cried out to them to stop. They were pulling up the new rice sprouts. They had spoiled Kona's farm, and now he would have no rice. The boys began to cry, especially Kona. However, Yanga gave him another small piece of the farm for himself, and then showed the twins how to tell rice from weeds.

One day the boys were with small Toang, Yanga and Flumo in the thatch shed on the farm. Yanga was cooking rice, and Flumo was working on a fence to keep out ground hogs. Their parents told the children to bring sticks for the work. Some were for the fence to surround the farm, others for the fire, and still others for the eaves of the thatch shed for storing the rice.

Flumo told small Toang to give Kona sticks for the fence. Toang gave him the sticks, but Kona tried to argue that they were not the right kind. Flumo overheard the argument and went to intervene. He told Kona that any kind of stick would be alright, just as long as they kept out the ground hogs that eat their rice. Kona was angry, because he had been sure he knew more than his sister. Moreover, small

Toang was laughing at him for trying to be too clever. Kona had enjoyed trying to divide the sticks into different piles, but he stopped it when he saw that his father did not like it.

Flumo was happier with Zena, who brought sticks for the fire and sticks for building the shed above the fire for storing the rice at harvest time. Kona had also tried to show Zena how to divide sticks, saying that some of the sticks were too green for the fire, but Yanga had laughed at him. She said they would burn soon enough. He shouldn't worry about such things. "Just watch and do what your sister does," she told him.

CHAPTER V

One Tooth

Cannot Make a Mouth

V: ONE TOOTH CANNOT MAKE A MOUTH

The twins had been with them four rainy seasons now. Flumo was sure the harvest would be good, but just a few days before his rice was to be cut, two of Yakpalo's cows broke through the fence, and began to eat as if they could never be satisfied. Yakpalo had built up a herd of eight cattle, by trading and marriage bargains, giving him great respect in the town. But these cattle were always causing trouble, particularly to the farmers. Moreover, Yakpalo rarely killed one to give a feast to the townspeople.

The cows had come very early, while the late night mist still hung on the ground. When Yanga arrived at the farm, she saw the hole in the fence, and guessed immediately what had happened. She left the children, and called to Toang to join her. They ran onto the farm, and saw the cows and the once heavy, bent rice stalks swinging free in the air. She cried out, took a stick and started to beat the cows. They ran, bellowing as they went. Toang ran to the farm shed to get her cutlass, but the cows had escaped by the time she brought it. She was so angry she would have killed them if she could.

Yanga and the twins stayed on the farm, to drive birds from what was left of the swelling rice, while Toang and small Toang went running back to town to tell Flumo what had happened. Flumo arrived to find Kona crying hard. The rice that he had watched and tended so carefully all that season was gone. Yanga did not cry, but was instead frightened that once again she would not have enough rice for her large family. She wasn't nursing now, but Toang and the boys ate more every year.

"Whose cows were they?" "Yakpalo's," she said. Flumo's face grew hard. He was still in Yakpalo's debt for the cutlass from two years ago, and every time he mentioned it to Yakpalo, Yakpalo passed it off as unimportant. Moreover, Yakpalo's nephew Togba was still too friendly with Yanga, even though he had a wife and children of his own. The marriage between Lorpu and the boy in Yakpalo's quarter was supposed to take place after the Bush School closed in two months, but Flumo had not yet decided whether to take the full dowry. Now this trouble was added to the load he had to carry. Yakpalo must take responsibility for the rice Flumo had lost.

Flumo hurried back to town. He knew that Yakpalo would be at the loom, weaving cloth for the townsfolk. Flumo went to Yakpalo and said, "The way owl sits down determines his share of the feast." The way he said it, his face guarded and blank, his voice quiet and steady, made Yakpalo realize Flumo was angry. Yakpalo asked how owl should sit down. Flumo said, "Owl should sit with all his children and watch them." Yakpalo knew then that someone or something of his had done wrong to Flumo. He asked which child of owl was not sitting in his proper place. Flumo answered, "The cows that sleep under owl's feathers."

At that point, Yakpalo's cows arrived back in town. One of them was bawling and walking heavily, favoring her left leg. "What have you done to my cow that she is walking so?" "What has she done to my rice that her belly is so heavy?" The men were getting angry. Yakpalo's nephew Togba ran to call the town chief.

The chief arrived to find Yakpalo and Flumo trading insults and accusations. The cow, however, was not hurt badly, and so the chief first quieted Yakpalo. He then turned to Flumo, who told how Yakpalo's cows had eaten his rice. The chief said that there was no need to carry the palaver further. Flumo and Yakpalo could settle the matter without carrying it to the chief's court. He, as their chief, would talk the matter out later that day. To carry it to court would mean that someone would be hurt, someone would lose. But to settle the matter informally would mean reuniting men who should be friends, and maintaining the harmony of the town.

That evening the chief called a few elders, as well as the *owner of the town.* The owner of the town was the chief's uncle, a wise old man who had once been chief himself. He was the grandson of Flumo's great-grandfather, who had founded the town. The men told Flumo and Yakpalo to sit on the ledge that ran around Yakpalo's high round hut. The chief and the elders sat on small stools sheltered from the late afternoon sun by the shade from the house.

The elders knew that there had been difficulty between the two quarters, starting from the first quarrel between Saki and Togba. It was time to end the problem. The owner of the town stood up, his fly whisk in his hand, and gave the blessing. He began, "We have gathered here safely. May we all depart safely. Men and women, whoever has a bad heart here and wishes any of us to die, may that person die so that we walk on his grave. If a man here climbs a palm tree, may he come down safely. We have come into this house to put cold water before these people. What we say here, may it put this house in peace."

He reviewed the history of the town, showing how the fathers and grandfathers of Flumo and Yakpalo had kept the town alive. He called on the ancestors, the very fathers and grandfathers he had praised so eloquently, to guide them today. He then broke a kola nut and offered the two halves to Flumo and Yakpalo, who ate them in silence. Flumo was still angry, but to have refused the offer would have put him in the wrong. It was a clever move on the part of the old man, Flumo thought.

The elders then urged both Flumo and Yakpalo to say all the things that had troubled them. The matters went back for several years. Not only were the disputes between Saki and Togba brought up, but also the delayed acceptance by

Flumo of gifts for the marriage between Lorpu and the young man from Yakpalo's quarter.

Flumo was urged to speak his whole mind, and reminded that nothing he said under the protection of the ancestors would be held against him. Thus he brought into the open for the first time the fear that had nagged him for years, the fear that Togba might have fathered the twins. Everyone knew about Togba and Yanga. Togba was called, and admitted he had slept with Yanga, but said he did not think the twins were his. Did they not look like Flumo, the same broad nose and jutting forehead? Once again he begged Flumo's pardon.

Flumo raised other insults, even his resentment at not being allowed to return the cutlass to Yakpalo. However, the town chief pointed out that friends must never pay all their debts to one another, lest the friendship end with the debts. Debt is a way of binding men together. The town chief pointed out that he too owed Yakpalo a goat from two years earlier, and he felt no need to pay it back just yet. The time would come when Yakpalo needed something, and he would turn to his friends. The town chief reminded Flumo, "One hand cannot work in place of two hands." He must not try to do everything by himself, even though he must know how to stand alone.

The town chief told the old story of the man who was wealthy and refused to make loans. He kept all his food, his goats and sheep and cows, even his wives and children, within his family. But one day the town turned against him. He refused to give a poor man a loan, and the next night his rice storage shed was burned to the ground. No one, not even the diviner, could find the guilty party. Yakpalo was not a man like that, the town chief said. He knew that "one tooth cannot make a mouth."

After the men raised other cases of suspected witchcraft and refused loans, the town owner spoke up. He agreed that Kpelle people sometimes do not work well together, that often there are quarrels. But he said that the Kpelle know how to preserve the town. Thus there was no need to judge the case, no need to pronounce one party guilty and the other innocent. He concluded, "Tongue and teeth must fight when a man talks."

Both Flumo and Yakpalo knew what he meant. There are always problems when men have to live and work together. Those who quarreled must, however, let the town's voice be heard.

Flumo and Yakpalo shook hands, snapping each other's fingers three times at the end. They promised to end the quarrel. Flumo said his wife would bring a gift for beating the cow. Yakpalo, however, offered something much more substantial. He said he would help the man in his quarter pay the complete dowry for Lorpu, and would add something on top to satisfy Yanga and Toang. In that way, the marriage could take place promptly after the Sande Bush School closed, and the two families, and with them the town, be brought together as one.

There was much applause and finger-snapping at Yakpalo's speech. Flumo had been outsmarted. Why had he not seen what would happen? He was jealous, but he had to smile. Yakpalo had turned a quarrel into a friendship, and had put himself in a very strong position in the town.

Some had mentioned Flumo as a candidate for the next town chief. Even Flumo had secretly hoped for the post. But, after today's quarrel, Yakpalo would surely be chosen. Flumo had no answer, no counter move to make. There was nothing to do but to put himself in Yakpalo's debt. It was well done – a man who could get out of trouble and at the same time increase his own family was a wise man. He would make a good town chief. Nonetheless, it hurt deep down inside Flumo. His rice was eaten, and he was outwitted by the very man responsible all in one day.

When Yanga came home from the farm that night, she reported that the cows had not eaten all the rice, even in the corner of the field where they had broken in. To be sure, all of Kona's rice was gone, and the boy, as he did so often, was still crying at night. But there would be enough food for next year, especially when Yakpalo gave them something to make up the loss. However, Yanga saw that, even though the matter was settled, something had hurt her husband. Someday she would know.

Town unity had been preserved, and now it was time to strengthen it still further by bringing the girls out of the Sande Bush School. Lorpu would rejoin her family, and soon thereafter be married. Already the parents of the boy had brought Toang a bright new kwii cloth and a white chicken, to show their good will.

On the day before the girls were to come out of the Sande Bush School, the town was almost empty. The twins noticed it, and asked where everyone had gone. They stayed with small Toang, while their mothers, Yanga and Toang, went away. But even small Toang did not know where the women had gone. During that day, the boys had only dry rice and bananas to eat. Their mothers came back at dark, and even then Yanga had little time for them. Something was about to happen, but the boys knew only that they were not getting enough attention.

The next day again there was no one in town. Yanga told the boys that the important women had changed their minds. She and Toang must be gone another day. Kona and Zena felt more and more restless, more and more upset about their mother's absence. Kona was particularly unhappy, always troubling small Toang about where their mothers were. Finally small Toang had to cuff him, and send him away crying. He ran back to watch, however, as the old women, all dressed in white, came solemnly into town. He stood nearby as they sat in front of the small thatch house in the center of town which contained the town guardian spirits, and then watched them again go behind the fence at the edge of town.

The next day it happened. Kona and Zena cried out with surprise when the roar of the gun broke through the early morning mist of dry season. Smoke rose from the distant forest, as if a town or a farm were burning. At the signal there were loud cries on every side. Men came out of their houses, dressed in their best country cloth robes. The boys were frightened, as they had been the night before, when they had heard the women driving a terrible-sounding witch from the town. Even small Toang did not know how to comfort them. She had asked her mother what was happening, and was told only, "You are too young yet – your time will come later."

Toang went with the boys to the center of town, where the chief's court had been newly rubbed with cow dung. Mats were spread in the open space around the palaver house, and it seemed that almost all the men and young children were there. Women kept coming and going, laden with clothes and ornaments.

At one side of town, a group of men were dancing and singing. Two men were at their head, beating *fanga drums,* held under their arms and alternately compressed and relaxed to yield varied tones. Before them went two men with a long pole, which they leaned against each of the houses in turn. The men, joined by occasional women, would dance before the pole, and then move on to the next house. They moved slowly in the general direction of the fence at the edge of town.

Noo ran to the group and danced excitedly and happily, until Yakpalo came to her, took her around the shoulders, wiped the sweat from her forehead, and pressed a British penny there. She danced away from the men back behind the fence, where the activity seemed to be concentrated.

In another corner, the delicate traceries of a belly harp and a mouth bow joined the tiny vibrations of a thumb piano. Only Saki, Sibie, and Yanga's brother Kerkula seemed able to hear the sounds, but they were content. The boys stopped to listen, and it seemed to calm them, even though there was noise on all sides.

Small Toang had her hands full when the boys left the musicians. They wanted to leave her, run to the center of the square to see what was happening, to play on the mats. She had to box their ears severely to keep them in place. Toang did not know what was coming, but she knew she had been stiffly warned not to let the boys run loose. They cried for a moment when she hit them, but then stayed obediently at her side. They knew from long experience that such beatings meant they must sit still and wait.

Kona and Zena had to wait endlessly, they felt. They could hear the women behind the fence, shouting to the girls to get ready, to put on their clothes, to be quiet. The girls had never been so close to the town, although the twins had often heard them singing in the morning or the night, singing with a quiet beauty from deep in the forest. Now they were just on the other side of the fence. Their town had been burned. Zena had pointed out to Kona that the smoke was still rising high above the forest. The girls had to come into town by night.

But still they waited, and the boys were hungry. Yet each time they asked small Toang for something, she would beat them and tell them to be quiet. Finally the boys saw women coming. At the front of the line was their second mother, big Toang. She carried feathers in her hand, and she came announcing something. The boys had not known that big Toang was so important in the Sande Society. Even small Toang had not realized it. But now here she was, at the head of the line.

The chief was there to receive her, and addressed her as the hawk who had carried the girls away to the women's Forest Thing, and now had come back bringing good news. The boys remembered having heard stories of this bird. Now here she was. The chief heard what she had to say, and repeated it to the people. They applauded, the drums sounded, and two of the younger women broke free from the crowd to dance a few steps in the open space. The chief quieted them again, and told Toang and the other lady with her that they should go for the girls.

They went back and then from behind the fence came the same women dressed in white the boys had seen yesterday, followed by all the girls the town had not seen for so long. There were girls from their own town but also girls from Yanga's town and from two other nearby towns. There were more girls than small Toang and the boys had thought could possibly live in the forest. Small Toang had never been behind that fence, because she had been told it was not time yet for the forest thing to eat her. All these older girls had been killed and eaten, and now they were alive again. Small Toang did not understand, but she was glad to see them alive.

She started to cry out greetings to them, but her uncle standing near her told her to be quiet. Had she been telling her little brothers to be quiet all this time, and she didn't know that lesson herself? He asked her, "Can bullfrog tell cricket to be quiet?"

Even had Toang greeted them, the girls entering town would not have answered. They walked bent to the waist, dressed in their finest clothes, looking at the ground. They had white chalk on their faces, and their hair was beautifully dressed with ornaments and braids. Toang wanted to reach out and touch each girl's hair, to hold and play with the beautiful small things she saw there. She wanted to wear the bright cloths that each wore under the *lappa cloth* that covered her shoulders. But she had to be patient – her time had not yet come.

She had seen her father, Flumo, making different things in the blacksmith shop. She could not go close, because only men could sit and watch and talk there. But she had caught the glint of colors different from the usual dark iron, the same red and white she now saw in the girls' hair. There were also ornaments the men had bought in Gbarnga or brought back from Firestone. To her the girls were beautiful beyond belief.

The older women zoes at the head of the line — Kona and Zena recognized them also, dressed in white — stopped before every house, and the girls had to stop and kneel down to the ground. Mothers and fathers danced around them, before them, beside them. Men fired rifles into the air. Women threw new clean rice over them as they walked. Drums boomed and rattled. Then the zoes would start the line moving again, until finally they reached the open space opposite the small thatch hut which contained the town guardians. The chief's house was on one side of the open space, and the chief's court on another. There the girls sat on mats, opposite the zoes. The head zoe then stood up and asked for the ancestors to bless the girls, and make them good mothers when their time came.

While the zoe spoke Toang's eyes were fixed on the girls. She knew that Yakpalo, her father's rival, had been weaving cloth for almost the whole year, and had thus not made a rice farm. Townspeople had brought him rice and promised him that he would not have to work, if only he would produce fine new cloth for their daughters. Toang had seen the women spinning thread from the cotton they grew in their gardens outside town. She had seen them prepare dye from leaves and bark, and dye the thread yellow, black and red, while some was left its natural white. The thread had then been stretched in long lines through the village and wound onto sticks to give to Yakpalo, who had woven it into bolts of cloth in strips the width of his hand. The cloth was mostly from the black, white and kola-nut-colored thread; for some special persons he put in a few lines of red.

Small Toang had learned some of the meanings of the colors from the older women. She knew that white pleases people, and binds them together. When Flumo, her father, had sacrificed to their ancestors at the twins' birth, it had been white — a white chicken, a white cloth, a white kola nut. When a stranger comes to visit, the white kola nut is the best sign of friendship.

Yet white is a frightening color also — the beautiful and the frightening are so close to each other, Toang felt. A tall, white, faceless *genii* had so frightened her uncle one night that he could not speak for a whole day. The water woman, who offers herself and wealth to a man in return for his children, has white skin and long, bare, white arms.

Toang had seen a man, white as any genii, come out of the forest the year before the twins were born. The man had stayed in town two nights, but only by the end of his visit could Toang overcome her fear and touch his skin. She had heard also that a white doctor lived in Mano country, and knew all the medicines of the Mano and more besides. Toang wanted, yet did not want, to see a white man again. Kona often asked her to tell the story of the white stranger, but Zena showed no interest.

Small Toang knew black as the color of darkness. It is an insult to be given a black gift. Yet even black things can be useful. Once Yanga's cousin had been told by old Mulbah that black dangers had come to her in the night, and that she must sacrifice a black chicken to protect her from those evil spirits. Also, black is the color of people as well as the color of the finest dye the old women can make, and so can be beautiful.

Red is the most frightening color, Toang thought. Even though black is the color of night, no one knows what red will bring. Only the most powerful zoe, the strongest medicine man, can wear red cloth. It is all right to mix a few strands of red thread in a chief's country cloth gown, or the cloth of a Sande Bush School leader. Toang saw a few girls with red threads in their clothes, and she knew they must be important girls. But an all-red gown would be a serious challenge to the most powerful zoes, and Toang had never seen one.

Toang knew that if a zoe offers a person a red kola nut, it is a threat. Yet the gift must be accepted to prevent worse trouble. Moreover, when Yanga had been sick two years earlier, old Noai had sacrificed a red chicken to the ancestors to keep the sickness from getting worse.

All these colors, as well as the neutral color of kola nut, go to make up cloth, to make the beautiful clothes small Toang now looked at. Life too is made up of good, evil, uncertainty, and the ordinary matters of every day. Her mothers had always taught her this, that she should never be certain of life and never trust anyone too much, not even her own family. Had not her second mother, Toang, tried to eat the twins in her dreams? The cloth that was woven for these new graduates of the Sande Bush School, the cloth that showed the intermixing of the elements of life, the cloth that Toang wanted for herself when her time came — this cloth now returned to town to show these girls were now women.

Yet some of the girls wore a different kind of cloth, bright but alien cloth brought up-country from the Liberian town of White Plains. This cloth did not have meaning woven into it, but it had its own strange beauty. It was cloth written all over with colors and pictures, cloth such as Toang's people could not make. The older people in town painted pictures on the walls of their houses — animals, people, and even designs which Toang could not yet understand. The chief's house, with its carved pillars at the front and its walls covered with paintings, was a wonderful place. But her people could not put pictures on cloth.

The new cloth wore out soon, but it was beautiful. And one could get it, not by the long, hard work of planting, harvesting, combing, dying and weaving, but merely by giving the people in White Plains palm kernels and coffee berries for it. Flumo had given his friends tools from his blacksmith shop in return for palm kernels and coffee. The men carried these to White Plains to buy Flumo enough cloth for Lorpu's new clothes, as well as gifts for Yanga, Toang, small Toang, and the boys. The men had travelled for three weeks to bring the goods, but they and Flumo felt it time well-spent.

Flumo felt somewhat strange about buying Lorpu this

new cloth instead of the country cloth they had always used. He excused himself by saying that Yakpalo was too busy to make cloth for everyone. However, he knew in his heart that he wanted to see the new cloth. Moreover, it would make big Toang happy — so little made her happy these days. Finally, he still did not like asking Yakpalo for anything. With the new cloth, he made a new wrap-around lappa shawl and head-tie for his daughter.

And now here was Lorpu in the line, her head bent down, wearing her new clothes, her pride showing through her enforced humility. Small Toang hardly knew Lorpu who had been in the Bush School, for three farm seasons, longer than Toang could remember. Yet Toang knew Lorpu by the beautiful cloth her father had brought, and by the most beautiful ornament she saw in the hair of any of the girls. How she wanted to be in her sister's place then! She showed the twins which one was Lorpu, but kept them from running to her.

The girls entered the square and sat in a half-circle on mats prepared for them, their eyes fixed on the ground. The townspeople murmured their approval, as rifles were fired and women broke loose to dance to the ever-present drum beats. Each family brought small gifts to the important women of the society, who were sitting on mats at the head of the line. Two women in white cloth were the most important, and behind them was old Noai, the medicine lady. Flumo took his present, ten round white British pence and a bag of kwii salt, and put them on the mat in front of the women.

Salt was important but hard to get. Toang had heard Flumo tell how a whole hamper of kola nuts used to bring only one bar of salt from the Mandingo people. The *Bassa* people made salt on the coast, but it was not as good as Mandingo salt. Even it, though, was better than the bitter salt the Kpelle made for themselves from banana leaves.

Today things were changing. The Liberians in White

Plains traded salt, clean, white, in bags, and much better than the bars of Mandingo salt. Even Mandingo salt could be bought in the new Gbarnga market, one bar for a hundred kola nuts, the same price as for a gown length of Mandingo cloth. Flumo could not help being glad that the Mandingoes had brought markets to Jorkwelle country.

Thus there was loud clapping when Flumo put a bag of new, white salt on the pile of foodstuffs before the zoe women. The men had bought it for him in White Plains, but had told no one about it. He wanted it to be a surprise to the women. Kona and Zena were very proud of their father at that moment.

Only those whose daughters had not returned from the Bush School failed to bring gifts. Flumo's aunt had been told her daughter would remain behind, and was grim-faced and dry-cheeked as she stood at the edge of the crowd. None would mourn with her today, but later Toang and Yanga would go to cheer her. A broken pot had appeared at her door that night, to confirm what she had already feared.

Then the chief stood up and walked the whole length of the line to inspect the girls, looking at them carefully, as if to make sure the women had trained them well. With him was Saki, Flumo's brother, the best musician in town. The town elders, including Flumo, followed behind. The smile on the chief's face showed his contentment, and his gift to the important women in white confirmed it. He brought two sheep and a cow, so that the people from all four towns might feast that day.

Before the feast could begin, the nephew of the chief, his sister's son, had to kill the sheep. He took the first sheep, talked to the spirits, put his hand over its mouth, turned its head to one side, and then neatly slit its throat. If the sheep had cried out, everyone would have suspected him of adultery with one of his uncle's wives, a great crime and insult to the ancestor spirits. He repeated the ceremony with the other sheep, and then with the cow. The town chief, the

nephew and old Mulbah then offered the animals to the ancestors, to the spirits who had protected the girls during their
three long years of separation from the village and to the high
God. The nephew then sacrificed a white chicken, so the
blood could flow over the dead animals, and Mulbah pro-
claimed himself content with the way it died.

Great steaming clay pots of rice were prepared, the
sheep and the cow were cooked in huge iron kettles, and the
people from all four towns ate in honor of the newly initiated girls. It was full moon, the harvest was in, the girls
were safely back in town, and so everyone, except the families whose daughters had died, danced and sang the whole
night.

The girls were soon released from the restraint of their
first inspection on the mats. They remained under strict discipline long after their return to town, but now they could
visit their homes briefly. But whenever they met an elder
they had to kneel and be touched on the back before they
could go on. And they must always appear in public bowed
to the waist. Only when the zoes gave them leave, could they
dance. Lorpu was relieved to be free for a few moments of
the discipline, and she danced freely and happily under the
full moon, her raffia skirt catching the dust raised by her bare
feet. She knew she was being watched. Her future husband
was there, and he came to her, wiped her forehead, and gave
her the first token of his love. She looked at him — and ap-
proved the choice.

The boys, forgotten for the time being, enjoyed the
celebration. Their mother was happy and gave them more
meat than they normally saw in a week. It had been a good
year and a good Bush School, and the town was content.

CHAPTER VI

Kwii Things

VI: KWII THINGS

During the next two years Flumo did not have so many requests for cutlasses, axes and knives as before. Tools he had already made were still in use. Moreover, many men were working at Firestone, and those who returned sometimes brought with them tools they had bought at the kwii markets. Nevertheless, his rice shed was full and his family well.

Every year the soldiers came to ask for more workers for Firestone, for road building, for work on the D. C.'s farm, for carriers for important Liberians traveling by hammock through the country. Some of the men in town were glad to go to Firestone. They could escape the other hard labor the government forced their fellow townsmen to do. Each man had other reasons as well. One had had a bad year on the farm, and hoped to earn enough money to buy his rice. Another man's wife was hard to live with, and he was glad to leave her and the children for a while. Still another wanted to earn the money to redeem his son who was working for Yakpalo to pay off an old debt.

All those who went to work for money were asked by their families to bring back "kwii things." The kwii were the coastal Liberians, those men who were black like Flumo but who acted like the white man who had visited their town the year before the twins were born. More and more kwii were coming up-country in their fine clothes, bringing with them new tools, new weapons, new foods, and new ways.

Yanga and Toang, like all the women in town, wanted the cloth, the pots and pans, and the ornaments the kwii had. But if the men bought these things, they could bring little else with them, and it was often hard for their families to find enough to eat. Flumo was sure they would be better off if they followed his example, stayed at home, and made their farms.

Flumo particularly tried to persuade Saki not to go back to Firestone, but Saki would not listen. He liked to leave town and be with the kwii. Moreover, he had a woman at Firestone, and she was very beautiful. It cost him money to keep her happy, but Saki believed it was worth the expense. He was sure none of the other men would tell about her, because they had their Firestone women too.

But just to be on the safe side he brought special gifts on his last trip: earrings for his wife, yellow and shiny; cloth to make his daughter a dress like the kwii children wear; pictures like those on the cloth for his son. These pictures were in what Saki called a book and could only be looked at and not used. Saki's wife could make no sense of it. He had to turn it over for her so she looked at it the right way. He laughed when his friends tried to look at it, but could not understand it.

One day Saki's little boy tore one of the pictures away from the book. Saki beat him for it, telling him that kwii people do not tear up pictures. But there was no way to put it back. The picture was spoiled now. Saki was going to throw it in the bush, when Kona begged him to let him have it, even though the picture by now was torn into five pieces, Kona spent the whole day looking at his picture, putting it together, and thinking what it might mean. Zena was not interested, but this was Kona's first real kwii thing. It had come from the white men at Firestone, and Kona wanted to know more.

Kona hoped his father would go to Firestone too, would bring back more of these wonderful things. But Flumo did not want to leave his town and family to work at Firestone, even to buy the kwii things for himself. Moreover, Flumo had joined his work group to make his own farm. The fact that fewer people wanted to buy his axes, his cutlasses and his knives, meant he had to do more work for himself. He hunted for meat in the forest. He cut palm nuts in the forest for palm oil and for the kernels he would try to sell.

Flumo's coffee was growing now, but he would have to wait two or three more dry seasons until it bore fruit. Times seemed hard. Flumo did not find as much joy in life with the town divided and many men absent. And the new pleasures of the kwii world were hard to get and too costly.

Flumo decided he must get something from the kwii people for himself. Other men come back with good things, and his wives were jealous. Thus when Flumo heard that his cousin was going to the big market in White Plains to trade, he decided to go with him. He collected his palm kernels, two large bags full, and persuaded Saki to help him carry his loads to the market.

Saki and Flumo and the other men made the week-long trip to White Plains, where a new store had been opened by a German. Flumo had never been into kwii country before, and he did not really like it. He saw kwii Liberians, soldiers, a German trader, and people from all other parts of the country, people speaking languages he had never heard before. He took his palm kernels to the German trader, and decided to buy a rifle. The trader took the two bags of palm kernels, and asked for one more to be sent the next dry season. Flumo agreed, despite the extra work involved, because now he too could have a kwii thing, one which would help him feed his family.

Saki went on to Firestone, and even tried to persuade Flumo to go with him, just to see the place. But Flumo wanted to get back to his family and his town. He had had enough of kwii people to last him for a long time, and besides he wanted to hunt in the forest with his new rifle, and show the people in town that he too was a man.

Yanga and Toang were pleased with the rifle and Kona was very proud. It would make hunting so much easier than using the bow and arrow, even when the arrow was tipped with poison to kill the animal quickly. He had already started showing Kona and Zena how to shoot arrows accurately. They and the other boys often played at hunting on the edge of town. They would shoot at trees, at leaves, even at birds in the trees. Kona rarely hit the target, but believed he could do better with his father's rifle.

Flumo soon took his rifle to the forest. He walked quietly, carefully, so that no animal might see him. He reminded his animal double, the bush hog, that he had never hurt it, and asked it to keep the other animals from being suspicious of him, so that he could approach them closely.

Flumo took other precautions as well. He had Kona and Zena bathe his gun in medicine before he went in the forest, since he knew that twins can bring good luck to the hunter. His membership in the exclusive Sheephorn Order of the Poro Society and the Snake Society would protect him.

The sheep horn, filled with onions and special leaves from the forest, pounded together with white clay, which protected him from robbery and accident, would keep him from the dangers of the forest. And new hunting medicine made by Mulbah would guarantee the success of this important first hunt with the new gun.

Flumo stalked quietly from the first gray before dawn in order to find what he wanted. A good kill would help his standing in town. A leopard had recently killed two goats belonging to Yakpalo.

If Flumo could kill the leopard, he could regain some of the reputation he had lost when Yakpalo had outsmarted him. He would put Yakpalo in his debt for helping save his wandering goats. He would have to give the skin to the chief, but the chief would honor him for it. The meat would help feed the hungry town. Even though he would have to give most of the teeth to the chief for his wives, especially the youngest and most beautiful who always traveled with him, Flumo could keep some teeth for his own wives and children.

And the claws would be his to give to Kona and Zena as medicine to protect them throughout their lives, to give them special status as children of an important man.

It was full morning when Flumo finally saw what he was looking for. He had killed a black deer on the way, but now he had his real prey. There, high in a tree above a stream, he saw the familiar gleam of gold and black. Another leopard might be nearby, and so he moved very cautiously. A leopard on a branch above him could drop on him before he moved.

So, with a brief prayer to his ancestors, to the spirits which stood behind his medicines, and to the high God who made everything and who had power over all spirits, all medicines and all animals, he moved slowly forward. Before him in a tree lay a leopard, half asleep after a night of hunting. He crept closer, until he had a clear shot at the dread animal.

He raised the rifle, took careful aim − and fired. The animal dropped with a great roar of pain and anger. Flumo had done his job well. The animal could not move, but looked up at Flumo with his eyes misting over with confusion, wonder and anger. The great beast lay dying as Flumo moved to his side. There was no one in his family whose animal double was the leopard, and so Flumo had no fear. And if it had been a human leopard, the beast would have taken human form before his eyes. Had it been a lesser beast, Flumo would have cut off the tail quickly, to make sure that it could not return to some human form. But, since he wished to preserve the skin intact, he took the risk.

Flumo had hit the animal just below the lungs, and the shot made a hole just above the stomach. He had missed the liver and the heart, where thought and breath have their home, and so the animal had not died at once. Instead the animal died from loss of blood, blood which can never be replaced once it is lost. As he watched the blood soak the ground, he wished he had killed it more quickly. But soon enough the leopard's eyes glazed and then closed.

The leopard was full-grown and heavy, a fine kill. Flumo

left the animal where he had shot it, and took back to town the black deer he had killed earlier. He left the deer in town for his nephew to skin, clean and cut into parts, and then took three men back with him to the forest to bring the leopard to town.

When the men brought the animal to town, they carefully removed the skin to honor the chief. Flumo was now glad he had shot it in the stomach, since the beauty of the back was not marred. When the skin was removed, the animal was cut up and the chief distributed the portions to the men of the town to fight over, after he had kept some for himself, and given Flumo and the other men who had helped carry it their part.

As he worked with the men to cut up the leopard, Flumo thought about animals and men. He knew that man is a town thing, while leopard is a forest thing, food for man. And yet he knew also that man and animal are one, since man can change into his double and back again. There in the leopard were the same kidney to clean the blood, the same liver to turn over in anger or to remain quiet in time of calm, the same nerves to carry blood and pass messages, the same testes to give children to the mother, the same brain to receive sensations, the same heart to cool the blood. He wondered again whether this leopard might be some man he knew — but he quickly put the thought out of his mind.

Yanga and Toang would dry the leopard and black deer meat over the fire in Toang's house, and then store it in the loft. It would be good for at least a month, before it became too spoiled to eat. Even so, there was not as much meat as Flumo would like, since he had given the kidney, liver, left leg, spleen and heart of the black deer to the medicine societies he belonged to, and had also sent pieces to his and his wives' relatives.

The Poro Society elders took their meat with thanks. It had been two years since the head zoe of the Sande Society had turned over the town and the forest to the men. The male Forest Thing and his wife had been for a long time now in the deep forest, but soon they would return. The men were preparing for the next session of the Poro Bush School, and there were only two more years to get ready. The meat Flumo gave them would help in the preparations for the time when Kona and Zena and the other boys would be initiated.

Flumo thought with pleasure of Kona and Zena coming into manhood. They had been with him for six farming seasons now, and in two more years they would be taken into the Bush School and become men, with men's names. No more would Flumo have to think of them as "Good-for-nothing" and "Dirt," or even as Kona and Zena. They had come to stay, and would soon be men. Strong leopard meat would help them grow well.

That night the family was full, even too full, with the meat from the feast. And there was more stored in the large clay pot of oil in the loft. There was new rice in the storage shed, and it was a time of peace in the town. The bush had been cleared and burned, but it was not yet time to plant the rice. The creeks were low, and the fish easy to catch, with the nets that Yanga and Toang had made during the days after the harvest was complete. The farm that Flumo and his work group had cut in the forest was large, and there would surely be plenty of rice for the coming year.

But then there came a surprise. Soldiers arrived in town to announce that the president of Liberia himself was coming up-country. The town chief had seen the old president at a conference held in Kakata three years before the twins were born. But now, for the first time, the president of Liberia was coming to Jorkwelle country. He would hold a big meeting at Gbarnga, and he expected all the important men to be present. The paramount chiefs, all the clan chiefs, the town chiefs, and all the town elders must come. Moreover, they must bring food so the strangers could eat well. The president had 40 people in his party, and they must be fed for a week. Finally, the town must send men to help carry the 10 most important people in hammocks.

It took eight men to carry one hammock, in two shifts of four each. The down-country people would carry the strangers to Gbarnga, but the Jorkwelle Kpelle must carry them back to Totota. This meant that every town near Gbarnga must send two men to help with the hammocks, and must also send 30 hampers of rice and other food. This would cut deeply into the supply that Flumo and his fellow townspeople had laid away for the coming year.

But there was no choice. The people had heard what had happened to people who refused to cooperate. The last town to refuse to put up the white cloth of surrender had been harshly treated. The Jorkwelle people had resisted longer than most, and Flumo was proud of them for it, but the resistance had been futile. The president of Liberia had finally forced all the warriors to lay down their weapons and had made the people melt them down to make cutlasses. He said he wanted work, not war. The soldiers had come into Jorkwelle country from Naama and Sanoyea, which had been the first areas to give up.

The president had told the people they could no longer fight wars, sell slaves, take prisoners, or even deal with important disputes. Flumo wondered to himself what slavery really is. Two of the three men that had been taken from the town to go over the great water to work had never come back. And the third still told stories of how he had been treated there in a country he did not know. Was that not slavery, Flumo wondered? And was it not also slavery that Kpelle boys sometimes went down-country and never returned? They were taken by coastal Liberian families and made to work hard, made to work without pay, and not allowed to return home. One important chief beyond Gbarnga was a rich man now because he had sold bad boys or men who could not pay their debts to people at the coast. The D. C. said this was against the law now, but Flumo heard stories that it was still happening.

The old president had come to Kakata, but two years before the twins were born he had quit his job. Some said that white men had made him leave the job. He had been sending too many people over the water, and many did not return. Now there was a new president, and this was the first time he had come this far up-country.

There was nothing to do but to receive him well. The townspeople agreed to give what the soldiers asked even though they knew the soldiers would keep some for themselves. Flumo himself had to give two hampers. Such demands were increasing every year, Flumo thought. He would have to make bigger farms to make sure his family had enough rice.

Flumo sent one man from his quarter to help carry the president's party, while Yakpalo's quarter also sent one. It was easier for Yakpalo to do so, since his quarter was growing. Just last week a young man from a nearby town joined Yakpalo's quarter, and was living with one of Yakpalo's new wives. Flumo's quarter, on the other hand, seemed to grow smaller rather than larger. He envied Yakpalo the new man who would help to make Yakpalo even richer than he was now.

Flumo could not see how to regain his standing in town. His own sons were still very young. And the other young men in his quarter were like Saki, fun-loving and worthless. They fought, they drank, and when things became too difficult for them, they ran away to work at Firestone.

The last thing Flumo had to give up for the president's visit was the meat he had dried and saved for his family, the very leopard and black deer meat that had cost him a day's hunting. No one else in his quarter had saved so much dried meat, and could give it to the soldiers.

CHAPTER VII

Cassava Grows
Only in Its Own Shade

The Chief hears a palaver

VII: CASSAVA GROWS ONLY IN ITS OWN SHADE

The loss of his meat bothered Flumo, and he was sure he would need more before he could leave to attend the meeting in Gbarnga. His family must be well-supplied during his absence. Thus he decided to go hunting once again before the president came up-country.

Flumo went out early one morning into the high forest. He was determined to shoot at least a red deer, if not a bush cow. He saw elephant rubbings high on one tree, but he realized that his rifle was not powerful enough for that. Moreover, Yanga's sister had elephant as her animal double, and he did not want to kill the animal that was her source of strength. She could do the work of two women in planting or harvesting rice, and everyone said it was because elephant was her double.

She had found this out because she had one morning wakened with a badly swollen foot. She told the diviner she had dreamed of walking in the forest, breaking down the trees as she went, and then stepping into a hole and twisting her foot. The only animal big enough to break trees, the man reasoned, was the elephant. Moreover, her swollen foot looked like that of an elephant. He decided her double had hurt itself, and made a special medicine that would cure both her and the elephant. The swelling went down, but now she knew the relation between her and elephant. Flumo would not hurt her, and so, even if his rifle had been powerful enough, he would not have pursued the elephant trail.

Flumo planned to set a trap for a bush cow if he saw no animals during the day. He had special medicine with him, and he also knew the right way to bait the trap. But first he must try his luck in the forest.

He went quietly and carefully. He wore his oldest clothes, the ones so colored they made him look like a bush hog. He sacrificed to the spirits of his ancestors and to the bush hog, and went out assured of his safety and invisibility.

Not far from town, he stopped. He saw something move in the bush. It was brown and large — perhaps a red deer. From a thicket of vines, he gave the call of the red deer, his rifle ready. An answer came. Another red deer, its voice somehow hoarse but clearly a red deer, called back to him.

He saw nothing move, but he was sure that the animal was in that clump of brush, over there. He called again, to make sure, and once more received an answer — but still saw nothing. It was odd, because usually a red deer would come to answer such a call. But he put the thought out of his head, raised the gun, took careful aim at the spot where he could just see a hint of brown, and fired.

There was a loud cry in answer, but the cry of a man, not an animal. Flumo froze with fear. What had he done? Had a man changed his body for that of his double, a red deer? He ran to the spot, where the crying could be heard, and there he found Yakpalo's son, Bono. His bow and arrows were beside him. He too had been out hunting, and his cries were intended to lure what he too had thought was a red deer into a position where he could shoot it. Bono lay, one arm limp at his side, blood flowing from it.

Flumo ran to Bono with horror. He had shot the son of Yakpalo, his rival. And yet if he had not shot, Bono would have shot his arrow, perhaps tipped with poison, at Flumo, and their places would have been reversed. What had happened, however, had happened. Flumo could not think what might come next — to himself, to his sons, to the boy he had shot.

For a brief moment, he looked at his rifle, and considered turning it on himself. He had heard of one man who had killed a friend with a poisoned arrow, thinking the man was an animal. He had then scratched himself with the same arrow, and had died alongside the man he killed. For a moment, he wanted to do likewise. But the thought of Kona and Zena stopped him. He had to accept what he had done in order to protect his sons, and give them a chance in life.

Bono was almost more a boy than a man. He had been born two years before Flumo's daughter, Lorpu. His father had paid the bridewealth for a girl who was still maturing. Bono had been sent that day into the forest to hunt.

Bono cried to Flumo to help him. He was dying there in the bush, he was certain of it. He could not move his arm. He begged Flumo to run to town to ask the chief to send men to carry him to town where they could save his life.

Yet Flumo realized that if he did not stop the blood, the boy would die while help was coming. Flumo knew that when the blood is all gone, the animal dies, and so does the human being. Flumo looked around him for leaves that he knew would stop the flow of blood. He mashed them together, and rubbed them into the wound on the boy's forearm. He plastered the wound with the leaves, and then tied them tight with still another large leaf and flexible vines. He tore his own shirt, and put it around the boy's arm, to make sure the bleeding stopped.

Flumo then marked the place where he had stood, and the place where the boy had been, measured the distance, and replaced the branches in the position where they had been before he shot the boy. He knew that the chief would ask the men to examine the place closely to determine that the shooting was not intentional. In this way Flumo made sure to protect himself.

Flumo reached town in late afternoon. The chief was in his palaver house, and Yakpalo and the other elders were with him. They were listening to one woman accuse another of poisoning her. The first woman had found a string of beads in her calabash of water, and witnesses said that the second woman's young daughter had dropped the beads in the water. The case was nearing resolution, as the daughter explained how she had accidentally lost her beads. But the case was put off as soon as Flumo called to the chief and told him what had happened.

The chief in turn called the elders, including Yakpalo, and told them what had happened. Yakpalo began to cry out, but checked himself. The word must not spread yet. The group of men took Flumo quickly to the edge of town, tied him with vines, and forced him to lead them to the place where the boy lay. He did so with haste, lest the boy die.

At the spot, the men found Flumo was telling the truth. He had not shot to kill a man. They picked up Bono, whimpering in pain, and carried him to an old farm shed near town where they would start treatment and discuss what to do next. They laid him on the ground inside the shed, and gave him water to drink.

The problem that faced them was serious. If the boy died, it would be very hard for Flumo. Yakpalo had other sons, but this was the favorite son of his head wife. They discussed the matter as the sun left the sky and it grew dark. Yakpalo himself then broke in, "What about the boy? Must he die while we talk?"

The chief acknowledged the father's wisdom by remarking, "Cassava can only grow in the shade of its own leaves." Some men still wanted to finish the palaver before they attended to the boy, but the chief prevailed, and called Mulbah the old medicine man. He found the right leaves and used them to clean and dress the wound. He commented that Flumo had also used good leaves, and thus had probably saved the boy's life.

Nonetheless the arm was broken, snapped between the elbow and the wrist. The bullet remained in the boy's flesh, but he could remove that easily. However, Mulbah himself was not able to mend the arm. They must go to the next town and call Togba Koli, the bonesetter. Mulbah pulled the bullet out of the boy's arm, while Bono bit his lip in pain. Mulbah packed the arm in leaves, and told Bono's father to feed him well that night and let him rest. The bleeding had stopped, but the boy must not yet move his arm.

Yakpalo, in grim anger, told the chief that Flumo would pay, pay dearly if Bono died. Flumo, tied securely with vines, stood silently. Nothing he could say would matter. The elders knew by going to the spot where the boy had been shot that Flumo had not intended to kill him. Everything now depended on the boy living. For now, Flumo could only wait.

The next day Yakpalo himself went to the next town to bring the bonesetter to live with the boy on the old farm site. No woman or child must visit there while he recovered, and the men who stayed with him on the farm must keep away from their women. There Bono remained for five weeks, while the farm was securely fenced against intruders, living as the bonesetter's own son.

Togba Koli, the bonesetter, broke the leg of a chicken when he arrived, and announced that the boy could use his arm when the chicken was once again able to walk. The bonesetter pushed Bono's broken bone in place with his finger and then rubbed the arm with white chalk. He pressed hot leaves on the arm and rubbed the wound with more leaves. He put more chalk on the arm, and then tied it tightly with strong, stiff piassava splints.

Every day during the next five weeks, Togba Koli treated the arm in this fashion. The pain was severe, but Bono did not cry out. In time, the swelling began to go down and normal feelings began to return to Bono's hand.

Then one day the chicken walked. The bonesetter noted the event, and removed the piassava split from the boy's arm. The skin was marked and scarred, and the muscles were weak, but Bono could move his hand. The only problem was that he could not control his two smallest fingers. The cord that tied the fingers to the shoulder had been cut by the shot and had not healed. Fortunately it was not the hand he ate with, not the hand he used to hold a cutlass, but still it would never be the same.

Bono returned to town to his family. The elders had released Flumo once they knew that Bono would live. But now it was time for Flumo to pay his debt to Yakpalo. The elders met, with Yakpalo and Flumo as the accuser and the accused. It was understood that if the boy had died, some member of Flumo's family would have been given to Yakpalo, or perhaps even killed. None would have blamed Yakpalo for taking such direct action had his son died, none, that is, except the D. C. who did not understand such matters. Had not Yakpalo been heard to say to Flumo, "Flies will show where your body is if my boy dies?"

However, the boy was alive, even though with two dead fingers, and so the payment to Yakpalo would be less. The elders hung their heads together, and decided that since Flumo had shot Yakpalo's son with a rifle, the gun itself must change hands, and be given to Yakpalo. Flumo must be washed, and the gun purified. In addition, Flumo must sacrifice a sheep and a white chicken to wash the blood from the land and give Yakpalo five lengths of white cloth, two white chickens and a large piece of Mandingo salt.

Flumo also had to pay the bonesetter. He gave him a goat, a white chicken, five lengths of white cloth, ten pieces of iron money, and a necklace of leopard and chimpanzee teeth. Flumo hated to give up some of the precious teeth he had taken from the leopard, but it was necessary. One must not refuse a bonesetter or make him angry. He could, if he wished, break the boy's bone again simply by breaking a chicken bone in his own house. Both Bono and Flumo were now under his power, and might even die if the bonesetter chose to make medicine against them.

It was not only fortunate that the boy had lived, but it was doubly fortunate that the bone had healed so promptly, since there remained only one week until the president and his party were to come to Gbarnga. When the time came,

Flumo and Yakpalo, the town elders and the town chief all put on their best robes and went to Gbarnga, the district headquarters, to meet the president. One reason for the visit was a report, which Flumo knew was true, that the D. C.'s supervisor of roads had taken much of the rice, palm oil and other produce collected for the government, and used them for himself. In addition, he had beaten two of the men forced to work on his farm so severely that they died. The report had been carried to the president by two clan chiefs, and he had come to investigate, as well as to see Jorkwelle country for himself.

Flumo had heard that the president was on the side of the people, and did not like them mistreated. He hoped this was true. Now they would find out what sort of man he was. The president had said they could bring to him any quarrels or difficulties they had, and he would try to settle them.

Flumo, Yakpalo and the other town elders arrived in Gbarnga two days before the president and his party reached the town. They used the time to greet old friends and to make new ones. They went to the large market run by the Mandingoes and bargained to sell the kola nuts they had brought. The Mandingoes had many houses in Gbarnga. Flumo was not happy to see strangers, who did not live like the Kpelle and who would not give their daughters to Kpelle men to marry, with land of their own in the very heart of Kpelle country. But the former president had forced the chiefs to give them the land. Flumo had often heard that they did not do their share of the labor in town. They said they had to pray to God whenever the town crier announced it was time to clean the road or the open space between the houses. It was also said they would not send their children to be initiated in the Poro and Sande Bush Schools.

But the Mandingo people helped the Kpelle in their own way. They had good cloth, tobacco, salt and money which they traded for kola nuts. What did it matter that the Mandingo believed the Kpelle had worn no clothes before the

Mandingo started their markets? Whatever they believed, Flumo used them to recover some of his losses during the year.

On the day of the president's arrival, messengers reached the town with word that he would leave his hammock to walk with his elders from the river into Gbarnga town. Flumo was impressed. If he could walk up that long hill from the waterside, he must be one of the people.

It was a grand celebration. Five masked dancers came out to perform for the president, two of them tall on stilts. Children crowded behind the dancers, and ran in half terror whenever the figures moved toward them. The stilt dancers performed what seemed to Flumo impossible feats, first on one leg, then on the other.

The president arrived at the expected time, and walked into Gbarnga with two of his elders and many other important Liberian officials. All the chiefs and elders from the outlying towns were there massed to greet him. The horns boomed out, and the drums broke against the sky.

The stilt dancers reared up to full height, and then sank low to the ground. The large Loma masked entertainer waddled from his seated position up to the president, and sank before him as if to show his homage. The *Vai* dancer, bright with colored raffia and with mirrors to reflect the sun which shone for the occasion, danced and wheeled and leaped before the visitors. The austere *Gola* figure, a mass of raffia topped by a faceless helmet mask, turned cartwheels in the dust, defying gravity for the president.

The council began by discussing the man who had abused his post. The president dismissed him from his job, requiring that he repay both the government and the people whom he had beaten. After he had produced the money from his private funds, he would be put in jail. Flumo and the other spectators applauded, amazed and pleased that the president would put one of his own people in jail because he had hurt Kpelle people.

The president settled other matters which had arisen, and then said he wanted to speak to every town chief individually. The chief of Flumo's town had much to say. He told the problems his people had with taxes. He said there were not enough men to go to Firestone and to work on the D. C.'s farm every year. The president nodded, and said he would deal with these matters.

He then pressed the chief further. Was there any problem within his village, any dispute he had been unable to solve? The chief thought, and then told of the feud between the two quarters in town. He reviewed the history of the troubles, leading up to the hunting accident. The president listened carefully, and then urged that Lorpu and the boy from Yakpalo's quarter marry right away.

He further suggested that a boy from Flumo's quarter should be sent to live with Lorpu, as if he were Yakpalo's son. The chief then said that Flumo had twin boys. The president thanked Flumo and gave him five round silver British coins, bigger than any Flumo had ever seen. He then said that one of Flumo's sons should live with his sister Lorpu in Yakpalo's quarter, and grow up with Yakpalo's family. This would bring the families together and overcome the hurt.

In return, Yakpalo should give a great feast to thank the ancestors, to honor Flumo for killing the leopard, and to show his gratitude that his son Bono was alive and able to work. After all, the president pointed out, the result could have been much worse. The ancestors, the animal double, and even the High God must have been with Flumo that day, to keep him from killing Bono.

The town chief, Yakpalo, Flumo and the other elders applauded the president's decision. It was true what they had heard. The president had showed his wisdom in bringing his people together. The soldiers, the messengers, the important kwii people and even the D. C. might be harsh men, who beat them and took their money from them. But the president was on their side.

The president's words were heeded. For the next year and a half after Lorpu's marriage, the boys lived together, and yet not together. They continued to play together, but they had different houses to go back to at night, and different persons to give them jobs to do.

Kona and Zena were twins, and thus had a special place in the town. They had power, and people went to them for help. They made medicine for rain to come or sometimes for rain to stop. It was even said that Zena could pick the right medicine from behind his ear.

The townspeople feared as well as respected the boys. When they played the game of passing a stone around the circle as fast as possible until one person missed, the other boys were afraid to knock Kona or Zena if he dropped the rock. They said Zena had made a boil to come on one boy who had hit him on the head. Everyone should know, thought Flumo, that you must never hit twins on the head. That boy learned the hard way.

The boys had power, but it was not clear yet how their powers would be used. Their mother was very proud of them, and continued to see and talk to Kona at Yakpalo's house. Even after she became pregnant again, she enjoyed watching them grow. She had lost two children since the twins, and this was her third attempt. She hoped she might have good fortune by staying near the twins.

She also had Flumo make medicine for the child to live, when she was sure she was pregnant. Flumo had her sit on the ground, and he brought his blacksmith tools from the shop. He put them in a rice fanner and killed a red chicken over them. He then put the fanner on Yanga's head, spat palm oil on a lighted torch and touched it to the tools.

He then shouted as if the medicine had caught him, just as the witch shouts if caught. He went on to say, "The town is full of witches. They are found in the air and on the ground, in the night and the day. Whoever tries to bewitch this woman, let this medicine catch him. When he is caught, may he cry my name, saying, 'Flumo, come and save me. I was the one who wanted to eat this woman's child from her stomach.' Let this medicine make his body hot as I am making it hot with this fire. May he not sit down or lie down. May he not sleep or stand up." He then spoke directly to the medicine, "When you catch a person, and I call upon you, may you answer me."

He and Yanga cooked and ate the chicken, and tied the feathers to the broken halves of the torch used to light the palm oil, and hung it over the doors to his house. This was the strongest medicine he knew, and he said it would keep Yanga and the baby safe.

The fact that Kona was in Yakpalo's quarter, and Zena still with his father, bothered no one except Flumo. Yanga felt that Yakpalo could give the boy some of the discipline he seemed to lack in his own home. He always asked questions, always tried to see deeply into things. Zena accepted the Kpelle world as it came to him.

Kona's new father tolerated Kona's inquisitiveness at first, but soon grew weary of it. He made sure the boy behaved properly. The first night in Yakpalo's quarter Kona asked for more rice and soup. Kona felt that he was not properly fed, and he was hungry. He was beaten properly for his greediness. In Yakpalo's house, Kona had to struggle with many other children to get his food, and he had to learn to be satisfied with what he got.

The twins still stayed together as much as possible when they were in town. Only when they had to go to the farm did they now part company. Everyone in town agreed it was a good thing. Each would learn to be a man, apart from the other. Perhaps Kona would even learn from Yakpalo not to ask so many questions, and to be more dutiful. For Kona the experience of Yakpalo's quarter was sobering. No one applauded him when he won at the game of guessing the number of feet on six sheep. He was one day accused of cheating in a guessing game, when he had figured out too quickly that the other boy was thinking of his mother's mortar. He had asked whether it was a town thing, and then whether it was a working thing. The other boys had said he was cheating. He must just try to guess one thing at a time, not try to find out what group it belonged to. And they laughed at him until he was in tears. He missed his mother. She never would have done that to him.

Zena too was able to do things well, but they were things that pleased his father. He knew the plants in the forest, and could answer the questions about different kinds of leaves and trees. Moreover, he knew everyone in the village well. In the game of blindfolding one boy and making him guess whom he touched, Zena always won. He might not be able to talk as fast as Kona, and pronounce words as well, but he could make things. When the big tree at the edge of town came into flower, he made the best spinning tops from the large red flowers.

It was a time of change in the town. Flumo and Yak-palo agreed that change is hard, that earning a living is hard. They could not buy the kwii things from Firestone. Yet they had to accept the gifts their friends brought, and it hurt to be in their debt.

Saki brought from Firestone a special present for Flumo. He brought him two boxes, one for his blacksmith tools and one for his clothes. Flumo had never used such things before, but times were changing, and he felt he had to change with them. The boxes had iron pieces to close them and locks to keep out inquiring hands.

A man had stolen openly from his neighbor last year and had been put in stocks in the center of town. This was a punishment reserved for the most serious crimes, such as rape or incest, and Flumo felt the man deserved what he got. But then another man stole a lappa cloth that belonged to Yanga. The town chief tried to stop the stealing, but he did not know how to deal with kwii ways. The chief began to think that kwii people had no sense of right and wrong, but those who had been at Firestone said only that they had different ways. What he thought wrong here in town might not be wrong at Firestone.

People who had been at Firestone would sue each other in the chief's court for the least matters. Up till now the harmony of the town could be kept by letting the elders hang their head together. But now these young hotheads, thought Flumo, wanted to take things into their own hands.

Then Saki said that Togba had stolen his knife, and Togba replied that Saki had borrowed rice two years earlier and never repaid it. They threatened each other. They even said they would take the matter to Gbarnga to let the D. C. solve it. Saki said he would wash his hands of Togba, would cut all ties between them.

To save a long and costly dispute, which might drag on for months, and which only the kwii people in Gbarnga would win, the chief quieted the boys. He even threatened that if he had to bring the case to his full court, he would sell one of them to the kwii people. Togba muttered that the chief could not do this any more, but had too much respect for the chief's authority to say it aloud.

Togba and Saki thus agreed to come to court in their own town, and accept whatever decision was made. Each made his case against the other and called his witnesses. The witnesses swore on medicine bought from Mandingos in Gbarnga that what they said was true. Everyone feared Mandingo medicine, and it was enough to frighten all witnesses into telling the truth.

Saki's witness said the knife had been in his house and insisted Togba had entered the house for something. Togba's witness in turn swore that he had seen Saki borrow the rice, which he never returned. Both then drank the medicine from a small, dirty spoon into which it had been poured from a bottle. Each had the spoon put on his head, after which the spoon fell to the ground. They swore that if they were not telling the truth they should fall to the ground dead just as the spoon had fallen.

The chief heard the matter, and then resolved it. He declared both wrong, and both right. Saki should have repaid the debt promptly, even though friends should not have to ask for such repayment. Saki should not have sued Togba. The chief said he did it just to show the money he had earned in Firestone. Togba, on the other hand, had taken the knife. He claimed he had only borrowed it until Saki returned the rice. But he should not have borrowed it that way. He should have asked for it openly.

The chief was relieved, because if he had not solved it, he would have had to refer it to Gbarnga, a costly and unpleasant process, or submit it to an ordeal. The poison ordeal he knew from childhood the D. C. had now declared illegal. The chief felt he would never understand these kwii people. They did bad things and called them right, and outlawed the old ways of the Kpelle.

The only ordeal still allowed used a red-hot cutlass. Mulbah would rub medicine on the legs of both parties, as well as his own leg, and apply the red hot cutlass to the legs of all three of them. Only the guilty person's leg would be burned. The method worked — the chief had used it several times. But it was not as effective as the old way.

Saki brought these locked boxes from Firestone to stop stealing. Flumo felt bad using them, but he wanted to keep his things safe. The trouble was that Zena could never figure out how to use them. Zena often helped Flumo in the blacksmith shop, and often went on errands. Before Flumo put the boxes in the eaves of the house and under the bed, Zena had known what to do. He would climb into the eaves if he needed a tool, or take a shirt from the basket under his father's bed. But now these locks and keys confused him. He was afraid of them and often forgot what he had been sent to get, or forgot how to open the boxes. Kona understood these new things better. Perhaps, Flumo thought, it sometimes helps to ask questions.

Flumo no longer smelted his own iron. None of the other blacksmiths did it any more, and he could get good iron in White Plains or from Firestone. Yanga and Toang now demanded kwii clothes, and no longer were willing to take all the time and effort to make clay pots when their husbands could buy iron pots from the market. More people sold their palm kernels, their rice, their kola nuts and their coffee to the German store in White Plains. Flumo's coffee trees would soon bear, and he would be able to be more independent, since the German would buy all the coffee Flumo could send.

Change continued to come to the town, despite Flumo's wish that it would stop. Soldiers came often for taxes, for rice, for lodging, for porters, for road-building, and for entertainment. Yet the chief was glad that the government took over the most serious disputes. There had been a murder in the next town, and the D. C. settled the matter and put the killer in prison. Men no longer fought wars these days, even though some of the older men regretted the great wars of the past were over, when men fought and killed other men over a kidnapped woman or a misplaced farm.

The town chief remembered with mixed pleasure and pain the great war before Flumo had married. Chiefs Wolomian and Biito had burned towns, captured booty and slaves, and returned with glory to their town and families.

He remembered the day when he, as chief of the land, had sent the warriors out led by their best belly-harp player to do battle under Wolomian. They had left the town with cries of hoped-for victory, jumping over the naked body of his daughter, who then stood up to cheer them on their way. He remembered how Wolomian's head wife had kept his war charms during the hero's absence. He remembered how his men had won a great victory and the other warriors had had to send a girl with a white chicken to acknowledge their defeat in battle. He remembered too how the final war had ended, how the sun had darkened while still high in the sky, revealing five stars in broad daylight. Wolomian and Biito had agreed to stop the war because of that sign.

The chief felt old now, however, and no longer could fight. The same Mandingoes who had come as medicine men to help them with their wars now bought kola nuts. The chief was inwardly glad for peace, even though as he looked at his old warrior sword, one he had saved from being melted down by the Liberian soldiers, he felt some of the heat of youth come to him again.

He realized that no longer would the Kpelle have to move on because of war. They had reached their last and best home. The Mano had forced them to leave their old town and great warriors to the north before that had driven them into the forest. Now they would no longer have to move, and they owed that to the justice of the Liberian government.

It was a world, the chief realized, where the young men could grow up in peace. The young men may be strange now. They may have new ideas. But no war chief kills them. He looked on Kona and Zena as they grew, glad they did not have to fight. They used tools and not weapons as they practised the arts of manhood. Their father Flumo had made them strong sharp cutlasses to teach them to work. They learned the uses of tools in farming, house-building, the blacksmith shop, making clothes, cooking food, trapping animals, and even playing.

The chief looked at his town with pleasure, pleased that it no longer rang with the shouts of death and fire, pleased that the boys like Kona and Zena could learn good ways. He had enjoyed the fighting, but those days were now over forever. Better to see Zena sorting his father's tools, and learning the proper use of each. Better to see Kona learning the art of weaving. Soon they would know the two worlds, the world of the forest and the world of the town. The chief understood and enjoyed these worlds. Only the third world, the kwii world, confused him.

The two years which remained before the Poro Bush School would open passed quickly. The town was at one again, for the time being its problems resolved. Flumo and Yakpalo grew to accept the president's decision. Flumo was pleased to have Zena with him, working the bellows and keeping the charcoal on the fire. Yakpalo was content to have Kona bring him lengths of thread, ten armspans of white and twenty of black, for his loom. New tools and new cloth were coming in, but the demand for the old had not stopped. And, most important, both Yanga and Lorpu delivered children safely, Yanga a girl and Lorpu a boy, whom she named after the president, to show her gratitude.

A hammock is a place of honor

CHAPTER VIII

Sitting Quietly
Reveals Crocodile's Tricks

Coming out of Bush School

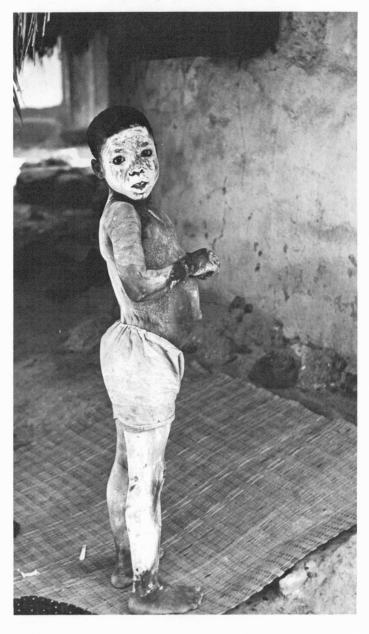

VIII: SITTING QUIETLY REVEALS
CROCODILE'S TRICKS

The rice was in. The men brought presents from Firestone for their wives, some extra money and stories of new things in the world. They told of the road soldiers were building beyond Kakata, of the stores and the things one could now buy even in Salala, of the strange ways of the white man at Firestone, and of the war between white men now in progress beyond the great water.

Saki brought with him cloth for the whole family, as well as a rifle for himself. Flumo did not like the rifle, but let Saki keep it. He is a married man now, Flumo thought. Flumo himself was finished with guns, but his young brother could keep it if he used it well.

Kona and Zena did not understand the activity around them. Every day the men worked long hours at the edge of the high forest near town. The boys wanted to see this work, just as they had seen and even helped in the work their fathers regularly did. But this time they had to stay in town.

They did not complain, however, because they had been brought up not to complain. Once Flumo had told Kona not to follow him to the forest. He had run after Flumo to beg him. His father had picked him up, hit him once hard, and sent him crying back to Yanga.

So this time they waited back at home with the women while their fathers worked. And, even when the work seemed to be finished in the forest, the town was still excited. Flumo told the boys their time had now come. In four days they would have to fight the Forest Thing. But until then every-

123

one would celebrate their coming entrance into the forest for the Poro Bush School.

Flumo worried that the twins were too young to enter the forest. They had lived for eight rainy seasons now. The other boys who now danced in the town were older, some of them even ready to marry and have children, if it had not been for the four years they must spend learning the ways of their people. But Kona and Zena were twins, were special. And so no one thought it strange that their father wanted them to join the society so early. Besides they were growing strong and straight, and seemed as ready as some of the older boys.

The boys made small wooden spears to fight the Forest Thing. All their relatives crowded around them to encourage them to make fine spears. The boys, however, didn't believe they could defeat the Forest Thing. They had often heard him singing in town when they ran to their house, closed all doors and listened in frightened silence. He sounded fearfully strong and powerful, but the unearthly beauty of the singing of his wife chilled their blood. How could they, small boys, even smaller than most who entered the bush, fight so terrible a being?

Their grandmother, Flumo's mother, encouraged them. She said it would be easy for such fine strong young men, her young husbands, to kill the dread figure. They must smooth the edge of the spear and sharpen it carefully, and then go in and strike off the head of their enemy. She especially asked them to pull out his teeth so she could use them for snuff bottles. She said that the teeth of the Forest Thing would make the snuff taste finer, and she was sure that her strong husbands, Kona and Zena, could do the job well. Saki echoed her words, and said that he wanted the skull of the Forest Thing to drink his palm wine, as warriors in the past had drunk from the skulls of those they had slain in battle.

The boys shivered as they heard these words. How could they be so manly, so powerful, so strong? How could they

kill the thing that was to bring them the new life of adulthood? But they promised their grandmother and Saki they
would try.

During those four days of dancing, all the boys who
would enter the forest slept in one house. Kona and Zena
were frightened and wondered why they were together again
after living in different houses. The older ones tried to show
their courage by making light of what would happen, but the
younger boys, including Kona and Zena, did not really believe them. They dared not say so, but they almost knew that
the big boys were quite frightened, too.

The boys never had stayed indoors like this, away from
their parents. After each day of dancing, they went back to
the house to listen. They knew the sound — it was the Forest
Thing. Usually he came late at night when they were supposed to be asleep, but now it was still early. The Forest
Thing came every night for their four days of isolation.

Zena felt his spear to be a source of security when he
heard the singing outside the door. But the second night he
could not find it. He called to Kona to give it to him, in case
the dread person should enter the house to find them. It was
dark and the boys in the house could scarcely see their hands
in front of them.

Zena asked Kona to pick up the thing and give it to him.
"What thing?", Kona asked. "The thing in front of you."
"The things are many." "The stick" — Zena's voice had a
tremble in it of fear and anger. Kona picked up a piece of
firewood which he could barely make out in the dark. Zena
half rose as if to hit him, but sat back. "No, the small stick."
Kona then realized that Zena wanted the spear he had made,
which lay on the ground in front of Kona. He asked Zena
why he had not said what he wanted. Zena did not reply —
Kona should have known what he needed.

Then the voices began again. Kona and Zena listened
carefully, from the dark and quiet of the house. The voices
seemed everywhere in town. The older boys said that the

Forest Thing and his wife could fly through the air, could be in many places at the same time. The boys believed it. They heard the cries, the strange slurred singing, and the terrible beauty of the voices, now at the edge of town, now in the forest, then next door, then across by Flumo's blacksmith kitchen. Time moved with fearful slowness.

And then the singing seemed to stop at the boys' house. There was a sudden silence — it seemed to last for many heart beats. Then came a pounding at the door. The voice called out, "Many boys are in there, and I need them. I will eat them in two days." The boys were frightened but knew that this was a time for them to be strong and silent — no crying now.

The voice told the boys they must show their worth, before they could come to the forest. He ordered Kona to crow like a chicken. Kona, in fear and eagerness, managed to gasp out a reasonable imitation. The terrible voice then said that all the boys must swim on the floor. They all fell to the ground and started squirming along the dusty earth. He then said he was sending in peppers to be their palm nuts, and they must eat them all. The door opened and a basket of tiny red peppers was passed in — and the boys without exception took them and chewed them up. Their eyes filled with tears, their throats burned and their skin became hot and sweaty. But they had to finish all, lest the Forest Thing catch them.

Their days were full of dancing and celebration. The boys were groggy with an unfilled need for sleep. But they had to keep going, had to submit to the encouragement of their friends and relatives. They knew the time was coming, and they were frightened. But they dared not show it. Kona wanted to cry, but feared that crying would mark him as a baby too small to go behind the fence into the bush, too small to be eaten by the Forest Thing. Zena was more sure of himself, but still feared what might be coming.

The next night and the night after, they heard the same noises, the same voices, the same commands. The boys knew that four days was the limit, that this must be the night. The end of boyhood had come for them, and they did not know what might be coming. They could not sleep, both for anticipation and for constant harassment from outside the closed door, where the terrible yet beautiful voices called them, harried them, beckoned them. The tasks they were given were more difficult than ever. They had to fly like birds in the house. They had to drink what the Forest Thing called spirit's milk — and it was terribly bitter. They had to sing like the frogs of the swamp.

And just when they felt they would drop with exhaustion, the voice told them to open the door and come out. It was time now to be men, time to enter the forest. And yet to open the door required a courage none of the boys felt he had. It took the biggest of them to make the move that none of the others dared make.

When they opened the door, the Forest Thing had gone, and its voice could be heard already far away on the other side of town. Outside the house they saw no dread thing, no terrible apparition, nothing but their fathers telling them to come, telling them not to worry. The voices now came from far away, first in the forest where their fathers had been working, then on the other side of town near the old medicine lady's house, then at the base of the great cotton tree which was the town's medicine.

The night soon would end. A faint grey behind the cotton tree showed that the deep black left in the sky would soon give way to dawn. At this time usually only the roosters would be awake, urging the people of the town to leave their beds and get to work. This night, however, the whole town seemed to be awake. Perhaps it had never slept.

Boys from every house in town, and happy, apprehensive fathers walked out of town on the path forbidden these past few weeks. A short way from town, at the edge of a clearing, was a fence of a type they had never seen before. Woven from mats with a beautiful cross-hatched design, it seemed almost a part of the forest itself. In the center the boys saw a low opening, and immediately to the left of the opening something that looked like a small thatch house.

When the boys reached the fence, they found most of the town there ahead of them. Men were ducking in and out through the opening, while women remained outside, dancing a special dance with rattles on their ankles. The youngest boys, who remained with their mothers, cried from fear, and Flumo's sons found it difficult not to let a few tears stand on their cheeks.

The women sang together before the fence. Their leader sang, "All zoes," and the rest responded, "Zoes, you are zoes." The leader continued, "This is my son you are taking," and the others responded "Take them all, and bring them all back." The leader urged, "Let my son not become a swimmer, let him not climb the palm tree in the sky," and the others repeated the chorus. As they sang, they all danced, and their feet raised dust from the ground and echoes from the surrounding forest.

The boys stood irresolute, with no idea what would happen, while the searing beauty of the voices — now behind the fence, now far in the forest, now in town behind them — both frightened them and drew them nearer. The twins were glad to see Flumo in the crowd, but he did not stand near them.

It was almost fully light by now. The boys could see the designs in the fence more clearly than they really wanted to. The low opening pulled their eyes. They could not forget it, even if they tried. And when the voice in a terrible roar called for the boys to come to be eaten, they realized that they would have to pass through that opening themselves. They understood the command, but nonetheless one of the men explained it to them in a clear voice.

The twins turned to Flumo, but he was no help. He motioned to them to turn back, as if to tell them to be men. They saw tears in their mother's eyes, back in the crowd of women, and to avoid letting the tears catch them also, they turned back to watch in frightened fascination.

The smallest boy was called forward. After him Kona and Zena must go. The boy had the same kind of small carved spear the twins held ready for fighting the Forest Thing. He didn't seem to be afraid, but the boys saw that his lip trembled. The Forest Thing's interpreter led him forward, talking to him quietly.

The voice from behind the fence shouted in a blurred roar, "Bring him," and the interpreter answered, "I bring him." Three times this exchange took place, and then on the fourth the interpreter pushed the boy through the hole in the fence. The great voice rose in triumph, the guttural slurring giving over to a high-pitched shout. The terrible, seductive singing of the Forest Thing's wife was now quiet, and in the silence there came a sharp crack, a cry of pain, and the carved stick, now broken, flew back over the fence. The voice sang that the Forest Thing had eaten the first boy. It said the boy had tried to fight him, but had brought with him only a little wooden stick that could do nothing. He called for more boys to come. He wanted to eat them all.

All this was too much for some of the little ones, who would not enter the Bush School for another two or three years. They ran to their mothers and cried without stopping. The mothers tried to push them back, make them men, but couldn't. After all, the youngest among them had seen only five rice harvests. Flumo's sons would have cried if they had not, out of fear and fascination, kept their eyes fixed on the fence and the opening.

Their turn came next. The Forest Thing's interpreter led them to the fence, as they held tight to their carved sticks. A warm and friendly hand on the shoulder, a brief firmness of the grasp, helped greatly as he pushed them through the hole to the other side. Their spears came flying back over the fence, in the view of the crowd. The twins were gone.

After the last big boy had entered, the wife of the

Forest Thing once again took up her song. She and her husband, those dread spirits of the forest, had eaten their fill. She sang, the unearthly beauty of her voice filling the air and filling the ache that was left in the boys' mothers' hearts. Now they must return to town to celebrate and adjust themselves to not seeing their sons. No woman could go behind the fence, except for old Noai, who had that privilege as head of the women's Sande Society.

That night the men came back from behind the fence to announce that there had been a successful initiation. They brought green leaves with them, some around their waists, and some to put on the roofs of the houses from which boys had gone to the Bush School. The leaves, Yanga knew, were smooth and soft and green, a sign that all had gone well. That night everyone who remained in town danced for joy, danced with satisfaction that their boys would soon be men.

Not for four years would the boys come out. Not for four years would they see their mothers, nor any other woman from the town except old Noai. Behind the woven wall was a world of men, a world where young men and boys grew to be real men, to be members of the Kpelle world, to be full human beings. For four years they would learn and grow, suffer and yet bear the suffering, share each other's pain and promise, and die together to childhood.

Yanga knew that some of the boys who had been eaten by the Forest Thing would never leave his belly. The terrible being who sang so beautifully could kill and perhaps not restore to life. She dreaded the possibility that a broken pot, or even two broken pots, might appear at her door, a brief, silent announcement that her sons would not come out again. If it happened, she must not cry, she knew that, as she would if one of her boys had been killed by a leopard, or died from witchcraft, or succumbed to fever. She knew that it could not happen for all the boys to return. Some had to satisfy the appetites of the spirits and the ancestors.

Yanga did not know the secrets of the boy's Bush

School. She had to be content with what she had learned in the Sande Bush School. But she knew that the boys would learn when to speak and when to be silent. "You cannot say it," they had taught her as a girl, and she had taught it to her sons. She had always told them to look straight ahead at the secret places on the road marked by bunches of grass tied to vines, and not to speak if they saw what they should not see.

Flumo too had tried to bring the boys up right. He had used proverbs in their presence, to accustom them to speaking properly. He had tried to teach them not to ask "Why," even though he had failed to show Kona why that question was wrong. He had let them make their own explanations of the things they had heard. And when they could not explain, for themselves and asked him, he responded simply, "I hear you." This was a response which he also taught them to use when problems arose.

Flumo feared what might happen to Kona behind the fence. Kona always asked the reason for things, always inquired into other people's business. He should have known by this time that silence or indirect observation was the best approach. No, he would always blurt out his ideas and uncertainties. He did not seem to realize that truth is what the old people say it is, not something that any young boy can explain for himself. Truth is truth, Flumo thought, but no young person can know it until he is told. Kona was always too free, moreover, with his news. When he saw something in the bush, he would run and tell everyone in the town, and not keep his news to himself.

The last thing Flumo told Kona and Zena the day before they went behind the fence was, "Sitting quietly reveals crocodile's tricks." They had to watch and wait and grow in order to come out men, with at least the seeds of adult wisdom. Flumo felt he had laid the groundwork for their manhood, but now they must make their own way, so that they could become proper Kpelle, proper members of the Poro Society, proper men.

Flumo also remembered that the most important thing he had learned in the Bush School was "You cannot say it." What he learned there, and how he learned it, he must never tell non-members. He had learned not even to discuss Poro Society matters with members in public. His sons must now learn this lesson, directly and seriously.

Flumo had heard about a Mano boy killed when he revealed secrets to the white doctor. He knew of no such case in Jorkwelle country, but it could always happen. The white doctor had been asking too many questions, and this boy had been willing to answer them. The case had shocked everyone. The Poro Society, Flumo realized, was not just a matter for the Jorkwelle alone, not for the Kpelle alone. It belonged to all the people, Mano, Kpelle, Loma, Gola, Vai, *Gbandi*. And they all knew not to tell the secrets. Likewise, they all suffered when this Mano boy told the white doctor things he could put in a book. Even the boy realized, too late, that he had to die.

The years passed. The boys grew. Kona and Zena and all the other boys in that small village in the heart of the forest learned to be men. They worked and played, talked and relaxed. They could not see their mothers and sisters and the other women in town, but they learned how men must relate to women. For now, however, the twins were glad not to have their older sister, Toang, and her friends to trouble them.

Four times the boys went through the cycle of wet and dry, the cycle of planting and harvesting rice. They and their fathers did all their own work, even though the town sent them food from time to time. It was a period of great peace for them, even though they heard faint rumors of war in the world outside.

Men from the town went to Firestone in greater numbers, because people beyond the water needed rubber. Kona and Zena saw their uncle Saki only rarely during those four years, since he spent most of his time at Firestone collecting the rubber for the kwii people. It was reported to the boys that the white men were fighting a terrible, cruel war, more terrible than any the Kpelle had fought. Kpelle people from Guinea had even gone to fight in that war, and many had not returned. Kpelle people in Liberia did not have to fight, and they thanked God for that.

After the fourth rice harvest, the pace of life behind the fence quickened. Those last few boys that tradition requires were brought to the fence and eaten by the Forest Thing. Smaller than the other boys, they had remained in town until the end. Four years earlier, they had run from the fence in tears. But now they were big enough to enter.

Kona and Zena understood now that the last boy to enter must kill the Forest Thing. All the others had lost the fight. But that last boy must win, so that the Bush School of the Poro Society could end.

The boys could hear dancing and singing from the town, when they went close to the fence. They could sense the coming happiness. The women danced before the fence and then again in town when the Forest Thing fought the last boys. Among them was Saki's son. Saki came back from Firestone for the occasion, and made sure that his boy went through the old ways of the Kpelle, even though Saki wanted him to be kwii someday. Saki's son, moreover, went behind the fence last, late one night, before the pepper bird had announced the coming of the dawn. Kona and Zena saw him come through the fence, and for once the stick was not broken. Surely that day the Forest Thing would depart.

The last thin crescent of the dying moon shone in the cold, dry-season sky. The boys had been awake most of the night, and now the day of return had arrived. Flumo and the other men who had been in and out of the Bush School to train the boys during those four years, now prepared them to re-enter the outside world. They painted each boy with white clay on his face, his arms, his upper body and his legs, and gave him a short raffia skirt to cover his nakedness.

Outside the fence, the sounds grew and the activity increased. The paramount chief had come from Gbarnga, and the clan chief was present also. The old town elder was seated before the fence, accompanied by the town chief and his quarter chiefs, Flumo and Yakpalo. The chiefs of the other towns that had had boys in the Bush School also held places of honor.

The boys heard singing outside the fence, and could even imagine that they heard their mother's voice. Kona and Zena could hardly remember what she looked like or sounded like. Some of the boys who had come in to the Bush School during the years after the opening remembered their mothers better. New rice, freshly harvested, occasionally dropped over the fence, as the women tossed the hard white grains from overflowing calabashes.

The boys were all reminded of the need for secrecy as they prepared to leave the forest. They were told that other boys, younger than they, had not yet entered the Bush School. They must not tell them or women or any strangers what they had learned. Yakpalo reminded the boys, "Pangolin showed leopard the way to eat him." They knew the pangolin, that strange animal who could protect himself by curling into a ball, letting his hard scales baffle his attacker. But if he opened up and displayed his soft underbelly, he could be eaten easily. If the boys repeated any of what they knew, they would be like the pangolin who unrolls himself and is eaten by leopard.

The sound of drums increased outside the fence. The boys knew the women were dancing, dancing for joy. They could hear their feet slapping against the ground, and they could see the dust rise over the fence. The rhythms grew more intense and complicated, as the noise became almost unbearable.

Only a few women held back. A broken pot had appeared before their doors, for some as late as the previous night, telling that the Forest Thing had chosen not to bring their sons back to life. He had swallowed them, and the ancestors had accepted their lives for the others who now returned as adults. These women swallowed their sorrow, and accepted the joy of the community. The joy was theirs only to share with others.

Then a silence settled over the waiting crowd. A space was cleared before the fence, and mats spread on the ground. Mulbah, the oldest and most respected of the medicine men in town, stood before the assembled people. He told them of their traditions. He warned them that the old ways were dying. He saw only trouble ahead. Even this very day there were men at Firestone who should be here rejoicing with their town. He told of Liberian schools, schools run by white men, who took children for many years. These children were eaten by a different thing, which kept them from becoming men. The old man warned the people of the town that the end was coming, and that he personally would die before he would accept these new ways.

But today the people must forget tomorrow's impending darkness, and do what their ancestors had done for as long as any man could remember. He was an eye-witness to this ceremony, and he could remember back many years before the Liberian soldiers had first come. And his own grandfather had been an eye-witness to it years before that. He said, "Sitting quietly reveals crocodile's tricks," and reminded the people that they should only believe what they or their elders have seen.

The old man spoke in words that brought chills of pleasure and fear to the twins. He spoke clearly enough, and yet there was a mystery in his manner, in the very choice of words. They had spent four years mastering that deeper and grander language they had heard in the forest, and had never before understood. Old Mulbah's words raised him up in the

eyes and hearts of the people, even if the women did not
understand everything he said. They only knew he was calling
on them to take back their boys from the Forest Thing and
welcome them to town. He said he had taught them as well as
he could. Not all the boys could return, but those who would
now be reborn were new people. They had new names, and
once again must learn to be part of the town, this time as
men.

The boys then heard the town chief step up and call
loudly to the Forest Thing. He was answered by a long,
slurred, guttural cry. The townspeople took up the cry in response. The boys knew the correct response, but their time
had not come to give it. The exchange of greetings and affir-
mations continued until the Forest Thing agreed to return to
the bush and only return when the next school opened many
years later. The women would have three years to prepare,
and then three years for school. Then the men could use another four years to get ready, before the Forest Thing would
once again return to eat the new generation of boys.

But before the Forest Thing agreed to leave, he would
have to test the spirits to see if now was the proper time for
his departure. The Thing would throw a basket over the
fence. If the basket landed face down, he would remain and
not release the boys: if face up, he would depart and leave
them in peace to re-unite their families.

The whole town stood in silent expectation. They saw
the basket rise in a slow arc over the fence, hang for a moment in the empty air, and then fall to the ground. The basket bounced once, and with the help of old Mulbah, landed
face up. He showed it to all the people present, and they responded with a loud cry of joy. The women rushed forward,
Yanga embraced Toang, drums started, and some even took a
few steps in dance.

But then the crowd fell back again. From the side of the
fence, through an opening newly made, there came a long
thin line of boys. They were bent double, their eyes on the

ground, each one's arms on the hips of the boy in front. Their newly-daubed white chalk contrasted with the brown of their raffia skirts. The townspeople gave way before them, as the line grew to fill the open space before the fence.

The first four boys sat down on a mat, with old Noai behind them. Her presence reminded everyone that a mid-wife is needed at a birth and these were new-born boys. They had a small basket for offerings. Yanga saw that one of the four boys was her own son, Zena. Her heart beat hard with gratitude. She had not seen him for four years. He was so big now. She hardly knew him, and yet she knew him. She ran up, and put a white kola nut in the basket. She wanted to touch the boy, to embrace him, but that time had not yet come.

Boys continued to come out, but Yanga did not see her other son Kona, whom she had once called "Good-for-nothing." She knew he would come, but still she feared. Per-haps the Forest Thing had decided at the last minute to keep him, had decided that, in fact, he was good for nothing. Per-haps he was sick and could not walk. Perhaps — but then he came, his head down, his eyes on the ground, his hands on the next boy's hips. He too had grown, even more than his brother. They were twins, but Kona was slightly bigger. Oh, he looked fine and handsome. She looked back at Zena, and her eyes filled with tears. She melted back into the crowd lest anyone see her cry.

After the boys had circled twice around the open space, they left as quietly as they had come, taking a road newly-cut in the forest. They would now wait in a freshly-cleared area near town until it was time for them to be washed and to re-turn to town. Their family could visit them, and bring them food, while they waited patiently for the right time to enter town, dressed in their finest new clothes.

After a few days in this place, the boys saw the first faint glimmer of the new moon. Mulbah and Noai agreed that the time would be soon. They together would lead the boys to the river to wash the white clay and all evil spells from their bodies. The boys would then put on new clothes and come into town to be welcomed at a great feast.

Flumo had prepared well for the great day. He had harvested the first coffee from the trees he had planted so many years before, and he received a good price for the fragrant beans. Coffee was scarce now that the kwii people were fighting each other over the water, and the Lebanese man in his new store in Salala was glad to get it. There on the new road Flumo saw huge trucks that the kwii people used to carry the coffee down to Monrovia.

With the proceeds, Flumo bought new clothes for everyone. He also bought new lanterns, shoes for the boys and iron for his blacksmith work. When Yanga saw the shoes, she asked, "Why should anyone want to cover up his feet?" But Flumo only laughed and replied, "We want our boys to look their best when they come back to town."

The boys, dressed in the finest clothes they had ever seen, arrived in line in the town. They followed a new path, to show that they had left the old life behind, that they were now different persons. To follow the old road would bring bad luck, they realized. The old man who had taught them so much was at the head of the line, carrying his sword left over from the days of the great wars before the Liberian soldiers had come.

Yakpalo fired Flumo's old gun to mark the boys' entry into town. Their eyes still on the ground, the boys walked bent double, gowned in new country cloth robes, with long tassled caps on their heads and bells on the tassles, and covered by country cloths and elaborately colored kwii cloths. The boy who had entered the fence first four years earlier led the line. Kona and Zena had followed him into the Bush School, and had to follow him during the whole time of their training. Moreover, they knew he would remain a leader throughout all their life, and they were jealous.

Kona and Zena were jealous also of Saki's son, who had

been the last to enter the school, just the night before they had left the fence. He too had a special position, as the one to kill the Forest Thing and drive him back into the deep forest for seven years. However, they realized that the boy did not yet know what they had learned during their years behind the fence. He would have to learn it informally at Poro society meetings.

The time had come to put jealousy aside and rejoice with the people of the town. All of them were together now, as they moved in a long, slow line to the center of town. As they walked they were welcomed by all the women, who danced around the line. The chief's wife danced as she had not danced for years, her every motion exciting the crowd. Her husband dashed to her, wiped her forehead, and helped her back from the line. The boys finally reached the center of town, where they sat down on mats in front of the chief's palaver house. Some of them had not seen the town in four full years, but they dared not look up yet.

The chief walked the whole line of boys, inspected them, and pronounced them well trained and ready to be members of the town. He then went to the heads of the Bush School, seated at the head of the line of boys, and gave them two sheep, two white chickens, white cloth, and white kola nuts, to show his thanks. He sat down, and the other people in town followed him to bring their gifts to the heads of the Bush School. Women tossed clean white rice and rice flour on the boys, and men gave them fresh water in a clay pot. The old man who led them responded, and then sent the boys to the house where they would stay for four days.

Flumo and Yakpalo came to visit their boys in that house. They brought them water to drink, since the house must have no pans with water in them, lest it bring bad luck to the boys. Flumo and Yakpalo saw the twins, and felt their renewed friendship grow. They shared sons now. The president's decision, so long ago, had been wise, and had united them, and with them the whole town.

The boys were no longer Kona and Zena, no longer "Good-for-nothing" and "Dirt." They were now new men, with new names. "Dirt" had proved clean and good. He was now named Sumo, because of his stature, slightly shorter than his brother. "Good-for-nothing" had shown his value. He had lived for a year and a half with Yakpalo, his father's one-time enemy, had been through Bush School, and had come out a tall, strong young man. He was now named Koli, to show that he had the strength of a leopard.

Sumo and Koli — two boys to carry on Flumo's line, and keep his family and ancestors alive. Sumo and Koli — two boys to make Yanga's heart happy in her old age, and to show that she was indeed a woman. Sumo and Koli — younger brothers for Lorpu and small Toang to be proud of, and big brothers for small Noai to look up to. Sumo and Koli — marvelous big boys they could all be proud of, especially small Noai, named for the old medicine lady who had healed the boys when they were sick. Sumo and Koli — the town was pleased with them, for they were twins, they were men now, and they would bring good fortune to all.

CHAPTER IX

Can Turtle Fly?

Elders welcome the boys

IX: CAN TURTLE FLY?

No dust rose from the forest paths the boys had followed when they came into town from Bush School. But the dust hung in the air in town during the four days of celebration. The boys wore their fine new clothes, although the dry season dust had begun to dull their brightness. The dust rose thick when family and friends danced at night in front of the boys. Clouds of red dust, stirred up by bare feet, clogged the nostrils, settled in the hair and aged the new clothes with a thin coating of red.

The whole town held the first feast. The chief killed a cow and two sheep, and every family killed chickens. The next day each of the two quarters in town held its own feast. And the final day every family welcomed its own children home. Only after that feast and after washing the dust from their feet could the boys visit their mothers.

For his own family celebration, Flumo had hunted in the forest the afternoon before and had killed a water deer, the meat the twins loved best of all. He had chased it with his hunting dogs into the big river on the edge of Mano country. The dogs had jumped in after it, barking and yelping and shaking their hunting bells. When they had cornered it, Flumo had killed the animal with a spear. At such moments, Flumo could not help regret his decision never again to use a rifle. It would have made hunting so much easier. But they all enjoyed the meat, and Flumo knew that the joy of celebration justified the effort.

Now the family could relax, after the final day of welcome was over. Even the twins could relax, freed from the constraints of the Bush School. From now on they must never violate the code of manhood, but otherwise they were free.

The forest trails were open and clear. It had not rained for over a month, and the swamps were low. The cold in the night and the dust in the air were lessening. Now the family could rejoice, let go, and visit friends. The boys looked forward especially to traveling to see relatives. Flumo no longer feared traveling. The tribal wars had long ago ceased, and peace ruled in the land. In the old days Flumo could not travel more than two days' walk from his home. He remembered one boy who had gone to Bush School with him. The boy had left with his parents to visit a distant town, but they were captured on the way, taken as slaves, and never seen again.

This time Sumo and Koli had no fear of being taken prisoner on the road. This would be the biggest trip of their lives. They would walk to Salala to see the new road, and see the strange and wonderful things of the kwii world there. Koli remembered still the many stories of the kwii world, of the white man, and now he would meet one for himself. Was he not Koli, the leopard? He knew white men lived at Salala. But he did not tell Flumo his plan. Koli had now learned one lesson. It is not good to say everything that is on one's mind.

Koli knew that he must get Yakpalo's permission before leaving. The president had given him into Yakpalo's care, and Yakpalo had the right not to let him go. Fortunately, Yakpalo agreed. He said Koli should carry his greetings to friends in Salala.

Flumo, Toang, Yanga, small Toang, Koli, Sumo and even their little sister, small Noai, left on the trail after a week of getting ready. They started out very early one morning, while the dry season mist still covered the tops of the trees and protected the travelers from the hot sun. It would soon be hotter than they liked, and so they enjoyed the cool of the morning while it lasted.

No dust arose from this trail. It was a relief from the dust of the town to be back into the cool of the forest, still far from the big road now being built from the coast up to Jorkwelle country. Saki told them of the red dust there, how he had come in just a small part of the usual walking time from Firestone to Salala in a tremendous, smoke-belching monster, noisy, dirty and dusty.

The new road cut through the forest, along the old path from Totota to Kakata, and was now half-way up-country. All along it, the red from the trucks and the workmen covered the green leaves of the vanishing forest. Soldiers, white and black, worked to build the road, which they said would help save Liberia from the German devils. The twins did not know what German devils might be, but they were glad to be safe from them.

Koli was particularly anxious to see this new road, even to eat the choking red dust that Saki told about. He too wanted to ride on the big truck. He wanted to see all the wonders that the white man could perform. Sumo laughed at him for it, said he did not believe in them, and said that even if they were true, such things were not for the Kpelle. But from what Saki had told him, it seemed to Koli that he might be able to enter that world, and take what it had to offer.

They heard a good-luck bird singing from the trees above them. Koli noticed it, and said he felt his good luck would now begin. He had finished Bush School, and he felt good entering into his manhood. He skipped and ran as he moved along the bush trail, although Yanga often had to slow him up for small Noai. He wanted to run, to find the world Saki was always telling him about.

Sumo seemed less interested. He watched the forest more than did Koli. He was the first to notice a column of driver ants moving across the road ahead, and warned small Noai not to step in them lest they bite her legs. He saw a bee's nest high in a tree near the road, and had the family stop while he climbed to bring it down to refresh them all.

He spotted a man high in a palm tree, tapping the tree for delicious palm wine, and he persuaded his father to ask for some. Soon he too could climb a palm tree, for nuts or palm wine.

Koli was restless with the talk of forest things. He challenged his brother Sumo to give him a riddle he could not answer. Sumo responded, "When an arrow flies, it does not come back." But Koli knew the answer to that one, and had often even applied it to himself, "A serious person does not rest until he reaches his goal."

Koli returned a harder one, "My father's bag was burned, but the handles remained." Sumo could not answer it — he had heard the riddle in Bush School, but had forgotten the answer. But his father knew it, and replied to Koli, "A town can be burned, but the paths leading to it are not burned."

Flumo then gave the others a harder story. He told of four brothers who one day met a beautiful girl. They all sought to marry the girl, but unfortunately she drowned in the river. Now it so happened that the men were named "Pick up bones," "Put bones together," "Put skin on bones," and "Put back breath." The men went to the river, and each did the work his name shows. At the end each claimed he should marry the girl.

Flumo asked his family to say who should have the girl. Each argued for a different person. Yanga said that without breath there is no life. Toang argued that there can't be breath if there is no skin. Sumo said that the bones must be together before skin can be put on. And small Toang insisted that someone had to pick up the bones first.

The argument went on until at last Koli insisted that his mother Yanga was correct. "Put back breath" must be able to do his brothers' work as well as his own, since in order to put breath in a person one must also be able to put the body together. Moreover, anyone can pick up bones and cover them with skin. Only a true zoe can put breath in a body.

The others had no answer for Koli, and acknowledged him the winner. He had told his answer well, and had illustrated it with motions showing the various acts of the brothers. And when he came to the final act of the zoe, his performance was so convincing that his mother was sure he must be the zoe in the family.

But Sumo would not be defeated so easily. He granted that only a zoe can put life in a body. But a zoe must also know about the forest. He asked Koli what makes a tree. Koli was stopped for a moment. He suggested the leaves, but Sumo pointed out that shrubs and vines have leaves. Koli countered with the stem and bark, but Sumo showed him that vines have the same. Koli had to give in. What makes a tree indeed? Sumo in triumph showed that rice and the giant cottonwood, both of them trees, are the same because both of them can stand by themselves, and have one main stem.

Sumo had showed he too was a zoe. He had met his brother's challenge with another. He had not had to use medicine. This was not the time for medicine, even though Sumo knew stronger medicines than Koli. Let Koli test him. He would not show everything he knew the way Koli did. Had he not often gone to the zoe tree in the Bush School to think on this matter? Had he not often listened as more important zoes boasted to each other of their powers? Had he not been shown by old Mulbah the way to walk in fire without being burned, the way to put his hand in boiling water without being scalded?

Flumo knew what was happening. He saw his boys testing themselves against each other. He warned them both. Neither must think he is better than the other. Neither must be like turtle, who thought he was better than the other animals in the swamp. Turtle asked the rice-birds to take him with them into the sky. The birds told turtle to grab hold of a stick with his mouth, and hold tight. The birds then picked up the stick, and flew off into the sky. After a while turtle grew tired, and his lips began to hurt. Thus he opened his mouth to ask the birds to take him back to the swamp. But, of course, he fell to the ground and was killed. "The person who opens his mouth too much will get in trouble," concluded Flumo.

Koli thought about what his father said, and agreed to respect others more. Sumo, too, agreed that he must not challenge his brother in the very areas where he had had special training in the Bush School. It was too much like boasting, and boasting gets all but the most powerful man in trouble.

Sumo was content to leave it at that for the moment. But Koli kept other thoughts in his mind. He felt somehow different, somehow better than his brothers and sisters. His father and mother always tried to stop him asking so many questions. But he wanted to find out about things, and he couldn't see anything wrong with it. He wanted to learn as much as he could about things. His elders had always put him down, and he did not like it. They had done their best in Bush School to make him like the others, and he had agreed for the time being. But his mother had always told him he would be a special zoe, and he felt that his special ability was to talk and learn. Why should they stop him?

He had had a dream two nights before they left Bush School. In his dream, he had been an old man, and had known the answers to all the questions the other men had put to him. He was sure this was his way in life. Someday, somehow, he would have the chance to learn more − and then he would show all his people what he was made of. He did not want to learn how to breathe fire and smoke, as some zoes could do: he wanted to learn how to know and breathe the truth.

They reached the half-way point between their town and the next. There they stopped so that each person could put another rock on the pile, which showed that their work was nearly done. Their town had cleared the path up to this point, and it was wide and spacious. Ahead the next town had the responsibility of clearing away the vines and branches that would overhang and then hide a path if they could. They had not done so well. The Forest Thing would have to come to their town some night soon to warn them of their responsibilities, before the Liberian soldiers did the same thing. Before the Bush School had ended, the Forest Thing had come to Flumo's town to tell everyone to clear the trail, and to tell each quarter to clean around its houses for the coming of the boys. This town had not had a Bush School for itself, since their boys had come to Flumo's town, but still they had their work to perform.

The family passed farmers beginning to clear the bush for their new farms. A women's work group was busy, in orderly lines, clearing small vines and shrubs away from the forest giants their husbands would later cut down. On another farm, the men were already at work felling the big trees, always careful to leave palm and kola trees. Nearer town men were digging up dry-season cassava to replace rice they wanted to sell. They had planted their cassava so that when hungry time came late in the rainy season, they would not have to go into the forest to dig wild yams or gather wild fruits or forest snails.

That night they arrived at a town near Gbarnga. They would avoid Gbarnga and its soldiers. They were received well and lodged in the stranger-house. Koli and Sumo were given presents of a chicken and a small hoe, because they were twins. They bathed and ate and rested well, in order to be ready to go on the next day.

However, the next morning little Noai was sick. She had diarrhea, and it would not stop. Flumo thought of staying in town to consult the herbalist, but Sumo said he had learned the right leaf in Bush School to stop her stomach from running. He ran into the bush and soon brought back three small red leaves. "They have to be very new," he told his father. He crushed the leaves and gave them to Noai to eat. She was soon able to continue the trip without trouble.

Flumo was proud of Sumo, prouder of him for finding the right leaf than he had been of Koli for answering riddles or stories. Koli talked too much and asked too many questions and was too clever. Sumo would be a true zoe, part of the forest and part of the town. He only said, "The turtle who knows how to swim lives longer than the turtle who tries to fly." Sumo felt a glow of pride at this. His time would come, and he would be a good zoe.

On the third day, they began to see more coffee, cocoa and rubber farms. And then shortly before dark they met soldiers working on the road. They walked to a new town where people of all kinds lived — white men, coastal Liberians, Kpelle men, people from other tribes.

The first man Flumo met said it was another two hours' walk to Salala. Why not rest there for the night? They agreed, but did not like all the strangers in Kpelle country. Yanga admitted she hardly slept that night, for fear those people who talked so strangely would hurt her.

They walked on the new road the next morning. Many men were working, some with cutlasses and hoes, but some also with great machines that roared and hurled dirt and dust in the air. Flumo was awed but wished he was back in the forest. And then, as they crossed the last river Salala appeared in the distance, a large town, larger than any the boys had ever seen. The D. C.'s house, the soldiers' barracks, the road and the trucks, the strange-looking Mandingo men with their long robes, the houses with zinc roofs, all appeared strange and wonderful to Sumo and Koli.

But more wonderful than anything, even the trucks, were the market and the stores. The boys gaped at what they saw there — more peppers and okra and palm oil and rice and ground peas than they knew existed. They saw cloth of all kinds, country cloth woven on small looms such as Yakpalo used and Koli was learning how to use, rich lengths of white and blue Mandingo cloth, and brightly patterned pieces of lappa cloth from England stored since the white man's war began. They saw tools which could put a blacksmith out of business, shiny and smooth and new. All these things put new ideas into Koli's head and made his home seem small and unimportant.

Sumo named the things he saw in the market — pots, shirts, knives, onions, pans, coconuts, cutlasses, headties, hoes, peppers, cups, bananas. There were so many of them he could hardly keep them straight. How could he ever tell his friends in town what he had seen? Koli said, "I know. Remember all the pots and pans and cups together. They are all alike. And so are the shirts and headties like each other. That will make them easy to remember." Sumo still wanted to argue. "That's not the right way to do it. I can remember the knife, the onion and the pan, because I cut the onion with the knife and put it in the pan. And I open the coconut with a cutlass. Koli's only answer was, "You can't remember things that way. Things that are alike have to be named together."

Once again, Flumo had to separate the boys, showing that each was right. Back in town it was right to think of what you could do with the things, but here in Salala maybe it was easier to remember things by putting similar ones together. But Flumo admitted to himself that he had not thought of Koli's way of doing it. Saki would divide the things Koli's way, he thought.

Flumo and his family had brought coffee to Salala to sell to the Monrovia traders. He also had some rice to sell in the market so he could buy presents for his Salala relatives. In the market he found he could sell 30 measuring pans of rice for two lappas of brightly colored cloth and a small knife. He emptied his rice into the large pan before the woman who sold cloth. He said he knew he had 30 pans full there, but the woman did not agree. So the woman took the small measuring pan she had with her and counted out the number. Flumo was triumphant — there were 31 in all. She agreed to give him a better knife than the one he had asked for, and the bargain was complete.

After they left the market Koli asked, "Why can't we take these things with us?" The traders seemed so very rich to him, since they had brought so many things to market. Sumo and Koli could not believe one person could own so much.

Flumo responded, "The spider web is not always for the spider." The boys understood. The market could catch a man like a spider web. And the web did not belong only to the market sellers. It belonged to the big people who brought the cloth and the lanterns and the buckets and the axes to Kpelle country.

The boys had never seen some things in the store. They found tall lanterns that could give as much light as the sun, and big pots that could make strong drink from sugarcane water. Saki had brought the first of this drink to town, and had proceeded to make a fool of himself with it. Flumo thought to himself that the Liberian soldiers and traders had brought cane juice to make his people weak.

Drink like that makes the kwii people crazy, Flumo told his boys. Saki had told of one kwii man at Firestone who did not like the way his wife cooked his food. His wife tried every possible way, until one night she got drunk on cane juice and burned his food, and then went to sleep and left it cold. He came home, ate the food, and told his wife how well she had done. The kwii have no sense, Flumo said, and he urged Koli and Sumo not to get mixed up with their business. "Let Kpelle go to Kpelle, and kwii go to kwii," he finished.

One more thing in the store caught Koli's eye. The store-keeper called it a mirror. Koli picked it up and looked at himself in it. He started to walk out of the store with it in his hands to show his father, who had gone with Sumo to the next store. Suddenly the store-keeper, a light-skinned Lebanese man, saw him and shouted. Koli was frightened and dropped the glass. It broke into a hundred pieces on the floor.

Koli could not find Flumo. He had stayed behind only a moment, caught by the magic of the mirror, now broken on the ground. The store-keeper shouted at him in words he could not understand. If this had happened before he went to Bush School, he would have cried. But now he was a man and had to stand for himself. The store-keeper called for a Kpelle man to talk his words. And through that Kpelle man the store-keeper said every kind of mean and ugly thing he could think of about Koli, who could only stand there and take it.

After he finished shouting, the store-keeper sent for a soldier to lock Koli in what he called the night-house. Koli tried to say that his father was right there in Salala, but the man would not listen. The man and the soldier, a Loma man, soon came back.

The soldier asked Koli, "Why were you stealing the mirror?," and hit him hard across the face. Koli tried to answer, "I was not stealing it, but only wanted to show it to my father." At that moment, Flumo heard the shouting as he came out of the next store. He hurried back and found Koli with the soldier and the storekeeper. He asked what was wrong, and soon had to agree to pay the store-keeper for the mirror and also to give the Loma soldier some tobacco as a white thing to show his respect for the government.

Koli had not stolen the mirror, Flumo knew that. It was stealing when a townsman had taken Flumo's rice to market and had used the profits to buy cane juice. Flumo had gone to old Mulbah for him to prepare a great curse against the guilty man if he did not repay the money. Mulbah had done so, but also reminded Flumo that the curse would come back on him if the man were not guilty.

Flumo knew his boys would not do that. Once Koli had killed and eaten a chicken that Yanga had told him to catch, because the chicken had given him such a hard time and because he was hungry. Flumo had beaten the boy and reminded him that "Rooster cannot crow in his friend's home." He must not take what is not his. Flumo had the boys' promise they would never do so, and he believed them.

But, stealing or not, Flumo had to pay for the mirror with the little money he received for his coffee. He had already bought presents for his relatives, and for Yanga and Toang and their mothers. But nothing remained for the boys, and all because of Koli.

Koli, however, did not think of the money. He could only think of how the Lebanese store-keeper had cursed him, and how the Loma soldier had beaten him. It was all for nothing. His father had come back and paid for the mirror and had given the soldier his white thing to make him feel good. But Koli saw himself as nothing but a little country boy. He did not know what these people knew. He could not speak their language. He could not own their things. He wanted his chance to be equal with them. But he did not know how.

The family left the market, and went to a small town just beyond Salala, where they found Flumo's relatives. All the townspeople were celebrating, since the Bush School there had just come out, and all the boys were in town.

Flumo's people welcomed him and his family warmly, and invited them to enjoy the feast with the other townspeople. They danced through the whole night, even though the moon was beginning to wane again. The dancing and feasting helped them forget the mirror, the soldier and the Lebanese store-keeper. Now they were back with their own people, and nothing bad could happen.

However, white people were here too. The trucks which brought their uncle Saki from Firestone to Salala, which brought mirrors and cloth, also brought other white strangers. "Why are they here? There is no store. Let them go over to Salala where the stores are." Flumo did not think it right that white men should enter this small Kpelle town.

Koli too saw the man, and felt his anger rising in his

heart. The man looked like the Lebanese store-keeper. "All these white people look the same," he thought, and he wanted to hate him. And yet he wanted to be like him, at the same time. He looked like the man in the picture Koli had saved from Saki's book. Men like that can do anything, even put their faces in a book.

Somehow the white man seemed to be friendly with the people. What did he want? He could speak their language fairly well, although not of course the Jorkwelle Kpelle that Koli and his family knew. Koli's first thought was that this white man might also want to beat him, but his second thought was that he had power. Koli was a zoe, and he must have power — yet not the power of the forest. He would take the power of the white man and learn to use it.

That night the man sought out Flumo and his family, and talked well to them. Koli said very little at first. He remembered what his father had said: "Pangolin showed leopard the way to eat him." Koli would not show his soft underbelly to this white man. He would not be eaten, the way his father's money and his own pride had been eaten that very afternoon.

The white man went on talking to Flumo about the new things in the town, and Koli found himself more and more interested in the talk. Indeed this man might be able to show him something about the world of the store-keeper, the soldier, the picture, the truck, the secret of kwii power. Koli began to ask questions: "Is it true you came in a truck? What do you sell in the market? How does a mirror work?"

The man smiled and began to ask Koli questions in return. The man's questions were strange ones, questions no one had ever before asked Koli: "What do you know about God? What do you want to do when you become big? Do you want to learn to put your words in a book so you can send them far away? Do you want to be able to count on paper like the Lebanese store-keeper?" This last question touched Koli. The white man could show him something real and helpful. If Koli could learn what the white man had to tell him, perhaps he could help his family not be fooled by store-keepers and soldiers.

The man also talked to Sumo, but Sumo wanted to learn the business of a zoe, not a white man. His people would show him their medicines and their ways of divining, things the white man did not know. Moreover, he could not see the things the white man talked about. Sumo stopped listening to stories about houses across the great sea and about a God higher than the sky who had become a man. Let Koli worry about such things.

Koli talked to his father and mother later about what the white man had said. He had stayed to listen long after the others got weary and left. He told his parents about the house for learning to do what the white man does. The white man had called it a skin-house, because the marks the white man puts on a white skin can carry his words anywhere. There he could read and even make himself a book like the one Saki had brought to town.

Yanga told Koli not to think about the white man's matters, but Flumo was willing to find out more. He too talked to the man the next day, and the man asked that Koli stay with him. He said he would teach Koli many things in his house, so that Koli would know more about God and would be able to do the things the white man does. Flumo didn't think much of the first reason — after all Koli already knew as much about God as any young Kpelle man might want to know. But the second reason sounded good. None of Flumo's people knew these things. Even Saki, who had worked so long at Firestone, did not know what the white man knows, did not have what the white man has.

But the white man wanted what Flumo could not grant. He wanted Koli to stay at the town, where he could go to school. The white man called his skin-house a school, just like the Bush School. But Flumo could not leave Koli behind at Salala. Not only did he belong to Yakpalo, but also to leave

Koli with the white man would violate what Flumo's people had always believed. Had not old Mulbah said as much when the boys came out from behind the fence?

Flumo told the white man that before he could make any decision, he would have to discuss the matter with all the elders in town, in particular with Yakpalo, the boy's other father.

The white man was unhappy, but had to agree. He tried to make Flumo promise that Koli could come back in a month. Flumo said only that he would try. He never promised anything if he could help it.

Before Flumo and his family left for home, the white man told Koli many more things. He told him about the towns he could see as he went toward the coast on the new road. Koli could travel on that road, ride in trucks that could carry a man farther in a day than he could walk in a week.

The new road grabbed at Koli's heart. He must one day ride on that road. As he and his family finally prepared to leave Salala and go home, Koli felt in his heart that he was already on that new road, already driving fast. Sumo, however, walked the forest trail with assurance. He would not leave the old road, would not give up what his people had given him. He would be a good zoe, even though Koli might find out the secrets of the white man.

Kwii kettles for sale

CHAPTER X

How Tall

Can Okra Grow?

X: HOW TALL CAN OKRA GROW?

By the time Flumo and his family reached home again, it was time to clear the forest for the next rice farm. Already the memory of the white man was beginning to fade in Flumo's mind. He remembered, of course, the Lebanese trader in Salala — that sort of anger did not disappear so quickly. But he had learned not to believe the kind of wild promise that the white man had made. How could his son know what the white man knows? Didn't everyone realize that the white man could fly, could send his voice a distance of ten days' walk, could use a machine to clear a road in one day that his people needed two weeks to finish? Already the promises the white man had made to Koli seemed ridiculous. Flumo hoped that Koli would realize the folly of returning to the white man's school, would forget about trying to do the impossible. No good could come of it. "Let Kpelle go to Kpelle, and kwii go to kwii," he repeated to himself.

Flumo said nothing about the conversation with the white man when he returned to town. He brought Yakpalo the good news that his cousin's head wife had borne a son, and that his cousin had taken a third wife. He told about the changes in the world, about the markets he had seen, about the reports that the motor road would soon reach Totota. He did not, however, mention the white man. It seemed too foolish.

Rather he prepared for the new farming season. Men needed new cutlasses, and not all of them were willing to buy the kwii cutlasses he had seen in Salala. Flumo had given in to kwii ways and brought iron from Salala, and he hammered

161

out the tools that were needed. He admitted to himself that he was glad he did not have to go into the bush to smelt iron for his shop. Those days were over now. He saw with pleasure Sumo in the blacksmith's shop early in the morning, preparing the fire and setting out the tools.

Flumo thought it good that Yakpalo was starting in earnest to show Koli how to weave. What he did not know was that Koli spent his time telling Yakpalo about his conversations with the white man, about all the amazing things he had seen, and about what the white man claimed could be learned in his school. Koli did not yet tell Yakpalo, however, that the white man had asked him to return to Salala, to go to school.

Yakpalo enjoyed talking to Koli at the loom. He too was interested in the white man and his ways. Yakpalo had always felt that Flumo was too stuck in the old ways, not willing enough to change with the world. Yakpalo had seen more of the world than Flumo. He had seen Firestone, although he had not stayed to work. He told Koli stories in return, and Koli almost forgot that he was supposed to learn weaving. Yakpalo had to remind him to watch the loom, to provide him the thread, as Koli looked off into space and thought about Salala, about Firestone, about the white man's world.

Sumo's education was not confined to the blacksmith shop. Sumo asked old man Mulbah to show him his medicines. Sumo's request had to go to the town elders, who agreed that he had the calling to be a zoe. Sumo went with Mulbah into the forest to gather and identify leaves, when he was not helping Flumo in the blacksmith shop.

Flumo needed Sumo to work in the blacksmith shop, but wanted Koli to help the men cutting the bush. But Koli held back. He seemed unhappy about something. Flumo had to threaten to beat him if he did not go to work with the others. Koli went out with the men, to do the work he could do, but he was not satisfied.

Indeed, Koli's heart was still in Salala with the white man. He still felt he should be riding on that new road, and the farm seemed remote and dull. He wanted to attend the white man's school. His father had said they would discuss the matter back in town. But two weeks had passed, and there had been no mention of the matter. The white man had asked Koli to return in a month — and a month was half gone.

Koli hoped that Yanga might help him go to school. She went with the men on the farm to cook their food and bring them water. One of Koli's jobs was to carry water from the river to the farm, and this brought him close to his mother after each trip. One day he summoned the courage to ask her to speak to Flumo about the school.

She was amazed. Was the boy still thinking about that? Didn't he know that his family needed him? And he was not their son alone. Yakpalo would need him to work on his big new farm. Yakpalo had taken a fourth wife, and had a large family to feed. Cutting such a large farm would be hard work. And when the rice was ripening, Koli could drive the birds away. There was too much work to do, and everyone needed Koli's help.

His mother asked him how he could think of going away to the white man's school. After all, he had finished school already, and was now an initiated member of the community, a man among men. In a few years he should think about marriage, and he must now show he could make a good husband.

Koli saw that Flumo would not send him back to learn what the white man could teach him. The way seemed closed. He dared not ask his father, especially after his mother had spoken as she did. She knew Flumo's feelings, even without asking him, after so many years together.

He decided to ask Yakpalo. The president had given him to Yakpalo many years earlier. Perhaps Yakpalo understood more about the white man than Flumo. Had he not listened to Koli's stories about talking to the white man? Yakpalo was an important man in town, certain to be chosen as the next town chief. Surely he would agree to let Koli go to the white man.

But Koli had to wait until his chance came. Three days later Yakpalo was to brush his farm, and Koli was expected to carry water for the men and help cut the bush. While they were walking to the farm, Koli finally got near enough to Yakpalo to ask the important question.

He began to tell Yakpalo about the Lebanese storekeeper who had beaten him and almost put him in jail. He told how children today needed to know the ways of the white man so that the Lebanese would not take advantage of them. And then he began to tell about what the white man had asked him to do. Yakpalo must have seen the white man's schools during his travels. This white man would give a Kpelle boy a chance to learn.

Yakpalo listened carefully. He did not want to see a boy from his town, particularly a boy in his own family, get trapped in the white man's ways. He had seen one of these schools at Firestone. Boys went in and came out different, came out like babies, came out talking and acting in a way no Kpelle man could understand. Everyone said that no good could come out of these schools. The boys who went to these schools could not be white men. Everyone agreed such boys became worthless kwii men who knew nothing, nothing about the Kpelle world and also nothing about the white man's world.

And yet Yakpalo was not so sure in his heart. Maybe these white people were not so different. Did they not have to eat and sleep like everyone else? Did they not sometimes get drunk, sometimes fight among themselves? Moreover, they did not know everything. One white man had come to Salala to show the Kpelle how to plant rice with a machine, and his machine had been lost in the swamp. Yet it was true that they knew some things he wished he knew. Perhaps Koli could really find out something about the white man and his world and life.

And yet Yakpalo knew that Flumo did not want Koli to leave. Yakpalo had told Flumo what Koli was saying at the loom. Flumo looked away, but Yakpalo knew he was concerned. He wanted his son at home, to be a man of his people. Thus Yakpalo could not agree for Koli to leave home and go back to Salala. Somehow in his heart he would have been content for the boy to go, but it would mean betraying Flumo. They had worked hard to become friends again. Yakpalo must not spoil that.

Koli was now more desperate than ever. Almost three weeks had passed and he was no closer to school than before. He knew from Yanga's face that Flumo would never let him go to school. He now knew that Yakpalo would not help him, despite his interest.

The only thing he could do, he decided, was to go to the white man's school by himself. He had heard in Salala of one boy who had run away from home to go to the white man's school. He would take that chance, leave home secretly, and not come back until he knew the white man's ways. If other boys had left their families without permission in order to go to the white man's schools, he too could do so.

Yet to leave his family, his very life, frightened him. Without a family, a man is nothing at all. No one in his town had ever left his family. And how could he come back if he had run away?

Only the thought of what he might bring back to his family from the white man's world drove him on. But he did not know what to take. He had little clothing, in addition to the fine new clothes his father had given him when he came out of the Bush School. He had no money at all, no food at all. And yet he had to go to school. So he put together his small pack of things, a bit of food from the meat dryer in his mother's house, and started early the next morning.

He got no farther than the next town. When he reached there he found that he did not know the way to Salala. He asked a man for directions, but the man knew Flumo and was suspicious. He told the boy only, "Rooster cannot crow in his friend's town," and then asked the boy if he thought he was a rooster already. He refused to help Koli, and instead took him back home.

There they met Flumo, who was totally unable to comprehend the fact that his son had tried to leave home. Why had he left home to live with a white man who made false promises?

Flumo started to beat his son properly, to beat some sense into him, when Yakpalo intervened. Yakpalo told Flumo to wait a bit. The boy was determined. Perhaps they should listen to him. Yakpalo told of his talk with Koli, and admitted that even then he had felt that the boy should have the chance. After all, the world is changing fast. Let Koli see that world, and learn for himself. He would come back to his people soon, after he had found what he wanted to know.

Yakpalo said he did not believe in the white man's school any more than did Flumo, although he was impressed with what the white man could do. Yet Koli just might find something useful to them all. Let him go. At worst, he would just find out his own foolishness, and would learn to be a better member of the town. This might be the right medicine to cure him of always asking questions, of always trying to learn things that were not for him to know. And, at best, he might really find out the secrets of the white man's world.

Flumo was furious. He had lost Koli many years earlier to Yakpalo. He still felt it had not really been his own fault. All the time and effort he had given to raising the boy would be lost if Yakpalo's word prevailed. It was true that the boy was now Yakpalo's. Flumo had tried to forget that fact during the four years of bush school. Now it came back to him with force, and he had to accept the fact that the decision lay in Yakpalo's hands.

The only thing was to appeal to the town elders, perhaps even to the elders of the secret society. This was the first time the town had been hurt by the white man's words. Flumo argued before the elders that Koli had been bewitched by the white man, and that he had lost his reason. He had tried to run from the town, when he had failed to get permission to go to the white man's school. No one ever took such a decision by himself, and especially not a child.

The only case anyone could remember was when a distant cousin of Flumo had dreamed of a water woman, beautiful with long white arms and round white face. He had gone to the waterside and there had found her ring, as she had promised. He gave himself to her, and promised to give up his wives and children for the wealth and power she would bring him. The woman came to him at night, white and terrible. His rice farm grew well, he earned more money than he had any right to expect when he sold his palm kernels — but soon his wife, and then his oldest child, sickened and died. Everyone said he had been bewitched by the terrible white woman who came to him in the night.

Flumo called on this precedent as an argument against his son going to the white man's school. He told how his cousin had grown rich, how no rice birds ever entered his farm, how he killed a big, meaty animal every time he hunted in the forest, how he could call down lightning when he wanted it.

Then Flumo pressed his point home. He reminded the elders that the townspeople had accused his cousin of witchcraft. Under heavy pressure, he had confessed to having a water woman. And, as soon as he made the confession, he went insane. Even at the time Flumo spoke, his cousin was in town. But he had no permanent home. When he was violent, people would put him in stocks, and soon release him to wander to another town. His hair was tangled with dirt and leaves. He often went without clothes. He could work hard, and so the people would feed him. Yet everyone knew that he was a man who had, by himself and without the help of friends and family, gone to the white water woman to be rich.

Thus did Flumo argue before the elders. If Yakpalo let his son go to the white man, Koli would be lost. It is one thing to go to Firestone to work. Many men in town had done that. But bringing home the few things that a rubber tapper earned was not the same as marrying the water woman or trying to be like the white man. For Koli to go to the white man's school would be for him to give up his people, to die as a Kpelle man. In fact, just like Flumo's cousin's wife and children, the townspeople would die if Koli succeeded.

Flumo reminded the elders of the rifle he had once bought from the white man. He had killed even leopards with it, but he had had to pay the price. He had shot a man. He who takes the white man's things must forfeit his own life or the life of his people. Koli might one day confess that he was guilty for going to the white man, but he would surely go mad afterwards. Flumo finished his argument by asserting, "Okra cannot grow taller than its planter."

Yakpalo agreed that it is true that okra can only grow as tall as the one who puts the okra in the ground, but he also pointed out, "When cassava sees its water, then it is easier to swallow." In order for the Kpelle people to live with the white man — and live with him they must, for there were more white men every year in Kpelle country — they must learn the white man's ways. Then the Kpelle man could swallow what the white man brings. Otherwise they would all be forced to accept the white man and his ways without any soup — and who can swallow cassava before it is cooked?

Yakpalo also pointed out that Koli was a twin. He reminded them that Koli had been bitten by a snake when he had been in Bush School. Flumo had wanted to get old Mulbah to bring medicine, but Yakpalo had told the people to wait. A zoe cannot die by snake bite, if he is a true zoe. The power of twins lies in the cassava snake, and since Koli had never eaten cassava snake meat, he would resist the poison. In fact, Koli had recovered quickly without medicine.

Yakpalo said that even if the white man were a snake, as the white water woman appeared when she came to Flumo's cousin, Koli could resist. Flumo had told Koli before he went to the Bush School, "Sitting quietly reveals crocodile's tricks." Yakpalo reminded the elders that the snake and the crocodile are brothers. Koli had learned about crocodile. Let him now learn about snake. Let him go to the white man and learn how to live with him. He will come back soon enough, and live with his own people.

The elders listened to the arguments. They remembered the president's decision so many years before. On the basis of that decision, they agreed that Yakpalo had the authority to let the boy go. However, they did not want any disagreement to reopen old hatreds between Flumo and Yakpalo. So they compromised by letting Koli go to the white man, to return one day as one of their own. And, if he can bring back the white man's wealth, let him give it to Yakpalo, and then be Flumo's son again.

This decision satisfied Flumo and Yakpalo alike. They then called Koli into the meeting, and talked harshly to him. He was wrong in running away. Koli agreed he had been wrong to go to the next town without warning his parents. But he denied he had intended to run away. He had only gone there to see his friends. He had meant to come back directly.

The elders murmured their satisfaction at his reply. They and Koli alike knew Koli had tried to run away. But his denial showed that Koli realized his action was wrong. He would not stubbornly affirm his decision.

The elders then gave Koli his task. As a man, an adult member of the Poro society, he must be loyal to his family, his town, and his people. He had two fathers — Flumo and Yakpalo. He had many mothers in town. He must remember them all. True, he would not have to make farm this year. He would not have to chase rice birds. He would not have to do his share of town labor. His fathers, Yakpalo and Flumo, had agreed to do his share of the work.

But Koli must continue to serve his people. He must try to learn the white man's ways, and come back home. He had spent four years in the Poro Society Bush School. So four years would surely be enough time to learn the ways of the white man, if it was possible at all, which they doubted. Above all he must not let the white man bewitch him, and make him into another white man. Some people in the town already believed he had been bewitched, but he must prove them wrong.

Sumo for a brief moment felt envy at his brother, who was being allowed to leave the town and leave his work. Sumo certainly did not want to go to the white man's school, but he objected to Koli leaving home.

However, Sumo gave it little more thought. Let him go. Sumo would learn to become a proper zoe. Old Noai, who knew all the leaves in the forest, had agreed to show him more leaves just as soon as the farm tools were all made and the farms cut. Old Mulbah had also agreed to allow Sumo to watch him work, and was willing to show him the art of divination. A twin zoe can see into the future, everyone said, and Sumo wanted to learn the methods of cutting lines into the sand to find what would happen, wanted to learn how to throw the kola nuts. Let Koli go to his foolishness. Sumo would live his life here in town.

Koli and Sumo had always been close, despite their difference. Even when Koli had been given to Yakpalo, they had not been far apart. Koli had, of course, spent time on Yakpalo's farm while Sumo worked on Flumo's farm. But each had always known what the other was doing. Now they felt a sense of loss. Koli was going to learn from the white man. Sumo was going to fulfil his destiny as a zoe. Each had the same thought — would they know each other when they again met?

That night, as Koli prepared to leave home, Flumo told him and Sumo a story about two birds. These birds had been hatched together, but they had flown from the nest and gone off to another part of the forest. They had not seen their mother for many years. But she had taught them a special language in the nest. One day they sang to another bird in that special language. The other bird answered with the same song, and by that answer they knew their mother.

Flumo said that his children were the same. They would also know each other when they met, because they had a spirit within them to keep them together. A family never drifts apart, because it has a common spirit and a common language. As soon as a man sees his brother or father or mother, or anyone in his family, he will recognize him as his relative. Flumo told Koli always to remember his family, always to sing the special song that belonged to his family. In that way, he would never be lost, no matter what the white man tried to do to him.

The town Elder speaks

CHAPTER XI

And He Has Gone

Gathering Leaves

XI: AND HE HAS GONE GATHERING LEAVES

The first step before Koli could leave for school was to make him protection medicine to add to the leopard's teeth he already wore. No child would be sent to such an uncertain and unknown future without medicine to ward off poison, witchcraft, accident and sickness. Flumo consulted the family's spirit stone and sacrificed a chicken to it. Old Mulbah made the medicine, with the help of Sumo. Mulbah insisted that it would work better if Koli's own brother, a twin zoe, collected some of the ingredients for the medicine he would put under Koli's wrist.

Mulbah made a neat, shallow cut on the inside of Koli's wrist, slipped the medicine under the tiny flap of skin, and then closed the fold again. It bled slightly but the medicine stayed in place. He warned Koli not to touch the flap of skin until the wound had thoroughly healed, and never to touch limes, so the medicine would keep him from harm.

Flumo could not accept Koli's foolishness, but the medicine quieted his fears a bit. And yet he feared the white man might have stronger medicine. Some people said that when kwii medicine comes, Kpelle medicine gets weak. If the white man wanted to harm Koli, he could do it easily. Flumo feared the white man, and half expected him to eat his son in the same way he ate whatever Flumo sold in Salala. Flumo never earned what he wanted when he sold his rice, coffee and palm nuts. This white man would surely be no different from all the others.

Now Koli had to get ready for school. Sumo was sulky and jealous as he saw the preparations. He almost regretted having helped make the protection medicine. He did not want to hurt his brother, but he resented the attention paid to him. Koli would not work on the farm. Koli ran away and was not punished for it. Sumo had always been the good boy, the one not to complain, the one to accept what the elders said. Koli, on the other hand, talked back to the old people, asked questions, refused to work. And now Koli got whatever he wanted to help him learn the white man's foolishness. Koli would take the fine clothes he wore at the closing of the bush school, a length of country cloth Yakpalo had made, a cutlass and a knife Flumo gave him.

More than a month had passed since Koli had seen the white man, and thus he was impatient to leave for school. But the family did not want to hurry. They had to find the right time, nor could they allow Koli to travel the forest road by himself. It was a good thing he had been stopped at the next town, that day when he had run away. If he had gone much farther by himself, the leopards, human or otherwise, might have caught him. The roads were usually safe from attack now, but a boy travelling alone on a lonely road was a tempting catch.

Yakpalo planned to take Koli to school. He wanted to sell country cloth as well as coffee berries he had picked in the forest. He was considering planting his own coffee, just as Flumo had done. But until then, what he could find in the forest would have to supplement his income and provide his family's needs for the coming year.

Moreover, Yakpalo wanted to see this white man, wanted to find out just what Koli would have to face. He had agreed for Koli to go to school, had forced the issue against Flumo. He gained prestige in town that way, but if anything bad happened to Koli he would lose. If Koli succeeded in finding out the secrets of the white man, the town would thank Yakpalo. Yakpalo had to know if he had made a wise choice.

Yakpalo started out early the next morning with three

of his sons, his second wife, his brother and Koli. Two of his sons had come out of Bush School with Koli and Sumo, and wanted to see the world. They were older than the twins, and ready to marry. The third son, Tokpa, was much younger, not yet initiated into the Poro Bush School, and fascinated by what Koli had told him of the white man and of the school in Salala. Yakpalo did not know this, or he might not have let Tokpa come on the trip. But Tokpa kept hidden his interest in the white man's school.

When the sun was high in the sky on the third day of their trip, the group reached the new road near Totota. They walked along the road, marvelling at the machines and the men, until they reached the town where Flumo had earlier stopped for the night. But this time they were not received well. Soldiers were collecting taxes from the people and forcing those who could not pay to work on the road. Yakpalo had not paid his taxes yet, and even if he had paid them he could not have proved it. Men on the road warned him not to pass through town and get caught.

So Yakpalo and his family followed a farm trail to bypass the town. There is more than one way to beat the soldier at his game, thought Yakpalo. They found it hard to avoid the town, since the farm trails did not connect to make a complete road. At times the family had to make its way through swamps that were not normally traveled, and once Koli almost lost his load into the swamp as he sank up to his waist in the murky water. Eventually they reached a little-used trail leading to Salala from the big river. It was thoroughly dark by this time, and so they were glad to be back on a proper path once again.

The family arrived in Salala after everyone had gone to bed. Only a few dogs were still awake among the houses. Yakpalo went to his relatives, who were living near the center of town, not far from the Lebanese store where Koli's curiosity had caused him so much trouble. They pounded on the doors and walls, until Yakpalo's cousin woke up and opened

the door to see what was the matter. He had not known Yakpalo was coming, but welcomed him warmly.

They brought bath water for Yakpalo, his wife and his
brother, but there was no way to fix a proper meal so late at
night, even though the waning moon had by now begun to
rise. The only thing to do was to bring out cold roasted cassava for the strangers, so that they did not have to sleep hungry. A small piece of dried fish was Koli's special twin gift.
Yakpalo's cousin gave Yakpalo his own bed, and he himself
slept on the floor, Koli and Yakpalo's brother beside him,
Yakpalo's three sons in the corner of the room, and Yakpalo's wife in the women's house.

Koli hardly slept that night. Hè was in a strange house.
He was tired and hungry. He had not bathed, and felt the
mud of the swamps and the dust of the big road on him. But,
most important of all, the next morning he would go to the
white man and begin to learn his ways. He dreamed, his eyes
wide open, of learning to read and write and by the end of
the year being able to earn all the money his parents wanted.
He saw himself driving one of the big trucks that had so
frightened him the first time he visited Salala. He saw himself in a store wearing a kwii suit with long trousers, giving
and receiving bags full of money. He saw himself ordering
that Lebanese trader to bring him a cold drink. He saw himself refusing to buy the best mirror from the Lebanese store,
because he had a better one sent to him from Firestone. All
these things he saw during that long, tired night in Yakpalo's
cousin's house.

It seemed forever before the rooster crowed, and the
family began to stir. While the sky was still gray, and the
morning mists had only begun to settle on the houses and
trees, Koli was up and off to the river to wash the dust and
mud from his body. He hurried back, and put on the same
fine clothes he had worn coming out of Bush School.

He was much too early for the morning meal which
their hosts had promised in place of the rice and soup they

had missed the night before. He could hardly wait as people went for wood, built a fire, washed and picked over the rice to remove rocks, cut greens, added palm oil and dried fish, and finally began to cook a grand welcome meal. Koli knew that he could not go to the white man without Yakpalo, but his impatience was hard to conceal.

Finally, after they had eaten, when the mists had cleared away and the dry season sun had acquired its full strength, Yakpalo said they would now visit the white man. He too looked forward anxiously to the visit, but he did not want to show it. Yakpalo and Koli, with small Tokpa hanging on in an eager way that disturbed Yakpalo although it did not surprise Koli, left to find the white man's house.

To Koli's disgust, Yakpalo insisted on stopping in town to greet the town chief, who was lying in his hammock sewing together strips of country cloth for a new robe. Yakpalo sat down and talked for what seemed an impossible length of time, exchanging news about Salala and Yakpalo's own town.

Finally they stood up to go — this time to the market. Yakpalo wanted to find who was buying coffee and country cloth. He saw two friends from up-country, who told him that prices were better in Kakata. And, of course, with each person he had to exchange greetings and find out the news.

It was this way all across town, until at length they reached the white man's house. There, next to the house, they saw boys like Koli putting sticks in place and tying them with vines for a new house. Was this the school? Koli's heart both sank and leaped — he was torn by opposite feelings. Would he be forced to work, and not have the chance to learn? Or were they building a fine big school, bigger than any house in his own town? Koli also saw that all these boys wore only short trousers as they worked on the house. And yet here he was, in his finest clothes, fresh from the Bush School.

And then they saw the white man himself, shouting at the boys, and ordering them to carry sticks, to tie them, to move faster. He was standing by a small truck filled with freshly cut house poles. Koli motioned to Yakpalo, and the two of them, followed by Tokpa, went over to the white man. He looked at Koli and didn't seem to recognize him at all. He was polite, but distant. His mind was on the new house. He asked what they wanted and who they were. Koli despaired. The white man had lied to him when he had said he wanted Koli to come to the new school. He did not even know who Koli was.

Koli managed to stammer out that he was the boy who had talked to him last month, that he had now come back to school, that he wanted to learn. The white man looked at him in confusion and some amazement, and then seemed to remember. He asked if Koli came from Totota, the son of the town chief. Koli was now sure the man did not want him in school. He only wanted the sons of important town chiefs. Koli, wearing his fine clothes, felt more out of place every minute. Koli only said that he was not from Totota, that he came from farther back, from behind Gbarnga, that he and his father had been in Salala last month, and that his twin brother had also been with them.

The twins were the clue. The man remembered them, remembered the evening when Koli had asked so many questions. He confessed that he had been certain he would never see Koli again, because his family had taken him back to town. But now he was glad he had come to school.

All this time Yakpalo stood without talking. He could see plainly that the white man lied and only used boys to build his house. Koli would learn nothing — Flumo was right. But his pride would not let him admit Flumo's rightness. He had to continue at least for a short while.

Yakpalo thus decided he would continue down to Kakata to sell his goods, where he was sure he could get a better price. When he came back, he was sure Koli would be glad to go home. Clearly there was nothing in this school business. But Koli must decide to return home by himself for the townspeople to understand.

The white man turned next to Yakpalo and greeted him. Yakpalo returned the greeting, but his heart was not in it. The man asked about Koli's father — he couldn't remember his name. Yakpalo reminded him, his voice full of scorn. He was increasingly certain that Flumo had been right. The white man seemed to sense that Yakpalo was less than friendly, but did not know why.

The conversation was fortunately short, since the white man had to return to supervising the building of the house. The other boys had all stopped working, and were edging nearer to Koli in order to hear the discussion. Some of them pointed to Koli's new clothes, and laughed. Koli wished he could simply disappear from sight, as he saw Yakpalo's mood growing, as he saw the white man's confusion and desire to get back to business, as he saw the other boys laughing at him. He wanted to go home.

But no sooner had the thought hit him, than he realized he could not go back now, if he wished to hold his head high. His brother Sumo would laugh harder than any of these Salala boys whom he did not know. No, he had to go through with it, at least for a short while. He told the man he would go get his things and come back. The man, quietly and as gently as possible, told him to come back wearing his everyday clothes. He could keep the good clothes in his box. What box, thought Koli, and groaned again within himself.

Tokpa lost much of his interest in the white man's school from this encounter. He saw that Koli did not want to enter and be eaten by the white man's foolishness and by the hard work the boys did to serve him. But he also saw that Koli had gone too far to back out now. He was only glad that he could stay with Yakpalo and not have to fight out of the trap like Koli.

Koli walked back to town with Yakpalo to get his

things. He walked more slowly now, no longer so eager. His dreams of the previous night seemed faint and foolish. What chance did he have of learning the secrets of the white man? He would only work for him and leave, knowing no more than before he came. Yakpalo said he would go to Kakata, stay for a week or so, and then return. Koli should remain at the white man's school until then, and could then return home if he wished.

Koli remembered his home, family, and the many good things of his life — but did not say anything yet. He was inwardly much relieved, however, that he had a chance to quit this foolishness. For two weeks the white man could show him the new ways, and then he could leave, knowing that all the fine words had not been true.

Yakpalo went on to Kakata, hoping for better prices. He had the time, since he had left his farms completely cut. Furthermore, Koli needed some time to realize just how foolish he was to stay in the white man's school. It would be better for Koli to go to Firestone to earn some money than to stay and build the white man's house for nothing.

Koli felt weak and alone as he saw Yakpalo leave. He gathered his few things together, changed from his fine clothes to his ordinary clothes, and bid his second father have a safe journey. He would see him soon, but even so he did not want to see him go. Hard times were coming, Koli thought. He asked Yakpalo to remember him, and come back soon.

It was a full three weeks before Yakpalo returned. He did not hurry, because it was not yet time to burn his farm. Yakpalo stayed in Kakata and saw the town. He even made a side-trip to Firestone to visit his relatives there.

Koli was both glad and sorry to see Yakpalo return. Now he would have to decide. Just a week earlier, he would have gone home with Yakpalo without hesitation. But now school had actually started. They had finished tying the roof poles on the new house, and then, while the carpenter put on the zinc roof, they had started to learn. The white man had put a book in Koli's hand, and had shown him some letters. At first the marks meant nothing to Koli, but now he could recognize and write his own name. He could make marks on a paper, and everyone else knew that these marks meant Koli. He had been given another name, and he now could write John next to Koli. The name meant nothing to him, but the white man liked it.

He was learning also about kwii things. He had been laughed at the first day when he sat down to eat with his hands. He had been given an iron spoon and told to eat with it. Now he could handle the spoon, and could even use the other tool with the four points to pick up his food. He could now laugh to himself, as he thought of his first, faltering efforts. He also enjoyed bathing with the clean white soap, so much better than the soap his mothers made for him.

He could now sort the things they used in the school into the proper groups. He washed the dishes and eating tools in the kitchen after school was over. He had to know where to put each thing, and he enjoyed seeing them go in the right places. People put things away so neatly here in the white man's school. No one in his own town did such a thing, no one perhaps except his father who kept his tools in one box and his clothing in another. He was already thinking how he would sort out his own belongings when he got back to town as a big kwii man.

So Yakpalo's return was a confusion to him. The white man's school was not so bad, nor did he really want to go home just now. And yet when Yakpalo came to Salala, Koli suddenly wanted very much to see his mother and his father, even to see his brother Sumo. His heart was torn inside him, and he did not know which way to turn.

Koli welcomed Yakpalo, relieved not to have to try to speak English, relieved not to be a schoolboy for a few moments. But Yakpalo made a mistake. He began to treat Koli as a small boy. Yakpalo was so sure Koli would want to go back home that he offended Koli with the unspoken assumption. Yakpalo seemed to be so very certain that coming to school had been an error, and that Koli had been wrong in the first place. If Yakpalo had only been quieter and less sure he was right, Koli felt he might have gone home with him. But, as it was, Koli's pride would not let him yield. His uncertainty melted, and he announced he was staying at the white man's school, staying in Salala.

Yakpalo's amazement knew no bounds. At first he thought of beating the boy, forcing him to come. But then he realized everyone would know he had forced Koli to come home, even after arguing so strongly for him to go to school. No, if Koli was to return home, he must take the blame on himself for his stubborn desire to learn from the white man. Yakpalo must not be blamed for a mistake, if he was to keep his status in the town. Let the boy continue in his foolish course. Yakpalo could not understand it, but he had to accept it, or else lose face in the town.

So Yakpalo swallowed his unhappy certainty, and bade Koli goodby. He left him another shirt, and some fish and palm oil in case the white man's food did not satisfy him. Koli looked at Yakpalo, hungry for his family rather than for fish and palm oil, but he said nothing. He forced back the few tears that were starting in his eyes, and told Yakpalo that he must stay in Salala to finish the task the town had given him.

Yakpalo arrived back home and tried to give as favorable a report as he could. He did not want to admit what he knew in his heart, that Flumo had been right, that Koli's going to the white man's school was a great mistake. So he told the people that the boy was learning many things, and even now could write his own name, as well as the new name the white man had given him. This caused a great sensation in town, and Yakpalo himself began to think less badly of the school. He was forced to praise the white man, because this helped promote his own cause.

Yakpalo in particular did not want to do anything to hurt his chances to become the new town chief. The old chief was very sick now, and people in town expected him to die soon. He had become ill while Yakpalo was gone, and had become gradually weaker. His family had built him a small thatch shed behind his house, where he could lie down and await death. They brought him food every day and washed him, but they did not make medicine for him. This was the time for death, for him to join his fathers. They only wanted to make him comfortable while he waited.

Yakpalo and Flumo were the obvious candidates for the post, as the leading men in town and in the Poro society. However, Flumo had never really recovered from the blows he had suffered years back, and there were fewer members in his family, fewer persons in his debt, than in Yakpalo's.

Yakpalo thus could not afford to admit Flumo had been right about Koli. If Yakpalo could not take care of one boy, particularly the boy given him by the now-dead president, how then could he watch over the town? So Yakpalo had to be his own witness in favor of Koli and the white man's school. It helped him that Koli had remained behind in Salala.

It was not a surprise when the next morning the town crier announced to everyone that the town chief, who had also been a great zoe, had gone gathering leaves. Indeed his family was tearing down the small shed where he had lain. Yakpalo and Flumo knew the meaning, knew that during the night the chief had died. He had lived a good life. Let him go now with honor.

The chief's family then began the wailing that seemed all too often to be heard in the town. Usually they wailed for young children, but this time they wailed for a man who had lived his life fully and richly. When a child dies, it is a time for genuine mourning. This time, Yakpalo realized, was more an occasion for joy than sorrow. Rain came that morning as if to confirm that the old man had died with honor. Everyone knew that the chief's spirit would go to rest in the town where the dead live. He would see his own ancestors, would join the living dead who still watched and cared for their families in town.

Only if the family did not give him a proper burial would the spirit of the chief cause trouble. Some had said that when Flumo's aunt had died the family had neglected some of the proper sacrifices, and so she had made Koli go to the white man's school to show her anger. Further sacrifices later appeased her spirit. And now the children in the family, when they finished playing a game, would give her something to keep her happy.

The chief's whole family, as well as the important people in town, gathered at the grave site two days later. They spoke to the old chief, reminding him that they had always wished him well, that they had taken care of him in his last days. The eldest son, tied by a long rope to his father's body, looked down into the grave and said, "Father, you have left us and gone to the true side. When you go, you should take your evil heart from us. If there is a home for man after death, we extend our greetings to all the old people. We are taking your spirit stone with us. If any member of our family is sick and you are responsible for it, and we call you through this stone, may you hear us. May all the children in this house be well. When we walk in the forest, may you not frighten us. If you do anything bad to us, we will call a spirit to catch you and eat you." After each phrase, the grave-digger stood in the grave and reminded the dead chief, "Hear this." At the end of his speech, the son dropped a white kola nut in the grave to show his respect. Each of the other important relatives themselves also spoke to the old man and gave him a token of respect.

The cord tying the chief's eldest son to his father's body was cut, close to the chief, to ensure a long life for the son. The grave was filled, and the relatives all put on green leaves picked from the brush near the grave. Now they would celebrate, although the chief's head wife could not keep back her wailing.

Four days later, there was a great feast at which they mourned and wailed the last time for the dead chief. Yakpalo gave a cow, and members of the chief's family brought another. Others gave a sheep and several white chickens. The old chief's nephew performed the sacrifices, and the animals died well. Old Mulbah washed the close relatives of the old chief, and then the feast began. It went through the whole day and night, with singing and dancing and rejoicing at the close of a good life.

And then came the time to choose the new town chief. The D. C. himself came to supervise the election. Flumo knew he really had no chance for the office, despite the hopes he had held for so many years, and so went to Yakpalo privately and promised his support in the election. In return, he hoped that Yakpalo would forget the past and, in particular, forget Flumo's old debts. He had never fully paid for the rice from the year his farm had failed, and, whereas the debt was no longer mentioned, as a matter between friends and equals, it bothered Flumo to remember the obligation. Flumo said to Yakpalo, "When leopard has plenty to eat, he does not ask tortoise for more food." Yakpalo indicated his agreement, and accepted Flumo's support.

On the day of the election, therefore, when the D. C. came to ask for candidates, Flumo surprised the town by announcing that Yakpalo was clearly the right man for the post. Flumo asked his supporters to leave his own line, even though a thin loyal line of friends and relatives had begun to form behind his chair in the center of town. Only one line of voters was needed, and Flumo first in line behind Yakpalo, confirming his election as the new town chief.

Flumo had to bear his disappointment. Not everyone could be a town chief. He had his wives, even though Yanga had found a lover to replace Togba. He had to expect it. She was getting older now, and felt she needed young blood.

Anyhow, the man paid the new $10.00 fine that the government had imposed, after she had acknowledged him as her lover. She had come back to Flumo, just as she had before with Togba. Flumo was less concerned about the whole matter this time than he had been before. Perhaps he was getting older, too.

Flumo also had his son Sumo to comfort him. Sumo's knowledge of medicine grew daily. A twin zoe was supposed to know these matters directly. Nevertheless, he followed Mulbah everywhere he went, and spent less and less time in his father's blacksmith shop. Flumo was not unhappy, because Sumo would become a fine zoe. But Flumo made sure that Sumo also spent enough time in the shop to learn to be a good blacksmith.

After the rice harvest, Saki returned once more from Firestone. He said he had seen Koli at Salala, and had been shocked at what he had found. He could not at first find the boy, but then learned the teachers were punishing him for disobedience. He had not done his kitchen work, and had been asking his teacher too many questions. So he found Koli behind the school cutting ten loads of fire wood as his punishment.

Koli had been glad to see Saki, and with almost visible relief had talked Kpelle. The school did not let the boys talk Kpelle, and Koli was tired to death of not knowing the right word for anything. He had run into town on many occasions just to talk to people, or had secretly talked Kpelle with his up-country friends at night in the sleeping house.

Koli had angered Saki with all his talk of kwii things. He was proud of how he could write English words on paper, and he boasted about how he only drank boiled water and ate with a fork. He wanted Saki to call him John, but his uncle had refused. And, worst of all, Koli had seemed embarrassed at having his uncle visit him, since his uncle was only a country person.

The thing that most concerned Flumo and Yakpalo was

that Koli had refused to come home for the dry season. He said he had to stay at school to work for the white man. He would come home, perhaps the next dry season. But now all the boys had to help build a new house for the white man. Saki was sure that was the only reason why the white man wanted the boys to come to school. But Saki could not force Koli to come home. "Wait until next year," Koli said. Saki could only hope that the boy's animal double and his medicine would protect him. Besides, harm could not come to a twin zoe.

Flumo listened to Saki's report, and was more sure than ever he had been right, that Koli never should have gone to school. But he could say nothing now. He only looked at Sumo, who had stayed at home to learn in the proper way. He was becoming a blacksmith and a zoe, and would be a useful member of the town. Flumo despaired that Koli would learn nothing of value to himself or his people. If only Koli would leave the white man's school, and come home to the real school, the only school in which one becomes a Kpelle, the school that was their life together.

The Town Chief

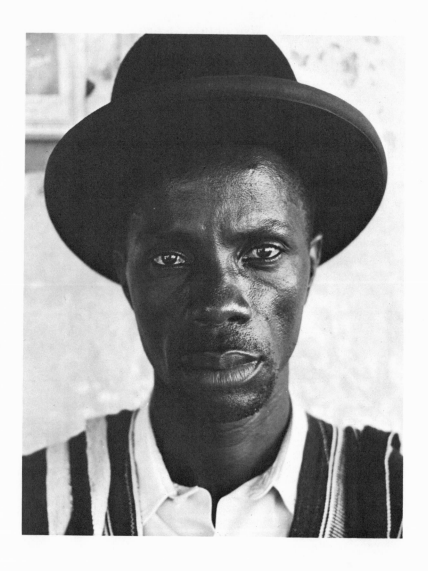

CHAPTER XII

Spider Stories

XII: SPIDER STORIES

Three years passed before Koli first visited home. Each year his family tried to persuade him to come back, but he had some excuse each time. The children were building a new house in which to learn the white man's knowledge. The white man had jobs for them to earn their school fees. Some of the other children even went to Monrovia with the white man. For Koli, his own town seemed so far away, so unimportant, and the new world of the kwii seemed the only reality of his life. He frankly did not want to go back home, did not want to be exposed to all the threats and persuasions of his family.

He missed his family. He realized that. But he saw them often. Flumo came to Salala twice during those three years, and once he brought Yanga and Sumo. Yakpalo came three times. Each time they brought coffee and rice for sale, and stopped at the school to see Koli.

Once Flumo found Koli praying to the white man's God. He and the other children were in church, talking English and singing the white man's songs. Koli had been embarrassed when Flumo came and stood at the rear of the church, but there was nothing he could do about it. He later told his father that the white man said those who did not know Jesus Christ had bad ways. Flumo's anger rose. He did not know this man Jesus Christ, but he knew that the Kpelle had good ways.

Koli was confused. He loved his father and his family, and he himself did not see anything bad about the way he had been brought up. But he could now speak and read English, and the kwii books told him about the white man's God, and how the savages must learn about Him. Koli did not believe his father was a savage, but the kwii book said so and thus it must be true. And yet he could find no way to say this to his father.

Another time Yakpalo came to the school and found Koli and the other children singing a different song. The new Liberian teacher was pointing to a large picture at the front of the room as the children sang the song. Yakpalo asked Koli about it later, and Koli told him they were learning numbers. Yakpalo asked him, had he not learned numbers already in town, working in the blacksmith shop, counting threads on the loom, selling coffee and kola nuts?

Koli agreed. He had done all these things and more, and he knew numbers. But he had to learn the kwii numbers, which were different. Kwii numbers were all written on a large picture, which the teacher called a table. It didn't look like a table, Koli admitted, but that was what they called it. And he had to learn to put the numbers together.

"How do you learn them?" asked Yakpalo. "Do you learn them by working with real things, as we do in town?" Koli admitted learning in the white man's school was very strange. The numbers on what the teacher called his table he had to put in his head, without understanding them, by singing this song. Right now, Koli said he knew the tune, but he really did not know the words. He wanted to know how to use the numbers, but most of the time they only repeated them or sang them.

"What other kinds of things do you learn?" asked Yakpalo. Koli went to get his book. He had one which showed how God made the world, and how plants and animals live. But the book had trees and flowers and animals he had never seen. Yakpalo asked if there were really such things. Koli was sure not, that the teachers were just telling stories.

Yakpalo began to understand. "These stories," he said, "are like the tales we tell in the village. Spiders cannot really talk, but we have stories about spider. In the same way, trees and plants and animals, and even people, don't look like this. The white man must be telling you these stories to show you how to behave in the kwii way."

But Koli did not agree. "The teachers make us remember every word of the story and repeat it, make us remember every word in the number song and repeat it. And the stories tell all the wrong things about how to live. They tell about animals going to sleep when the air gets cold and the water turns to stone. They tell of children leaving their parents to get married and live all by themselves in little houses and raise two or three children. They tell how men like to fight wars. They tell of a white God who says that a man can have only one wife." So much of it seemed nonsense to Koli, and yet he and his fellow students had to repeat every word the teacher said.

Koli told Yakpalo a story to show the foolishness of the white man's books. The teacher brought a big picture of a chicken, which he called a hand, and started telling about it. He said the picture showed a big red hand, when they could all see that it was a hen. The teacher had asked them what kind of hand it was, and they had had to tell him it was big and red. He would have beaten them for complaining.

Another time the teacher said that spider had six legs. Koli himself told the teacher that spider had eight legs, and even offered to bring one to class. The teacher, who was helping the white man, told Koli to see him after class and not make any more noise. And after class the teacher beat Koli hard with a stick for thinking he knew more than his elders.

That at least Yakpalo could understand. He reminded Koli that beating a child helps him know he is a child. He was sorry the teacher did it because of the number of legs on spider, sorry also that the teacher told unimportant stories about spider, when he could tell real spider stories to show the children how to behave. It was not the number of legs on spider that mattered, but rather his greediness, like the time when spider wanted to go to feasts in two towns, and had each town tie a rope around him and pull it when the feasts were ready. They had pulled at the same time, and had almost cut spider in half. Koli knew the story, and agreed he wished kwii stories were like that.

Koli showed Yakpalo the school, showed him the house where he and all the boys lived. There Yakpalo met Koli's new friend, Zangba, a Bassa boy from across the big river. Koli and Zangba had given each other gifts to show they were real friends, and they helped each other to wash their clothes and cook food late at night.

Yakpalo was suspicious of the boy, and asked Koli why he was living with these foreigners, who didn't know the Kpelle way. The boy did not speak Kpelle and had been brought up with those lazy Bassa people who always steal. Koli replied by telling the new president's order that the people in Liberia should come together and all be one people. Yakpalo had heard the order, but still he did not like Koli being a friend to Bassa people.

Koli showed Yakpalo the place where he slept. A mattress of straw wrapped in a cloth, and covered with the same country cloth Yakpalo had given him, was set in a wooden frame. All the boys had this type of bed. Under the bed Koli kept the box Flumo had given him for his belongings. The box was locked, just as Flumo's box was locked.

Yakpalo asked to see what he kept in the box. Koli showed him his clothes, including the white shirt and black short trousers that all the students had to wear. He also showed Yakpalo his fine clothes from the closing of Bush School, the same clothes he had worn that first day in school. Since that time, he wore them only when they told stories and acted them out before the other students.

Koli also showed Yakpalo the things he had collected since he had come to school. He had put them in special places and wrapped them in cloth. He had his utensils in one place, his knife and cutlass in another, his medicine in an-

other, his books and papers in another. Yakpalo was pleased
to see that Koli had not forgotten everything. He still knew
how to keep his things in the Kpelle way.

The bell then called Koli to eat, and he took Yakpalo
with him to the large house where the food was served. There
was a big pan of rice on the table, and another pot of soup.
Each boy brought his own small bowl and spoon, and each
dipped his food from the pot and ate it on his own plate.
Yakpalo asked why they did not pour the soup over the rice
and all eat together. Koli could only say that it was not the
white man's way to eat as the Kpelle did.

The boys prayed to God before they ate. Yakpalo asked
later why the white man did not make sacrifices when he
built houses or cleared the ground, but instead prayed when
he ate. Koli admitted it seemed strange, but the white man
did it that way. He was strange in many ways. Koli simply
had to learn his ways, as the town had told him to do. And,
as for sacrifices, the white man called them bad. They should
no longer make sacrifices and feasts for the ancestors, since
only God could help them. Yakpalo was angered at this. How
could they forget their ancestors, those who had gone before
and continued to help them all, including Koli. Did he want
to bring trouble on his head? Koli could only respond that he
took it as true that the old ways were wrong.

After they ate and cleaned up the kitchen, Koli did his
work, and Yakpalo watched. Koli was to cut grass around the
white teacher's house. Koli told Yakpalo that when he had
first been given the job, he had cleared away all the grass and
left the ground bare. The teacher's wife had been so angry
that the teacher had to drive Koli away from the house. Koli
had said he did not understand. He had done the job the way
he had always done it at home, in order to make the town
neat, and not leave all that trash there. But the white man
said grass was one thing and trash another, even though Koli
could not see the difference. Koli had asked, "Would not
snakes come, and the school be dirty, with all that trash

around?" But he learned what the white man wanted, and he only whipped the grass to make it short, and pulled out one kind of grass to make room for another.

Each time one of his fathers visited Koli, he tried to persuade the boy to come home. But Koli kept saying he was too busy, had no time, had too much to learn, had too much work to do. But finally, at the end of three years, he agreed to go home for the dry season. He would go when his uncle Saki came from Firestone for the harvest season. The girls were getting ready to enter the Sande Bush School, and Koli wanted to see his sisters, small Toang and small Noai, enter the Bush. He had to bring something for his sisters and mother, something to make their hearts glad as the girls entered the Sande society. He found an old picture book that the white man had discarded, and took that for his sisters and mother.

Saki arrived at Koli's school at harvest time. He wanted to be back home when the moon was full and when they brought the new rice in. There would be dancing and playing and everyone would be happy, particularly because the girls would open the Sande fence the next month. Saki wanted to hurry, wanted Koli to go with him the next day.

But Koli told his uncle he had to take his tests for the year next week. Then he could go. Saki went to the white man to persuade him to let Koli leave, but the white man agreed with Koli. Koli had to stay. The white man did not really want him to go home at all. He told Saki that Koli should stay in Salala. Let him go back to his town when he finished school.

But Koli's uncle would not agree. So he waited in Salala until Koli finished his tests. He asked Koli about the tests, how the people measured him. Koli said he had to repeat all the numbers the people taught him, had to tell all the stories in just the words he had heard, and even had to write stories about his own town.

His uncle looked at him in amazement and suspicion

when he heard that Koli was writing stories about their town. "What do the white people want to know those things for? Why aren't they teaching you about the white man's ways? Does the white man want to learn about our town and then take it from us?" Saki was sure that the people in town would not like it if they knew Koli was telling the white man about them.

Finally Koli finished his tests. The moon was beginning to wane, and Saki was angry that they had lost time, and would not be in town for the harvest, the dancing and the feasting. But Koli said that instead they could all celebrate at Christmas next week, when the moon was dark again.

His uncle asked, "Why should we celebrate anything if there is no moon?" Koli explained that Christmas celebrated the birth of God's son. His uncle had never heard that God had any son, and asked if this were another one of the white man's stories. Koli said, "No, it is true. God has a son, and he came to help people live better." Saki did not really believe it, commenting only "Tell it to the elders and the big people in town."

When the two of them reached home, the family received Koli as a dead man come to life again. Some of the townspeople actually believed he had been eaten by the white man, and were very surprised to see him again. They made a special feast for him, with new rice, freshly-made palm oil, greens and pepper, and a goat newly-killed. All the members of Flumo's and Yakpalo's families ate together.

Sumo did not like the attention paid to Koli. His fathers never made such a feast for him. He considered putting poison in Koli's cup, but changed his mind, since everyone would know he had done it. So he went to the celebration, still angry. His father had to call him aside and explain that Koli had been to the white man, had lived to tell about it, and was now home, knowing everything the white man knows. Now he would help his people, and so they must celebrate.

Koli trembled when he heard these things. He planned to stay home only a few weeks, and go back to school after Christmas. But now his family were talking as if he were here to stay. How could he persuade them that he must learn more? If he stayed in town now he would forget everything, and be just like Sumo, a stupid country boy. He must learn much more to be like the white man.

But for now no one was willing to discuss Koli's future. They were enjoying the present moment. They had filled the rice kitchens for the year ahead. Soon the girls, including Toang and Noai, would enter the Sande Society Bush School.

More significant, the people needed to watch Koli carefully first. They wanted to see what had happened to him, what person he had become, before they could think about the future. He was a big boy now and could even father children. It might be time for him to marry, but the families had to look at him carefully first.

Koli proved irresistibly attractive to the younger boys in town. He seemed to be a kwii man already. He talked English to those who had been at Firestone, and he claimed he could say his ideas so much better in English. He brought books, and he would often sit outside his house reading. When the boys asked him to show them what was in the books, he would tell them they were too young to understand the writing. But he would show them the pictures of the far-off mysteries of the white man's country.

Some of the younger boys began to want to go to the white man's school also. Saki's son, the one who had been last to enter the Bush School, told his father that he wanted to go, that he did not want to be the last to enter the white man's school. But Saki beat the idea out of him, and the boy gave it up, for the moment at least.

Tokpa finally had the courage also to ask his father if he might go to school. Yakpalo was not sure. He had been sure when he visited Koli that the school was nonsense. But he also saw that Koli stood and talked in a new way, that he could talk intelligently about the kwii world, and even do so in English.

In particular, Koli seemed certain of his future, and Yakpalo felt himself drawn to what the young boys found so attractive. Moreover, Yakpalo, as town chief, feared that Flumo's son might one day displace him. It might be good for one of his own sons to understand the white man's matters. He would have to think about the possibility.

Yakpalo noted the cleverness Koli showed in discussing with Sumo a riddle about two men who went out to find wives. They each brought gifts with which to marry the girls, but both gifts were bad. The first offered sickness *and* a bad name, while the other offered sickness *or* a bad name. They told the father of the first girl they met to accept one of the suitors or be killed. The boys had to tell which man the girl's father would accept.

Sumo said he would choose neither, and let the men kill him, since both gifts were bad. Koli, however, said he would choose the man who offered sickness *or* a bad name. It is better to have only one bad gift than two, and also better to be alive than dead. Koli said he would take a bad name, marry his daughter to the man, and hope in the future to make a good name again. The man who gave the riddle agreed that Koli had spoken wisely and had understood its meaning.

Yakpalo was impressed as he heard the boys debating the case. Koli had grown more clever, even if less respectful, during his three years at the white man's school. Sumo muttered that no one would ever give gifts like that when getting married. He did not want to think about things that would never happen.

One problem with Koli, however, was that he would not work. Yanga told him to cut firewood and he said educated men do not do such things. Besides he had cut wood all year for the white man, and he was tired now. Flumo picked up a stick, ready to beat Koli if he refused. Koli went out, but did not want to, and brought back only a small load after a long time in the forest.

And then, when the time came to make farm, Koli announced he had to go back to school. He thus raised the question that everyone had tried to ignore. Toang and Noai had entered the Sande Bush School, and town life was returning to normal. Flumo and Yakpalo both planned large farms that year, to feed their families and to contribute rice to the Sande girls. Both needed Koli's labor. He was tall and strong — but lazy.

Thus when Koli said he was going back to school, his fathers refused. He had to work, and then they would think about school. Surely three years of school was enough to learn of the white man's ways. He should stay, build a house, and think about taking a wife. And when the family needed someone to talk with the white man, someone to help them sell coffee, someone to argue with the soldier when he came to town, Koli would be there.

Koli could not agree with his parents. He knew he must spend many more years before he learned what waited for him. Moreover, only a little of what he had learned thus far made sense to him, even though he would not admit that to his family. Perhaps more years of school would help. He even thought of going to the new high school on the other big river after he finished at Salala.

His fathers finally agreed for him to go, but only after he helped clear the two farms and re-thatch two houses. He could not run away again, he knew that. So he submitted to the discipline. And he found that the discipline included not just the two farms — he had to help clear farms for all the men in Flumo's work group. He was now getting worried — there were ten farms to clear before they would begin to thatch the two houses. He had no idea how long it would all take.

Two times the moon waxed and waned as Koli worked,

and the third moon was on the increase. Koli knew school would have begun by now, and believed the white man would forget him. They had finished cutting the farms and were thatching the second house. As soon as the work was done, he would have to hurry to school. He would beg someone to give him money so he could take a truck to Salala, now that the road was finished as far as Gbarnga. He would save two days that way. He had never taken a truck before, even though he had seen many at school and some of his schoolmates had traveled by truck to Monrovia. However, he was sure he could do it, despite his fears.

When they finally finished the work, Yanga and Flumo gave him the clothes he needed for school, as well as a calabash of palm oil and a hamper of rice. Yakpalo gave him a new country cloth, as well as the money to ride a truck from Gbarnga to Salala. Yakpalo himself had to go to Gbarnga to sell coffee and palm nuts. There were now Lebanese stores in Gbarnga as well as a new big store run by a man from Germany. There Yakpalo could buy all the things before sold only in Salala.

So Yakpalo went with Koli to Gbarnga. After he sold his goods in the German store, Yakpalo took Koli to the end of the road, where the trucks would start their journey downcountry. No truck was ready to go back to Salala yet. However, one man told them that a truck would be coming that afternoon, and then go back the next morning. They must wait overnight and see what would come.

In mid-afternoon, a heavy, old truck, loaded down with goods for the Lebanese trader, came from the coast. The driver, dusty and swearing, got down from the truck and unloaded all the wonders of the outside world. He brought cases of smoked fish from the ocean, boxes of soap and sugar, drums full of kerosene for the kwii lanterns now so widely used, bundles of zinc for roofing houses, long bolts of cloth, and even a large copper still for making cane juice. Koli had seen all these things in the stores in Salala, but he had not seen so many at such close range. He watched with awe, thinking of all the money that went to buy the things.

The next morning the driver packed the truck full of all the produce the Lebanese trader had bought from the Jorkwelle people. He had bags of rice, coffee and palm nuts, as well as five cows who were complaining loudly of their fate. A few persons could ride on top of the load.

Here Yakpalo left Koli, his small bundle with him. The trip would cost Koli fifty cents, a huge sum in his eyes, but worth it because he reached school quickly. The last Yakpalo saw was the truck lurching down the hill to the river, with red dust billowing up behind to settle on the green leaves. Koli was clearly frightened, but he hung on firmly, his hands tight to his load. He looked and felt very small, perched on top of the bags of rice. The road home was now the road away from home, a road which carried him at a pace Koli had at one time not believed he would experience in his whole life.

CHAPTER XIII

Red Deer and Kwii Pig

XIII: RED DEER AND KWII PIG

It was three more years before Koli came home. When he arrived in Salala a third-grader, after completing primer, first and second grades, he wasn't sure exactly how old he was, although he thought he was perhaps 15 years old. At least the white man, after asking him questions about his life in town, made that guess. Not that it really mattered much, but these white people liked to give everyone a number.

Koli arrived at school two weeks late, and the white man was angry. He made Koli do punishment work at the school. He made gardens for the Liberian teachers, preparing the ground for okra, beans and eggplant, and he planted flowers all around the white man's house. It did not seem right to Koli to have to work again when he reached school, since the reason for his being late was that he had been helping his parents. But he accepted the discipline and the work, and he did what was required.

By now Koli was one of the big boys of the school. He had entered the school in its first year, and so his was the highest grade. Many new boys were coming now, some from as far up-country as Koli. None had yet come from his own town, although Yakpalo had not actually refused Tokpa that permission.

Some of the new children who came to the school were not yet initiated into the Poro or Sande societies. This year the Sande Bush School was opening, and some said the Forest Thing would eat the young girls at the white man's school. These girls had lived at first with the white man's wife in the big house. But now they had a house of their own with a coastal Liberian woman to care for them. Last year it had worked, since no one in Salala troubled them. They had been sufficiently crazy to go to the white man's school, and they were not big enough to marry.

But now the girls were supposed to enter the Bush School. In Koli's town the first group of girls had gone behind the fence before Koli came to school, but in Salala they were just getting ready. The people had begun to celebrate in town. Those girls who were to enter gathered together in one house. The older women rubbed themselves with white chalk, and danced for three days.

Then late one night the whole group of women in the town left for the forest, and took the girls with them. The town was empty the next morning, the girls safe in their new homes in the forest. Only the very young, the sick, the pregnant, and the school girls remained in town. Some of the girls in the white man's school had come from other areas, and so were not under local authority. But the school girls from Salala feared they would be forced to enter the bush.

In fact, two school girls disappeared with the main group that first night. And the next night, another one was gone. The remainder waited in terror lest the Forest Thing come and eat them. The white man was concerned. He might lose all his girl students, so he brought them to stay with his wife, until he could reach an understanding with the officials of the Sande Society.

Koli never did learn the decision, but high government people came from Monrovia to discuss the matter. The girls remained in school, quiet, terrified, and cut off from their families and friends. Perhaps one day they too would enter the Sande Society, perhaps even toward the end of the Bush School three years later. But for now they remained outside.

Koli looked back at his first three years in school. His townspeople believed he must by now know the secrets of the white man's world. Koli had bought more time by promising to go and learn all the secrets, but he realized in his heart that he still knew almost nothing. He had memorized many things, knew the multiplication tables, could read and write about winter and railroads and apples, about snowballs and circuses, but he did not know how to be a white man. At the same time, while he was in third grade science, his brother Sumo knew more about leaves and herbs than he did, and his father knew far more about farming and about the ways of animals.

At least he felt that he was becoming more clever, more observant and more able to describe things than Sumo. Last vacation, his father had been talking about the type of cutlass people now were buying in Gbarnga, and the old-style cutlass he could make. His father had pointed out that the new cutlass was sharper and shinier at first, but did not last as well. Koli had said all the kwii things were like that. The cloth was fine to look at, but it wore out soon. The knives opened and closed, but they could break easily and would not stay sharp.

It was also the same when one traveled. The kwii trucks got there faster, but the traveler was tired and dusty when the trip was over. Sumo didn't care about all these differences, didn't worry about how kwii cloth, kwii tools and kwii travel are all somehow the same, and yet all different in a definite way from the old Kpelle tradition.

Koli knew he wanted the kwii things, even though they did not last as well, even though he felt unsatisfied when he used them. He was ashamed to use the country knife his father gave him. The white man did not use a knife like that. He wore his country cloth shorts only when he had to, when the kwii shorts had worn threadbare and he couldn't beg any more from the white man. No pictures in his school books showed children wearing country cloth shorts. And the big ones wore long trousers. Koli had one pair now, and he felt very important when he wore them.

Moreover, the speed and noise and red dust and choking smell of the truck he had ridden to school seemed to Koli so much grander than the quiet, clean air, and the green forest of the bush trail. Sumo said he liked the forest better, but Koli really didn't believe him. The white man had forests, but he lived in cities, or so the books told Koli.

During these three years Flumo visited Koli twice and Yakpalo four times. Koli liked Yakpalo better all the time, while he was beginning to be ashamed of his own father, Flumo. Yakpalo was a town chief, and people were saying that he might even be made clan chief. On the other hand, Flumo was old and unsuccessful. The bad luck that had visited Flumo for as long as Koli could remember had not changed. Some people were beginning to say that Koli himself was the witch. If a twin was not a zoe, he might be a witch. Koli had heard that rumor several times on his first visit home, but he tried not to think about it.

Koli wanted his family to be important, to be kwii, to do things in modern ways. He wished his father would wear shoes when he came to visit. Yakpalo always carried western shoes and put them on when he reached Salala. Koli saw that his father would always be a kind of slave to the white men, doing what they wanted and not leading his people. Flumo's visits upset Koli, and he almost wished his father would stay at home.

Yakpalo's visits were different. Koli even looked back with pleasure to the time he spent in Yakpalo's house, even though Yakpalo had often beaten him when he did not do the right thing or when he asked too many questions. When Yakpalo came to the school, Koli was proud to be seen with an important man.

On one of Yakpalo's visits, he arrived dressed in his chief's gown, with a black kwii hat on his head. He had been called to a council of chiefs in Kakata, and three of his sons, including Tokpa, were going with him to carry his loads. He carried an umbrella, which he used to support himself, and in Koli's eyes he made a fine sight.

Yakpalo told Koli that he had been invited to join the kwii man's secret society. Koli did not know much about it, but he had seen them going to meetings in their black suits and black hats. More and more of the chiefs were joining this society, so they too could belong to the kwii world. It cost $50 for a country man to join, far more money than Koli had ever seen, but Yakpalo had managed to raise the sum.

Yakpalo understood what was in Koli's mind when Koli proudly introduced him to all his friends. He was flattered that the boy admired him, but he did not want Koli to forget his real father. Yakpalo knew that he should be careful now that Flumo had fallen in the estimation of the town. If Yakpalo pushed home his advantage and degraded Flumo still further — for example, by encouraging Koli to reject his real father — then Flumo might not continue to support Yakpalo, might become an enemy, might even resort to witchcraft or poison against him. So it was in Yakpalo's interest to advise Koli that Flumo was his real father, whom he must respect and obey.

Flumo once again put pressure on Koli when his sisters Toang and small Noai, now not so small a girl, were ready to come out of the Sande Bush School. Koli had been so small when Lorpu came out that he could remember nothing. Flumo and Yanga had told him about it, but now Koli wanted to see the ceremony for himself. He liked Toang, who was big now and ready to marry, and he accepted small Noai, although she always bothered him when he was at home.

So when Flumo came to Salala that dry season to bring Koli home for the closing of the Bush School, Koli did not object too much. He knew he was big enough now to return to school even if his family did not agree. So he went to town to pay his respects to his family, to see the closing of the Bush School, to welcome his sisters, and to give his father the honor that Yakpalo had said was so important.

But Koli met the same problems at home as before, now much more intensely. He was a big kwii person now, at least in his own eyes, and he did not want to do any of the work the townspeople asked of him. And yet he knew he must cut bush with the men. He felt ashamed to shed his long trousers and put on the torn country cloth shorts and tattered singlet of the bush farmer. He did not want to eat out of the same bowl with the other men on the farm, or even with his own family. He only wanted to drink boiled water, even though he had to make do with what he found. He wanted to wash with the clean white soap he had used in school. He preferred to stay in town and talk with the men who had been to Firestone, and to impress the younger boys who crowded around him to admire his clothes, his books, his kwii haircut.

And, more than anything else, after the Bush School closed and the girls were back in town, he enjoyed talking to Kuluba. When Koli and Kuluba had been small, their parents had talked about marriage, and now it seemed a real possibility. Kuluba had come out of the Sande Bush School with Toang and Noai. She was beautiful, fresh, new, ripe, so much more attractive to Koli than any of the girls at the Salala school.

Sumo, too, found her attractive, but she only saw Koli, with his long trousers and his ability to read and write and talk of the wide world. Sumo had been nowhere, and knew nothing but the blacksmith shop, the Poro society and the herbs he helped Mulbah collect.

Kuluba never tired of hearing about Koli's trip to Monrovia just two months earlier. He went in the white man's car — no truck, this one, but a box on wheels which traveled smoothly over the road, and did not force the riders to eat dust. One could close in the box with windows of glass he could see through. And the car went like the wind as it carried them to Monrovia.

Monrovia itself was like nothing Koli had ever seen or Kuluba had ever thought about. It was on the ocean, that huge, frightening expanse of water which made the big river look like a rivulet of rain running out of the town after a hard storm.

But the city itself was even more frightening. There

were cars and trucks everywhere, and if one did not watch carefully he would be killed. All the men wore black suits and tall kwii hats and the women wore gowns and beads and bracelets. There were houses on top of houses, with people living on top of people. The cars drove on roads hard like rock, and smooth like a carefully rubbed house, only finer.

Koli spoke of the market bigger than his whole town, with more people than he had ever seen, all crowded together selling rice, pepper, greens, oil and fish. And they sold also the most wonderful kwii things, cloth, mirrors (Koli remembered with a pang that Lebanese trader), medicines, combs, whatever a person could want.

His stories about the kwii world kept Kuluba always in Koli's company. And Sumo watched with increasing anger. He had hoped to enjoy Kuluba's attentions and company also, when she came out of the bush. He felt he was important, too. Was he not almost as good a blacksmith as his father? Had he not gone farther in the Poro society than Koli? Did he not know as many medicines as Noai, and almost as many even as old Mulbah? Was he not strong and tireless?

But none of these qualities attracted Kuluba. Some said that Koli was a witch, and Sumo almost agreed. He was a witch with long trousers and kwii ways. A twin should be a zoe, but if a zoe uses his powers only for himself, then he becomes a witch. And clearly Koli had bewitched Kuluba into forgetting that Sumo was alive. Perhaps Koli had sold himself to the white man's spirits, or even to the water people in Monrovia, and had come back to town to ruin his family as well as this beautiful girl.

Sumo knew he could not get any help from his mother. Yanga was just as attracted to Koli as the girl Kuluba. And the men in town would not understand. They hoped Koli would bring them money and status, when he finally learned all the kwii ways. And so Sumo's anger could only grow and swell inside him, as Koli made a big show in front of the other boys, as Koli avoided work on the farm, as Koli walked around with his books and his long trousers, as Koli talked to Kuluba. Sumo watched his brother closely, and it made him sick.

Thus Sumo understood when one night Koli and Kuluba quietly walked from the center of town to the old house where the midwife had once practised her craft, the very house where Koli and Sumo had been born, so long ago. The midwife had died two dry seasons earlier, leaving the house empty. It was beginning to break apart, and the old lady's brother's son planned to tear the house down and build another on that spot for his second wife. But the house still stood at the edge of town, empty and — for Koli and Kuluba — inviting.

Sumo knew what they were doing when Koli and Kuluba slipped away from the center of town. He walked a safe distance behind them, listening to them talk about the amazing things that Koli had done and seen. Sumo remembered his father saying, "Sitting quietly reveals crocodile's tricks." He also remembered the other saying, "Pangolin showed leopard the way to eat him." Perhaps Sumo was the pangolin, but if he watched and waited he might be the leopard also.

He saw Koli and Kuluba go to the old house and then, believing no one saw them, slip quickly into the house. Sumo felt his anger and envy rise as he heard the small moans of pleasures from inside. He left before Koli and Kuluba came out, but not before he had determined to do something about his brother. He would show who was the pangolin, and who was the leopard.

Sumo was friendly the next day. He would wait his chance. He even offered to play a friendly game with his brother. It was the familiar game of malang, a game both played well. Sumo was sure he could beat Koli, since Koli had not played much at the white man's school. This could be a way of telling Koli he should not feel so big.

The game opened as usual, each boy having four seeds in

the six holes on his side of the board. Each attempted to build his town, by collecting seeds and putting them in his hand. Koli, however, soon found that he had miscalculated his seeds. He decided to play them out and start over. He had not thought far enough ahead in his computations, and he saw that his brother had a good chance to fill his hand with the critical number of 24 seeds, which would enable him to gain an easy victory when he played them out. As a result, Koli played the seeds from his hand to disrupt his brother's plan, and started again to build his town.

Twice each of them redistributed his seeds in order to gain an advantage over the other. It was bad strategy to move too rapidly to defeat the other. But Koli forgot, and thought his chance had come. He played out his seeds, and won four of his brother's seeds. Koli was now ahead, had made the first capture, was for the moment safe on his side of the board, and thought he could win.

But Sumo continued to play a waiting game. He offered tempting captures to Koli, who took them not seeing Sumo's plan. Sumo had 24 seeds in his hand, and was toying with Koli, waiting until he emptied his side of the board in the effort to capture seeds.

When this happened, Sumo emptied his hand of its seeds, one in each hole, beginning on his side. They went around the board exactly twice, ending at the last hole on Koli's side. He cleared the board, leaving Koli nothing to play. The game was Sumo's. The onlookers applauded and Sumo smiled within himself.

Koli congratulated his brother on the victory, and left to talk to Kuluba again. But Sumo smiled within himself. Let Koli make the first capture. It would not help him. Sumo now could control the moves, could see to it that Koli lost the game in town. He was not quite sure how he would do it, but he knew there would be a way.

Sumo went to see old Mulbah. Mulbah did not deal with evil medicines, but Mulbah knew many charms. Mulbah had showed some of the simpler ones to Sumo, so he would understand and avoid them. Remembering what he had learned, Sumo decided to get Mulbah's help to put medicine on Koli so he would lose his power to fool the girls and boys in town, and so Kuluba in particular would come to her senses.

He asked Mulbah about the matter in an indirect way, "Can kwii pig make red deer look foolish?" Mulbah replied, "Only if kwii pig has made medicine." Sumo then asked what medicine would help red deer get back his status, and Mulbah agreed to help him. No names were mentioned, but Mulbah understood and sympathized. He too did not like how Koli was breaking up the old ways and falling into the white man's traps, traps which he was now using to catch everyone else in town.

Sumo had to find some of Koli's hair and excrement, which he would mix with certain leaves and herbs and boil up to make a strong medicine against his brother. Mulbah never asked the identity of kwii pig. He only wanted to make sure that no serious harm was done. When the medicine was complete, Sumo must put some in Kuluba's food to make her lose interest in Koli.

Mulbah knew also that Sumo wanted to gain Kuluba for himself. So he asked Sumo, "How can red deer live without water deer's sister?" Sumo replied, "It is hard for red deer to be alone." So Mulbah told Sumo to find some clothing that the girl commonly wore, and also to bring a strand of her hair, and a calabash full of the water where she washed herself.

The clothing and the water were easy, but the hair was a difficult assignment. It was no problem to cut a snip from Koli's hair, but Kuluba was always with Koli or else in her mother's house. Thus Sumo went to Kuluba's older sister to bring him a hair. The older sister, settled and married, also felt Koli was a witch, and so she agreed to help Sumo, and also to speak for him to Kuluba when the time came.

Kuluba's sister put both medicines into Kuluba's food. And now Sumo felt content to sit and wait for the results. He became frightened, however, when Koli became ill. His eyes had turned yellow, he was vomiting and weak, and he lay in his mother's house as if he might die. Sumo had not wanted his medicine to work so well. Clearly what he had put into Kuluba's food had caused Koli to fall seriously ill. He rushed to Mulbah for help, and told him in full what had happened.

Mulbah said the medicine had worked that way, because Sumo had mixed hate with the other ingredients. He should not have done so. He must now go to Koli and confess his hatred, and then try to make medicine to cure him. If Sumo was a real zoe, and not just an apprentice, he could cure his brother, as well as bewitch him.

Sumo came to his mother's house, where Koli was lying, weak from his jaundice. He did not want to enter. This was the hardest thing, to tell his brother he hated him. It would be much easier to make the medicine to cure him. Twice he started to leave, but the consequences frightened him more than the task he had to perform.

So Sumo entered his brother's room. He told Koli, "Red deer once hated kwii pig." Koli knew that his brother was saying something important. Otherwise he would have spoken more directly. So he cast about in his memory for the meaning of the words. He also used indirect speech at school, but the words they used were different. He was unsure what message lay inside these country words.

The clue, he realized, was Sumo's mention of kwii pig. These animals had recently been brought up-country, and a few already lived in their town. They were dirty and lazy and fat, and ate the food that belonged to others. They were like the bush hogs that Koli so much enjoyed eating, but they were different, in the same way that kwii tools were different from country tools.

Koli reasoned out what Sumo was saying, and concluded that the remark referred to himself. He did not know the right thing to say, could not think of the right indirect response. Had he been with his schoolmates, he would have known how to answer them, without being too direct. But he had been apart from his brother for too long, he was sick, and he felt his brain was not working well.

He said to Sumo, knowing the words would hurt, knowing that he left himself vulnerable, "Why do you hate me, Sumo? Is it because I go to school?" Sumo could not reply with such directness, but said only, in haste, "Either kwii pig should leave water deer's sister alone, or should learn the ways of bush hog." And then, confused because his brother had broken the rules of discourse, he continued, "Let me go fix medicine for you."

Koli had begun to worry about his illness. He was thinking how he could reach the hospital at Ganta or the nurse at Gbarnga or Totota. He knew that he was too weak to walk there, and he knew also that his family would not carry him to a kwii doctor. He no longer trusted these country medicines, but he had no alternative. He had to accept Sumo's offer, especially now that Sumo had confessed hatred. He knew that Sumo must have strong reason, but he could not imagine that Sumo had made medicine against him. He could only accept the help, with gratitude.

Sumo went to the forest to find herbs. He must not consult Mulbah on this case. He had to prove himself now, by curing his brother. There was a special force binding Sumo to Koli, for good and for ill. He had to use that force, but also use the proper forest plants.

He mixed the leaves and barks he found in the forest, according to what he knew of the yellow disease. He brought leaves from the plant called blue-wing manure, rubbed them in water and collected the liquid. He found a very small palm tree and uprooted it, and removed the branches and bark. He took the hard stuff in the center and boiled it for a long time. He gave the two liquids to his brother, sure that these would cure him. He also made a sacrifice, just as Mulbah would do, of a red chicken, to counteract the unintended witchcraft. He would not tell Koli about that, because for some reason Koli seemed to think that sacrifices were bad. Let Koli believe what he wished. The sacrifice was necessary if Koli was to recover.

Koli was weak and vomited for two more days. But then he began to improve. Koli was not sure at first whether it was because of Sumo's medicine, or whether time had healed him. He knew that the white man in Salala would deny the power of the country medicine, and would be angry at Koli for having taken it. But he felt better, and he began to think his brother was a strong zoe. He was not just a stupid country boy. Sumo had cured him, and Sumo had showed him the white man did not know everything. Koli had been sick and was now well.

Koli also realized now that he had been fighting Sumo his whole time in town, and that Sumo had proved stronger. Sumo's hatred had been Koli's undoing, and his kwii ways had not helped him. Koli thought back to the malang game. There he had moved to capture Sumo's seeds too rapidly, and Sumo had outwaited him. And now in this illness Sumo had won another game. What other victories might Sumo win? Koli realized he had become kwii now, and there was no turning back. He had to face the conflict with his brother as well as he could, even if he did not win it.

CHAPTER XIV

He Who Plants Kola
Picks the Fruit

XIV: HE WHO PLANTS KOLA PICKS THE FRUIT

It would soon be time to cut farms for the new year. But first Flumo told Koli to begin to build his house. "What for?", thought Koli, but he knew the reason. His father knew he liked Kuluba, knew he had finished six years of school. By building a house, Koli would commit himself to remaining in town. Koli had to agree, especially since Yakpalo had ordered him never to disrespect Flumo.

And yet Koli knew that he would never live in the house. He had to return to Salala for the last year of elementary school. He could not drop out now. And if he did well, the white man would help him go to high school at Muhlenburg on the St. Paul River. He could not live at home any longer, could not marry Kuluba, even though he liked her very much. She knew nothing of western ways, would insist that he make farms and settle in town. He had to find a kwii girl to marry.

But whether or not he would live in it, Koli collected poles in the forest to build his house. He insisted, however, that it be in the kwii style, with four walls, and the inside divided into four rooms and a long passage-way. Flumo could not understand this plan at all. He asked, "Why should a family want to cut itself into parts? Since we all belong together, why not live together?" Koli said a man should have his own room, where he could keep his things. A family should keep their cooking things away from the place where they slept, since a house is more than just a place for sleeping. Flumo couldn't understand, but accepted it as the kwii way.

They set the corner poles in the ground, and made the

223

distances between the two opposite corners equal. They used other poles to build the outer and inner walls as well as the roof. They wove supple but sturdy vines between the poles to make the walls firm and able to receive the mud. Koli insisted that they leave window spaces for each room, even though Flumo once again could not understand the purpose. This time Koli only answered, "It's the kwii way."

While some of the men were setting the poles and threading the vines through to make the walls and roof, others went to the swamp to cut thatch for the roof. And after the framework was complete, they thatched the roof. It was much harder, felt Flumo, to put thatch on this four-sided house, than on the round house he lived in. But he could not argue, since this was Koli's house.

After the framework and roof were complete, it was time to daub the house with mud. Everyone gathered for a day of hard work. Koli and Flumo gave them palm wine and cane juice to smoothe their throats and loosen their muscles. The children carried calabashes and buckets of water from the river to mix with the dirt the men had dug. The men then loaded the wet dirt on the backs of the small boys to carry to the house, where more men waited to put the mud in the spaces between poles and vines in the wall. They put also mud on the inside walls which divided the rooms, although many men complained that these walls were not necessary.

When they had daubed the entire house, the feast began. Yanga and Toang cooked goat soup, with potato greens and fish on the side. Everyone was well filled with palm wine and cane juice, and everyone was covered with mud. All dipped together into the common pot to enjoy the meal. Even Koli enjoyed the occasion after his first two long draughts of palm wine, and after he got over the shock of seeing himself covered with mud. And when the feast was ready, Koli, for the first time since he had returned to his town, was happy to eat out of the common pot with his family and friends.

The house would dry while they cut the farms, and then

the women would bring fine dirt from a termite hill, to rub a smooth and long-lasting coat on the surface. This final coat of mud would fill the cracks left by the drying dirt, and would make the house strong. Then doors — and windows, despite Flumo's reluctance — would be hung, and the house made liveable.

But Koli was determined that he would be back at school before they finished the house. He would work on the farm until shortly before it was time to leave, and then tell his family he was leaving. He told Yakpalo privately that he must go back to school, and he could see that Yakpalo accepted the fact. Yakpalo believed the old ways were in fact now dying, and was glad a son of the town was in school. He did not understand the white man's school, but by now took what Koli said as true. Koli would have to understand it for him.

Yakpalo thought about his experiences in Kakata and Firestone. He had joined the kwii secret society, but he felt out of place. The kwii people knew things he did not know, and he was too old now to find out. He was not happy, because he liked the old way of life in their traditional Kpelle country. But he could see change coming, and he knew his people must somehow meet the change. And thus he assured Koli he would support him when he told the people he had to return to school.

Koli was concerned about being late for school. Yet, just when he was ready to tell his family he was leaving, soldiers came to collect extra taxes. The townspeople said they had paid their taxes. In the dispute, which lasted for a week, Koli proved useful to the town for the first time, by quoting the law to the soldiers, and threatening to report them to the D. C. in Gbarnga, the same D. C. whose son was his friend in the white man's school. Faced with this threat, the soldiers reduced the amount they asked for.

When the soldiers left, Koli told his family he must return to school. Flumo said he had been there six years now, far more than any boy ever spent in the Poro Bush School. He must surely know everything about the white man's business by now. His ways with the soldiers proved that. But Koli insisted he must learn more, in order to be more help to his people.

Koli found it easier to leave because Kuluba was avoiding him. She seemed embarrassed and shy at his presence. Sumo was delighted that Kuluba had grown cold to Koli, but he too could not seem to get close to her. Perhaps one medicine had worked, but not the other. Koli was relieved that Kuluba did not press him to stay, although he wondered why she was so distant, so shy.

It was finally Yakpalo, always Yakpalo, who decided Koli was right and who persuaded the others to let him go to school. He told of his trips to Salala, and of what he had seen there. He said that Koli was becoming a big man in school, and that he would be better able to protect the people against soldiers, if he attended school longer. And he finished his speech by announcing that this year his own son Tokpa would go with Koli to school.

Koli was as amazed as everyone else. He knew Yakpalo had gradually changed his view of the school. But he had not expected Yakpalo to agree to let Tokpa go to school.

After long discussion, the people announced that since Yakpalo was their chief, and since he knew more about the kwii world than any of them, they would accept his word. He in turn replied that he wanted the last son of his head wife to be a kwii man also. He saw, from his trips to Gbarnga, Salala, Kakata, Firestone and even Monrovia, that the future was with men like Koli. And he wanted his son to be part of that future. He was glad that Koli could take Tokpa with him to Salala, to show him the ways of the kwii world and protect him when he got into trouble.

Yakpalo himself agreed to go to Salala with the boys. Tokpa, who had not yet been to Bush School, was nonetheless a big boy. In a few years he would be ready to marry, and when Bush School opened next he would leave the white man's school for the real Kpelle school. But for now let him attend the kwii school. So Yakpalo took Koli and Tokpa to Gbarnga.

At Gbarnga the three of them found a truck ready to go down-country. The road was now complete from Monrovia all the way to Ganta. Trucks were more and more finding their way up and down the road, and some traveled simply to carry people. Yakpalo, Koli and Tokpa put their loads in the back of a truck, and sat on a crude wooden bench under a heavy cloth covering. Tokpa was frightened, but dared say nothing, lest his father change his mind about sending him to school. The truck lurched and bounced, and the red dust filled their lungs, but in less than half a day they were in Salala.

After greeting his relatives, Yakpalo went to the white man to talk about Tokpa and about Koli. He admitted to the white man that at first he had doubted the school. He still did not understand what went on in the school, nor did he believe the things the white man taught Koli about God and about the world. He could only take them as true, since the white man had power.

But whether or not he could understand the kwii world, he wanted his sons Koli and Tokpa to know these matters. The kwii people were changing the Kpelle world, and his boys must understand the changes. He wanted Koli and Tokpa to grow up, knowing more than one small town behind Gbarnga. He wanted them to be able to do all the things he could not himself do.

He talked to the white man about Koli in particular. The townspeople had agreed, on his urging, that Koli could have one more year at school, but after that no more. Koli had told them that he needed one more year in order to finish the school at Salala. Yakpalo was certain that he would then be a complete kwii man, and that the white man would have no more to teach him.

The white man did not answer for a moment. And then he risked the truth. He told Yakpalo that Koli, although disobedient and rude, was a good student and must learn more than they could teach him in Salala. He must go down to Muhlenburg on the big river, and there attend the high school. He would be at the high school for six years, and after that he might even go to Cuttington College, just last year opened near Gbarnga. There he would study for four more years, in order to become the complete kwii person. The white man realized that this must seem strange to Yakpalo, that a person could go to school for so many years. But the kwii world demanded it of anyone who was to be truly successful.

Koli was staggered by this idea. What could a person do in school for so many years? He knew he had much to learn — but ten more years seemed impossibly long. But he kept quiet. Yakpalo too was amazed — and expressed his amazement. He said that Koli was a man now, had a house in town, could make his own farm, had a beautiful girl waiting for him. He couldn't go to school for his whole life. Perhaps, Yakpalo suggested, he might take Koli and his own son Tokpa back home that very day.

The white man argued that Yakpalo should not do anything so rash. Wait until the end of the year, and then decide. The white man said he would himself visit the town at the end of the school year to see the elders and persuade them. Koli had learned very little so far. As a school boy, he did not have to do the work the government demanded of every adult male. He was getting free food and clothing from the white man. He could talk big to the soldiers, who themselves had no schooling. But this was only a beginning of what he could do if he stayed in school. He urged Yakpalo to give the boys a chance to become what he himself said he wanted them to be.

Yakpalo did not agree or disagree. He accepted the white man's offer to discuss the matter in town the next dry season. Until then each would keep his own counsel, and not make a decision. Let Koli finish this year at school, and let Tokpa begin. They need not decide until later.

The year started well enough. Tokpa entered the primer class, and Koli was one of the three boys in the sixth grade. The other two were from down-country. One was the Bassa boy from across the river, the same boy that Flumo had warned Koli against. The other was the son of the D. C. in Salala. Only Koli was a true country boy, and thus the white man wanted to make sure he went as far as possible in school.

However, not long after school started, Kuluba's father and Flumo both came to see Koli, not on a trip to sell rice and coffee, not on their way to work at Firestone. They appeared before Koli with serious faces, and Koli was frightened. They obviously had something important to say. Flumo began, "He who plants the kola nut must pick the first fruit." Kuluba's father continued, "Without rain, the rice cannot grow." Koli was at first bewildered, but then realized they were speaking of Kuluba. She must be pregnant.

Hot and cold ran together across Koli's back, and up into his hair. Surely Kuluba was pregnant, and surely he was the father. The time was right. But what now? He couldn't leave and go back to marry Kuluba, take care of her, and have relations with her to ensure that the baby would be born without problems. He knew his people expected him to take care of her until she delivered and that he and his family must care for the girl and the baby.

But he could not leave school. He had made up his mind not to marry Kuluba. She knew nothing of the kwii world, nor could she go to school, now that she was pregnant. Koli would marry a kwii girl, like that girl in the fifth grade, even though she was not half so attractive as Kuluba. He thought back to Kuluba, with her long neck, thick legs, long hair, smooth face, smooth skin, and small eyes, and his heart went out to her. But he could not marry her.

He thought fast and hard, and found no answers in his

230 RED DUST ON THE GREEN LEAVES

mind. And then he remembered Sumo, who had spoken about water deer's sister that day when Koli had been so sick. And so he said, "The planter's brother can water the ground and pick the fruit." His father questioned him closely. Was he really willing to give Kuluba to his brother? Kuluba wanted him back, loved him, would marry him, would give him children. Koli swallowed hard again, determined to finish school. "No," he said, "let the planter be without kola nuts — he does not need them now." Koli surprised the men with his determination, as well as his manly command of indirect speech. He had learned *something,* at least.

Flumo and Kuluba's father talked the matter over, and then said they would ask Sumo his feelings. If he was willing to take his brother's responsibilities, they would be content. They knew Sumo liked Kuluba. But they were not sure if he would accept her as his wife, now that she was pregnant for Koli. And yet, there were some advantages, since Sumo now knew that Kuluba could bear children for him. The men told Koli they would carry his word back to town, and if they did not return to Salala, Koli would know that Sumo had agreed to marry Kuluba.

The year came to a rapid conclusion, and Koli did well in his studies. No word came from town concerning Kuluba, and so Koli, although hurt deep within himself, was relieved to be able to finish school. The white teacher was more than ever determined to have Koli go to high school. Thus, when the school year ended and Koli graduated, the white man and Koli left for Koli's town to discuss the matter. They took a truck to Gbarnga and from there walked to Koli's town. Koli feared that the white man might have to be carried in a hammock, the way big men from Monrovia had to be carried. But this white man was strong, and could walk almost as fast as Koli.

They reached the town shortly before dark. Yanga and Toang were just returning from harvesting the rice. The crops had not been so good that year. Rains had come early, perhaps too early, and had been irregular during the growing season. The women had put too little rice in the storage sheds for the coming year, and so were not pleased to have a white stranger eat their small surplus. But they had to greet him and welcome him to the town, not only because they must receive all strangers, but also for the sake of Koli and Yakpalo.

The stranger was given a room in Koli's new house, now finished. Koli used one room and the white man a second. No one lived in the house, since Flumo was hoping still that Koli would return to town and live there, even though he had not married Kuluba.

The next day, after talking about many things, about the white man's country, about Monrovia, about the school, about how Tokpa was doing in school, and about the harvest in town, the white man said he must now talk with Flumo and Yakpalo about Koli. He did not want Koli to be with them at the time, but he wanted to discuss the matter in secret and seriously. The white man amazed Flumo and Yakpalo with how well he could speak their language, even though with a Salala accent. But he was still too direct. A white man could never know how to talk important matters properly.

But they could not expect a white man to have the sensitivity of a Kpelle man. In order to settle the matter, they had to talk to him on his own terms. It was important to do so now, and so the men agreed to a private conversation.

Koli and Sumo sat together while the older men were talking. The night before, Koli had gone to see Sumo and Kuluba and Kuluba's son, who had been born just two months earlier. Koli had felt, but had kept well hidden, a surge of pride and gratitude at seeing the baby. It was his son. He knew he could father a child, and he was glad of that. But yet the boy was not his son. It was Sumo's son now, and no one would ever mention the fact that Koli had fathered it.

Koli also greeted Kuluba, but no smile of recognition

passed between them. That matter was finished. Kuluba had married Sumo, and seemed content with it. Flumo had paid part of the bridewealth for Kuluba, and promised the remainder after another year had passed. Yakpalo had encouraged Kuluba's parents to accept the part payment, since it gave Yakpalo more authority to have Flumo in debt to a member of his quarter. Debts are often more useful unpaid than paid, thought Yakpalo.

So when Koli met Sumo the next day, there was no further thought of the rivalry over Kuluba. Sumo was satisfied that his medicine had worked, and that by waiting he had triumphed in this as well as in the malang game. And Koli was satisfied that he could remain in school, and that he was himself able to have a son.

There was little the boys could say to each other. They had been so close as children, but now they belonged to different worlds. Each had won something, and lost something. But they could not discuss what they had won or lost. Instead they could only ask about small things, about the weather, about medicines, about the road. Talk soon came to a halt, and each sat with his thoughts, as the older men continued their discussions.

Koli reflected on the town, on Kuluba, on his son, on the fact that Sumo had things now that he, a kwii man, could never have. He had allowed Sumo to take from him something beautiful, because he had gone after it too rapidly. Perhaps he should have encouraged Kuluba's father to send her to school. He had accepted immediate gains in return for long-term losses, just as he had in the malang game last dry season. He had not thought ahead. He had planted the seed last dry season, but his brother had harvested the crop. He had failed to understand the ways of his own town. He seemed to himself less and less of a Kpelle man. Perhaps he was a failure already, like his father.

No, his only hope was more school, where he might continue to learn the white man's ways. Yakpalo had been right about those who went to the white man's school — but Yakpalo had not realized where they went wrong. They quit too soon, before they understood the new ways and after they had forgotten the old. If he stopped now, he would indeed be like a baby, ignorant in the ways of white man and Kpelle alike. Koli knew now, and he hoped Yakpalo also knew, that he had to finish the white man's school, if possible go on to Cuttington College, if he was not to remain outside both worlds, a lonely failure.

The white man returned with Flumo and Yakpalo. Koli knew immediately that they had not agreed. He also knew that the white man must win. He would go back to school regardless of what his fathers said to him. He knew it would be hard, and he must not weaken. It was the only way to prevent Sumo winning everything.

Flumo approached Koli and told him that the white man wanted him to leave his family. The white man tried to break in to defend himself, but Flumo motioned him to stop. Koli could not deny, said Flumo, that he was hardly a Kpelle man now. He wasn't a kwii man either, and never would be. But he could still learn to be a Kpelle man. It was not too late.

Yakpalo was clearly torn. He agreed with much of what Flumo said, but also understood what the white man told them. It seemed mad to Yakpalo that any man, any where, should have to go to school so long. Koli must know most of what the white man could teach him. He did not want Koli to go to Muhlenburg and become like a coastal Liberian who could not use an axe, could not swing a cutlass.

Yakpalo also argued that he needed Koli in town now, to be his son. Flumo had made the offer that if Koli were to remain in town, he could be part of Yakpalo's family, and perhaps prepare to be an important person in town, even the chief one day. Yakpalo's own daughter, who had also come out of the Sande Bush School last year, could be his wife, if he wanted to stay. She was a good girl and would make Koli a wife he could be proud of. Yakpalo urged Koli, for Flumo's sake and for the town's sake, to think twice before rejecting this chance.

But Yakpalo's pleas lacked conviction, and Koli sensed it. Flumo knew his mind, and spoke it forthrightly. Yakpalo supported Flumo, for the sake of town unity, and also because he half agreed. But he also half believed Koli and the white man, and so his final word was that the decision must be Koli's, and Flumo had agreed. Now both men looked at Koli expectantly, as he gathered himself to make his decision.

In some ways he wanted to yield. His love for his father and his loyalty to his people were important. His father had spoken more vigorously and passionately than he had for years. Koli felt youth and strength return to Flumo, and he feared that a negative decision might break the old man again.

But then he looked around the town, compared his own house with the houses he had seen in Monrovia, compared farm work with the work that educated people did, compared his own father with his friends' fathers, some of whom were district commissioners. Koli too could be a D. C. someday, perhaps even more, if he continued in school. And then he could really help his parents. No, he would go back with the white man.

It was his choice. And now he made it. Flumo said Koli would one day be sorry, with neither family nor town nor life of his own. Flumo looked old and tired, as he accepted Koli's decision. Let him, if he wished, go his own way. But he must never forget his people, never forget what his father was now saying, never forget he was a Kpelle man.

Koli agreed. He would come back from Muhlenburg to see his family. He would even bring his family gifts, when he began to make money for himself. He would help other children in town go to school. In particular, he would help young Tokpa in any way he could. And he would never forget his family, no matter what the white man's school taught him.

Koli knew that a man without a family, a man without a town, is not a man.

Koli prepared to leave the next morning with the white man, on his way to Gbarnga and then to Salala. Koli would work at Salala during the dry season and then go to Muhlenburg. He had to work in order to earn the school fees, since it cost more money than he had ever seen to go to high school. But the white man had promised to help him if he would work during the vacation. A church in America would provide the money, and the white man would use it to send Koli to high school.

Sumo watched, and called an uncertain goodby, as Flumo, Yanga and Yakpalo walked with Koli down the road to the gate leading out of town. The goats who browsed near the gate could not get out — when the farms were growing they would cause too much damage. But Koli went through the gate, aware of the damage he was doing and yet hopeful he could make it up one day. His mother held his hand a moment, and then let him go where he would. His father shook his hand, snapping fingers harder than Koli had remembered. And Yakpalo told him to remember, always to remember.

As Koli walked out of sight into the forest, Flumo turned to Yakpalo and Yanga and told a story about a warrior, a dog and a leopard. A hunter had brought a leopard cub from the forest into town, after shooting the mother. The people in town played with the leopard cub and did whatever they wanted to it. And then one day a dog came up and sniffed the leopard cub all over. The dog thought nothing of playing with that young prince of the forest.

The warrior saw the dog sniff at the leopard. He hesitated a moment and then took out his knife and cut the dog in half. He then began to cry. The people asked him why he cried. He said, "I know that when I die, people will do to my children what that dog did to the leopard's cub. If the leopard's mother had been there, the dog would fear the leopard too much to touch the cub. This is how people fear the warrior. When he is alive, no one will play with his children. But when he dies, they will do with his children what they like, and no one will lift a hand to help the little ones."

Flumo began to state the meaning of the story, but Yakpalo cut him short. "We know what you mean. Our sons are from the forest, and now have gone to the white man's town. It is late for us, for you and me. Yet the leopard's cub may grow, and one day find his place."

The three turned and walked back to town — Yanga to cook rice, Flumo to work with Sumo in the blacksmith shop, and Yakpalo to hear a dispute. All they could do was to live the lives they had made for themselves. Koli, whose name means leopard, had made a different choice. God willing, he would find his way, and not merely be the white man's plaything.

EPILOGUE

FOR THE KPELLE AND OTHER FRIENDS

A fence without the strength to fend
Off non-initiates — a mere
Device of palm thatch one can bend
Aside and enter in to hurt
And pry but not to mend
The fragile elegance that curt
And rude inquirers violate
So easily.

        I come, alert
To beauty, yet afraid to wait
Till beauty trusts that I will not
With probing coarse directness sate
My hunger, taking what I sought
For my own pleasure to embrace
And fix in artifices wrought
In my own image.

        Let me face
The beauty that first drew me here
And listen without giving chase
Lest openness be lost in fear.

GLOSSARY

BASSA. The second largest language group in Liberia, living south of the Kpelle, but completely unrelated, and reaching to the coast.

BUSH SCHOOL. A secret training session for boys and girls, administered by the two main secret societies but not simultaneously.

CALABASH. The dried half of a gourd, used for holding liquids.

D. C. District Commissioner, appointed by the Liberian government to administer a rural territory.

FANGA DRUM. A drum with an hour-glass shape, laced with strings which can be tightened and loosened as the drum is held under the arm in order to produce varied pitches.

FERNANDO PO. A Spanish-owned island off the coast of Nigeria where Liberians were taken to work in the 1920's.

FIRESTONE. The rubber plantation introduced by the Firestone Rubber Company in the 1920's and bordering on Kpelle country.

FOREST THING. The leader of the principal secret societies, not supposed to be a human being.

GBANDI. A language group located in the north portion of Liberia, bordering Sierra Leone, and closely related to the Kpelle.

GENII. A name, adapted from the Arabic, for an amoral, trick-playing spirit which lives in the forest.

GOLA. A large language group to the northwest of the Kpelle on the other side of the St. Paul River, but unrelated to the Kpelle.

JORKWELLE. The dialect of the Kpelle language spoken around Gbarnga, among the last Kpelle groups to submit to Liberian authority.

KOLA. The nut, either red or white, of a forest tree, which is used in many ceremonial ways.

KPELLE. The largest language group in Liberia, located in the north-central part of the country, perhaps 250,000 in number, with an equal number in Guinea.

KWII. A term referring to any westernized, modernized person or thing, whether Liberian or foreign.

LAPPA. A cloth, two yards by one yard, usually made from brightly colored imported cotton cloth, which serves as a wrap-around garment for women.

LOMA. A small language group to the north of the Kpelle and closely related to them, which made up the bulk of the old Liberian army.

MANDINGO. A large language group located primarily in Guinea and Mali, which has brought Islam and trade to Liberia and other coastal west African countries.

MANO. A small language group east of the Kpelle and closely related.

ORDEAL. A procedure for determining guilt or innocence by using some dangerous substance, for instance, poison or a hot cutlass. If the accused party survives the ordeal, he is presumed innocent.

OWNER OF THE TOWN. The senior elder of the town and the man with the last word in all serious disputes.

PALAVER. A word which comes from the Portuguese meaning dispute or debate, and which refers to one of the most common forms of social interaction in Liberia.

PANGOLIN. A mammal with a hard scaly back but a soft furry under belly that curls into a ball when attacked.

PORO SOCIETY. The secret society to which all adult males must belong, and into which they are initiated in the Bush School.

SANDE SOCIETY. The secret society to which all adult females must belong, and into which they are initiated in the Bush School.

TOWN. A term used in Liberia for a farm village.

VAI. A large and proud language group on the northern coast of Liberia, distantly related to the Kpelle, and possessors of one of the few independently invented scripts in Africa.

ZOE. A person with supernatural powers, usually inherited, which he is expected to use for the good of the entire community.